Regr

By

Kathy Kingsley

Chapter 1

Wednesday 28th July 1996.

Laurie woke with a start. She shot bolt upright in bed and peered at her bedside clock. SHIT - 8am!! Damn alarm, she thought, why the hell hadn't it gone off? Today of all days, for God's sake. "Rich, wake up...Rich!" she shouted loudly, looking over at her husband. Rich was fast asleep, lying flat out on his back, dead to the world. "For God's sake, wake up," she shouted again, giving him a hard shove on his shoulder. "The alarm hasn't gone off...AGAIN...what a fucking day to do this to me," she added in exasperation.

Laurie was not normally given to swearing but today was Cara's first birthday.

She had planned to have a relaxed breakfast, watching Cara open her presents, with her two sisters looking on in adoration and helping her play with her new toys. The perfect family. But who was she kidding, she thought as she scrambled out of her warm bed, threw on her dressing gown and raced into the bathroom. Now she had forty five minutes to get her girls up, washed, dressed, fed and out of the door, not forgetting the fact that she, herself, had to make some sort of attempt to look half reasonable!

She looked in the bathroom mirror. God, - her hair, shoulder length, newly blonde streaks shining through, was all over the place, sticking out in all directions. She must remember to try to smooth it down whenever she lay on it, said Frankie, her work colleague and closest thing to a friend she had. Frankie was always giving advice, wanted or not! The only thing was, Frankie was childless and seemed not to have a clue about Laurie's life with three children under the age of six to look after.

1

How could Frankie comprehend really? Laurie worked full time and had a job she thoroughly enjoyed, but trying to hold down a job, keep three children alive...(let alone thriving,) keep house and...oh yes...keep a husband happy too...well, she wished she had the answers.

She needed to get into the shower, three minutes in there would have to do. That would allow her ten for her hair and five for her make up.

At least she knew what she was wearing! Clothes being important to Laurie, she always planned her outfits the night before and had already ironed her top and trousers. She had some new sandals which she was looking forward to wearing too. Okay, the trousers were a size fourteen, not her usual twelve, (Laurie not having managed to lose her pregnancy weight yet.) With the first two, her weight had just naturally dropped off, but not this time. Probably stress, Laurie thought wryly. But hey, she wasn't bad really, she didn't look *too* bad, all things considered and she had three beautiful children as well as a job she absolutely loved. Who said you couldn't have it all!

If she got dressed in five minutes, she would have roughly twenty five minutes to get the girls up, washed, dressed and fed...OMG!!!

Rich, meanwhile would not have given a thought to any of this and she knew that when she surfaced from the bathroom, Rich would be dressed, munching on some cornflakes and would simply grab his briefcase and walk out of the house as usual at exactly 8.20 am, leaving her to it!

Sighing heavily, her mind wandered back to Cara's birthday.

We'll open her presents tonight instead...she's only one anyway, she won't know any different. Her two sisters will, of course, and she knew Sarah would be most indignant about it. Sarah was five, going on thirty five and Laurie knew that Sarah would have no problem whatsoever telling mummy off once she realised the morning was not going to go to plan.

Laurie dried herself quickly and ran naked into her bedroom. She pulled on her bra and knickers, grabbed her hairdryer and started to blast her hair on the hottest setting.

"I'm off Laurie, see you later," shouted Rich from downstairs.

"Okay," she shouted back.

She knew him well, she thought. Six years married, three children later and he still kept the same routine. How nice, she thought bitterly. How fucking nice for him!! Where was this damn rulebook that said she had 100% responsibility for everything and he just went to work?! She went to work too! Had he forgotten his kids this morning? Did he not think it might have been nice just to see if she wanted any help at all? God forbid, maybe even bring her some cereal or a cup of tea! She was feeling herself getting more and more het up. For goodness sake, stop it, she told herself firmly. She was getting way too stressy and, anyway, it was never going to happen. It never has yet, so why on earth should she expect anything different today?

She knew Rich. She knew him well. He was a man of order...tradition. He brought in the bacon, so to speak, and she was his wife. He actually considered himself a new man...Ha, she thought. A new man because he ALLOWED her to work!

Fucking laughable really.

It was time she had a chat with him, time to clear the air a little. She needed more help around the house, more support, and actually, unless she spoke to him and asked for it, she knew she wouldn't get any.

Why should he? she asked herself. If someone did everything for her, she would just lap it up. How nice that would be! Maybe she should have been born a man. Just her to think about, a well paid job and a wife that did everything! A meal cooked for her every evening...oh yes...and shirts that miraculously appeared in her wardrobe, freshly washed and ironed. Wow. All she would have to do is change the odd light bulb and take out the rubbish! Still, it wouldn't do to muse for too long, it wasn't about to happen.

Smoothing down her hair, she quickly applied her lipstick and walked into her daughter's bedroom.

Sweeping the curtains open, she peered outside. It was a beautiful sunny day, not a cloud in the sky. What a shame she was working. She had tried to get the day off but to no avail. A daughter's birthday didn't seem to count as important enough as far as her supervisor was concerned. Never mind. She would try to grab an hour outside at lunchtime maybe. No...not maybe, she WOULD. She didn't get much opportunity for time to herself these days and an hour of sunshine midday with a good book was just what she needed.

"Wakey wakey," she sang. "Come on, up you get girls. We have literally NO time this morning so here's your clothes. Get them on as quickly as you can and then come downstairs for brekkie. Sarah, come on love, can you hear me?"

"Yes mummy, I can," answered Sarah as she yawned loudly and rubbed her eyes. She then proceeded to grab her knickers from the pile Laurie had put out.

"As soon as you are dressed, help Marie will you?

"Yes mummy," answered Sarah obediently, always accepting of her elder sisterly duties.

"Good. That's Excellent. Right then, I'll see you both downstairs in a jiffy."

In the kitchen Laurie set out two cereal bowls and two glasses of milk. Right...all she needed to do now was grab Cara and warm up her bottle. Chocolate milk...her favourite. It would have to do as there was no time for anything else this morning. And anyway, Cara loved her bottle, chocolate milk especially.

She flew back upstairs, into Cara's bedroom. Cara was asleep. Bloody typical, thought Laurie as she opened the curtains. Saturday or Sunday, Cara would have been fully awake by now, screaming for attention. It's as though they have an inbuilt radar! Laurie couldn't remember the last time she had enjoyed a lie in. It always seemed to be the crack of dawn every weekend, although, to be fair, she had often taken Cara downstairs, plonked her on Sarah's lap and stumbled back upstairs to try to catch an extra half hour's sleep. She didn't feel too guilty. Maybe she should, but Sarah never seemed to mind and she knew Sarah also benefited by raiding the biscuit tin knowing mummy would not say a word when she did eventually surface. How could she really? And so, this silent deal happened on many a weekend...biscuits galore for Sarah and another half hour or two for mummy! Perfect!

Laurie picked Cara up out of her cot. "Good morning Sweetheart, happy birthday," Laurie whispered to Cara. She loved it when Cara was like this, all docile and sleepy, so she took the opportunity to lie Cara against her shoulders, taking in that lovely baby smell. Well...it would be lovely, she thought wryly, except for the stinking nappy. Glancing at her watch, Laurie sighed deeply. There were only ten minutes until they all had to be out of the door, there was no time to dress Cara therefore. She would just change her nappy quickly and pop her in the car as she was.

Lizzie, her childminder, was brilliant like that, she never made Laurie feel at all guilty. She always seemed so calm and in control, just very accepting of whatever state the girls were in when they arrived, Laurie losing count of the times they all turned up in their pyjamas.

After changing Cara's nappy, Laurie lifted her onto her hip and carried her downstairs, planting her in her bouncy chair. She grabbed her bottle and lodged it onto the colourful plastic teddies that were attached to the bouncy chair, supposedly to entertain a baby, thought Laurie, however they were perfectly placed for the bottle to lodge in between them and tip sufficiently into Cara's mouth. Not that Laurie would ever let on to her health visitor, she would most certainly disapprove!

Knowing the routine, Cara happily grasped the bottle with her two podgy hands and sucked at it greedily.

"Right, come on you two, have you finished your breakfast?" Laurie enquired, looking over at Sarah and Marie.

"No mummy," Sarah whined. "The milk smells stinky," she grumbled, looking all indignant.

"No it doesn't, it's fine," Laurie said, picking up the milk and taking a big sniff. Oh, perhaps not, she thought, looking at the date on the label. 26th July...oh shit! "Oh well, never mind," she said brightly. "Daddy didn't seem to notice this morning, he has had it."

"WELL. I. DON'T. WANT. IT," stated Sarah, glaring defiantly at her mummy.

"No, me no want it eaver," added Marie, with the same indignant look, copying her sister as she always sought to do.

"Fine," sighed Laurie. "Leave it then. Come on, let's get your shoes on, coats too. Sarah, help Marie, will you love? I'm going to put Cara in the car and then come back for you two. We have NO time this morning so no messing, hurry up!"

Laurie was hoping her teacher's voice would cut the mustard and get them both moving.

Picking up Cara, Laurie opened the front door and ran to her car. Opening the back door, she placed Cara, none too gently, into her car seat, giving her the bottle she hadn't yet finished. Then, remembering the foul smell from just a few seconds ago, she snatched the bottle from her. "No, Cara, the milk's gone off. Sorry darling, you will have to wait until we get to Lizzie's."

Seeing her milk disappearing from view and understanding the word "no" Cara burst into angry tears, screaming as loudly as her little lungs would allow. Great...another disaster of a morning, thought Laurie despondently as she raced back inside.

"Sarah, Marie, come on! Now!" Laurie shouted from the hallway. Sarah walked solemnly out of the kitchen, coat on, buttoned, bag in hand. Marie followed, her coat dragging on the floor behind her. "Come on you two," Laurie said softly. "Let's hit the road."

Marie's 'T' shirt was inside out, her hair uncombed, but apart from that, they had done well this morning. "Well done Sarah for helping Marie this morning. I don't know what I would do without you, poppet. I *do* love you. You're mummy's little helper aren't you?" Smiling, Laurie locked the front door and helped both her girls climb into the car, fastening Marie's seat belt before closing the car door gently, thankful that Cara's shrieks had subsided.

Just as Laurie was backing out of the drive, Sarah shrieked "Mummy, mummy!"

"Yes darling, what's up Sarah? Jeez, you scared me half to death! What on earth's the matter?" asked Laurie, feeling quite exasperated.

"Cara's birthday! It's Cara's birthday and you've forgotten! She hasn't opened her presents, we haven't sang "happy birthday" to her," wailed Sarah, tears streaming down her cheeks. "You forgot mummy, how could you forget?" she asked reproachfully.

"Whoa, whoa, calm down, will you Sarah? We haven't forgotten, it's just that we were all too late this morning. I promise tonight we will all sing to her and have a lovely birthday tea, how about that?" Laurie asked, praying that Sarah would accept her promise. "And we can sing to her now if you would like?"

7

Silence from the back seat and a good thirty seconds ticked by before Sarah replied. "Okay, mummy."

Thank God for that, thought Laurie as she turned out of their close onto the main road, all quietly singing "happy birthday" to Cara, who was now urgently sucking on her thumb, clearly deriving some comfort from it, having had her bottle snatched away from her so violently.

PEACE...thought Laurie. Peace and quiet. So Calm too...how lovely. She must remember to sing to them more often. It seemed to work quite nicely, Laurie thought contentedly. "Happy birthday to you, happy birthday to you, happy birthday dear Cara, happy birthday to you," sang all three of them in perfect unison.

Chapter 2

"Morning Sue, morning all," smiled Laurie, walking past all her colleagues who were already at their desks, head down, well into their day.

It was 9.30am and Laurie had negotiated a later start due to Cara's birthday. Bloody stupid idea that had been, she thought as she sat down at her desk. She should have negotiated an early finish instead, that would have been far more sensible. Now, all she had achieved was to give herself more stress by knowing she had half an hour to make up this week, at some point, as well! Oh well, she sighed, picking up her headset, placing it over her head and preparing for her first call. "Good morning, kay's catalogue, how can I help you?" she chanted in a sing-a-long voice, attempting a smile at the same time, as per her team leader's instructions only yesterday.

The morning went quickly, the phone going non-stop and Laurie threw herself into it. This was why she liked work. It was ordered, everything had it's place. If she placed a piece of paper on her desk, it stayed there! No little hands messing everything up. No shouts for mummy at all! It was wonderful really, she loved the order of it all, and let's face it, it WAS only work, not life and death. Just catalogue orders and chatty banter on the odd occasion with some of the nicer customers. She particularly liked the old dears who would keep her on the line for as long as possible, bless them. She was probably the only person many of them spoke to all day, so she would never try to cut them off, no matter how many times her team leader told her off for it.

Placing the headset on her desk, she grabbed her bag and, gesturing to Frankie who was sitting in the next cubicle, she mouthed "park?" to her. Frankie was busy confirming an order, blue jeans, size 18, LZ1347, and therefore simply nodded. Smiling at her, Laurie strode out of the office, walking along the corridor as quickly as possible, eager to get some fresh air.

Buying her favourite sandwich at 'Greggs', she walked along the high street and into the park. It was still a beautiful day and Laurie nabbed the first empty bench available to her that was fully immersed in sunshine. Stretching out her legs, she sighed deeply and looked at her watch. Forty five glorious minutes...not too bad, she thought...all to herself! She unwrapped her 'bacon and egg' sandwich and took a large bite. Closing her eyes, she felt the beautiful warmth on her face and body...absolutely perfect! Peaceful too, the park being far enough away from the main road to block out most of the traffic noise. She could even hear the birds chirping in the trees above. It would be lovely to be a bird, Laurie thought. What was that saying? Free as a bird...that was it...yes...how lovely that would be. Maybe she could come back as one in another life?...

"Hello," boomed a male voice, instantly breaking her daydreaming. Laurie opened her eyes and peered up at Mike.

"Hello," smiled Laurie shyly.

"Can I join you?

"Sure," answered Laurie, moving over a little to give him plenty of space to sit down.

Mike had joined the company two weeks previously and Laurie had only spoken to him briefly when introduced on his first day. He was about late thirties, she decided. VERY nice looking. Tall, dark, very sexy...dangerous therefore, she told herself. "How are you finding the job?" she asked casually, not wanting to give him the impression she was nervous at all around him

"Okay," Mike said slowly. "Always takes a little time to get into it, doesn't it? Getting to know everyone an' all. At the moment I feel very much like the new kid on the block, you know, a bit 'Billy no mates,'" smiled Mike, sounding a little lost as he looked over at her

God, those eyes, that slow smile...wow. She felt a stirring down below and shifted uncomfortably on the bench. "Yes, I suppose it is a bit strange at first. Still, we're a nice enough bunch and you will soon get to know everyone."

"Yes, I'm sure I will," he acknowledged. A few seconds of uncomfortable silence followed.

"It's a nice day isn't it?" they both said in unison, causing them both to laugh out loud.

"Hi," shouted Frankie loudly. "Sorry I'm a little late," she added, plonking herself firmly in between the two of them. "Couldn't get that last customer off the bloody phone," she moaned. "Anyway, I'm here now. Hello Mike," she smiled. "How's it going?"

"Good thanks," answered Mike as he stood up to leave. "Well, I'll leave you both to it," he said as he began walking away.

Laurie stared after him. What a lovely man, she thought. He seems really nice too...gentle...she thought. Yes, that's how she would describe him...gentle.

"Well," said Frankie. "Give me all your news, how are you Laurie? We haven't had a catch up in a long time...oh...and isn't it glorious weather too? Mmm, beautiful," she sighed, closing her eyes just as Laurie had done when she first arrived. She was totally oblivious to the fact that she had barged in and effectively driven Mike away.

Oh well, probably for the best really. He was far too nice, far too interesting. Maybe Laurie should avoid him in future for her own good! "It is beautiful isn't it?" she acknowledged with a sigh. "And I'm fine I suppose. Just the normal shit that seems to happen every day at the moment.

I need to get more organised and then life would be so much easier!"

"Yes," Frankie agreed, far too readily for Laurie's liking and Laurie knew she would now be listening to Frankie for the whole of her lunch hour, happily advising Laurie on how she could improve her lot in life.

Laurie closed her eyes, enjoyed the sun and simply allowed Frankie's words to go over her head. It was far easier that way, she thought, smiling to herself.

Chapter 3

It was just after 6pm when Laurie arrived home that evening. Cara had fallen asleep on the ten minute journey from Lizzie's. Laurie picked her up out of her car seat as carefully as she could and ran inside with her, placing her very gently on the settee. Marie, too, looked all droopy eyed. Only Sarah looked as though she had any life left in her for what Sarah was describing as Cara's 'birthday tea.'

Helping Marie out of her summer coat, Laurie looked over at Sarah who was busily jumping up and down in a very excitable manner. "Yaay, Cara's got pressies to open," she chattered happily. "Yaaaaaay," she added for good measure, dancing around in the hall.

Laurie let out a heavy sigh. She was exhausted. "Yes, Sarah. Just give mummy a minute. I've got to fetch in all the stuff from the car first and then at least let me get a cup of tea...I'm dead thirsty." Starving too, she thought miserably. Laurie had eaten nothing since lunchtime and was feeling quite irritable as a result. She should know better, she chided herself. She could easily have had a snack this afternoon with her cup of coffee but vanity took precedence and she was never going to get back to her size twelve unless she was quite strict with herself.

The trouble at work was they all ate rubbish...chocolate, sweets, biscuits. All were readily available from the vending machine and *cake*...well, that was almost a daily occurrence. It always seemed to be someone's birthday! No-one ever thought to bring in anything healthy, she grumbled. Unless Laurie was super organised and took in an apple or a banana, she could never just put her hands on something decent. So...as a result...she ignored all the fattening treats, feeling super superior to Frankie who always indulged. Not just one chocolate bar either...oh no...one in the morning and another in the afternoon! She didn't seem to care. Mind you, she WAS a size sixteen! She seemed perfectly content with it though, Frankie being one of those rarities in life...a woman who was not obsessed with her figure. She had a healthy approach to food and always had a sunny disposition which Laurie reckoned was probably as a direct result.

Laurie meanwhile felt her irritability deepen as tiredness crept into her bones.

She ran back to her car and grabbed three overloaded bags from the boot. Cara's bag was stuffed to the gills with nappies, extra clothing, toys etc..

Struggling to shut the boot with one hand, she breathed a sigh of relief as she saw Rich's car pull up. Thank God for that, he's not late. Smiling at him, she waited for him to get out of the car, briefcase in hand. "Oh brilliant, Rich, Thank *you*," Laurie cried. "I thought you said you were going to be late tonight?"

Rich smiled at her, taking Cara's overstuffed bag from her. "I know, I shouldn't have left really, far too much on, but never mind. Here I am, ready for anything you ask me to do...well...you know...sort of, anyway. Don't take it literally!" he joked. "How's your day been?"

"Oh, fine, same as ever, too much to do, no time to do it. Anyway let's go in. According to Sarah, we now have a massive party to enjoy."

Rich groaned. "Oh right, yes, of course...Cara. Does Sarah realise she's only one and she won't give a shit? Can't we just pack them all off to bed and grab ourselves some quiet time?" Rich smiled as he said this, knowing full well it wasn't going to happen.

"Not with Sarah in charge, no way. Let's just go and enjoy. Come on Rich, throw yourself into it," she encouraged as they walked up the drive together.

"Happy birthday to you, happy birthday to you, happy birthday dear Cara, happy birthday to you," sang Rich, Laurie and Sarah in unison. Marie had fallen asleep whilst Laurie had been unpacking her car and could not be woken, despite Sarah's best efforts.

Cara, having been prodded awake again by Sarah, had been placed in her bouncy chair and at least had her eyes open, a bemused look on her face. She rewarded them all with a gummy smile and grabbed at the pretty wrapping paper, crumpling it in her fingers, totally fascinated by it's feel and texture. She was oblivious to anything else but the crumpling sound she could hear as she held it to her ear

Diving into a piece of chocolate cake, Sarah went quiet, the only sound being "Mmm,mmm," as she happily tucked in.

Laurie looked over at Rich, also tucking in as though he had never been fed. Peace, she thought. She treasured these moments, they didn't happen often enough. Cara was content with her wrapping paper, Sarah with her cake, Marie asleep and Rich smiling. "Love you," she mouthed, smiling at her husband.

"Love you too," he replied, his mouth stuffed with cake.

"Love you too, more!" she mouthed back, smiling. Yes...okay...soppy, she knew, but it was something they had always said to each other, right back from when they had first met in their late teens.

And something not said often enough anymore, she thought sadly, remembering this morning's fiasco and how angry she always seemed to be with him lately.

"Right, come on Sarah, time for bed. It's seven o'clock already. Mummy and daddy still need their tea and I've got loads of washing and ironing to do. *And* its another early start tomorrow. So come on, chop, chop." Laurie clapped her hands together as she jumped up, picking Cara up out of her bouncy chair and running upstairs with her. She entered the bathroom and turned on both of the bath taps.

15

Placing Cara into her cot briefly, she walked back downstairs to fetch Marie.

Marie was absolutely fast asleep and Laurie was faced with a dilemma. Wake her up to bath her? Or just put her straight to bed?

She'd wake her, she decided. She needed a bath...No, she wouldn't, she may not fall back to sleep. She'd put her straight into bed. How about her nappy? Laurie questioned. Marie was dry in the day but couldn't be counted on not to wet the bed still at night. Oh, sod it, she decided. She would just put her straight to bed; give herself half a chance of a quiet evening. Picking her up carefully, she slowly walked upstairs into Marie's bedroom and gently placed her in bed, covering her with her pink duvet and placing her favourite pink silky blanket into her little fingers, just in case she DID wake up. Marie LOVED her silky 'blankie' as she called it, and Laurie noticed how often it calmed her almost immediately in any distressing situation.

Calling Sarah into the bathroom, encouraging her to climb into the bath, Laurie walked through to Cara, smiling lovingly at her as she picked her up. "Come on, little one, let's get you bathed."

Cara was quite an accepting baby in many ways, maybe because she had to be! The youngest of three, she was certainly not spoilt in any way and the needs of the eldest two always took precedence. And Cara, even at only one, seemed to accept this status quo without complaint. And it's a good job she did! thought Laurie as she tenderly removed Cara's babygro, vest and nappy and placed her into the bath with Sarah.

8pm and all was quiet...Bliss...All three asleep. The best time of the day, mused Laurie, sipping on her wine as she prepared the 'spag bol' for them both. Her girls all safe, snuggled up in their beds, it was a wonderful feeling and if she could stop time, right now, just for a few hours, she certainly would.

Rich came up behind her, placing his arms firmly around her waist. "Mmm, you smell nice," he mumbled softly, kissing her neck after sweeping her hair away with his hand.

Not now, she thought. Please...not now. Laurie felt exasperated with him but she didn't want to hurt his feelings. "So do you," she replied, turning to face him. "Now, how about you pour yourself a glass of wine and go sit down. Tea will be two minutes, that's all."

Rich groaned. "Really? Can't tea wait?" he asked as he grabbed her around the waist again, nuzzling into her neck.

"No Rich, no, it can't wait. I'm starving. I need food...and now!" she added, just in case he had misunderstood.

"Okay, okay, no worries. Just a thought. Don't get your knickers in a twist!" Rich shrugged his shoulders and did as he was bid, sitting at the kitchen table and taking a deep slug from his glass of wine.

The meal was gorgeous, and, together with a couple of glasses of her favourite merlot, Laurie was feeling decidedly mellow. Thinking back to the fiasco this morning, she remembered her resolve to 'have a chat' with Rich. When is it a good time? she pondered. They were both in a good mood at the moment so, in one way, why spoil it? They could have a perfectly lovely evening together. Maybe even some sex! That would be nice...follow on from Rich's earlier attempt. They could move into the living room, undress each other, put some romantic music on in the background and enjoy some real slow, sensual lovemaking for once. Crikey, she couldn't remember the last time they had done that! Certainly not on the settee! It was now always a 'quickie', in bed, just before falling asleep, exhausted, Laurie peering over to the bedside

17

clock afterwards to work out how many hours sleep she was going to end up with, girls not withstanding.

So, she deliberated... That would be lovely - however hadn't Frankie said only recently that, in order to get any satisfactory solution to an issue, you should only go into battle when you were BOTH in good moods? Give yourselves the best chance to have a calm, sensible discussion like proper adults without resorting to screaming and throwing insults around. Yes...she *did* recall Frankie saying exactly that and it WAS time, Laurie knew, to be honest with him. She couldn't continue as she was, something had to give and she needed more support. In fact, what she needed was for her to feel they were a couple...in this together...and both pulling their weight.

"Rich, we need to talk," she said gently, looking across the table at him.

"We do?" questioned Rich, his eyebrows raised. "That sounds ominous, don't think I like the sound of this." He took a deep breath, folded his arms in what Laurie perceived to be a very defensive manner and leant into the back of his chair.

How could she put this the best way? She didn't want him losing his rag as he had a tendency to do whenever he felt criticised. Oh, what the hell! She would simply have to go for it, she thought nervously.

Taking a deep breath, she began. "I need more help." There...she'd said it! Lifting her eyes to look over at him, she could see Rich was stony faced, his mouth one grim, straight line. He stayed quiet, clearly waiting for her to continue. Laurie took another gulp of her wine. Oh well, in for a penny, in for a pound. "This morning, for example, you just got up and went to work, you didn't even think to bring me a cup of tea!" Laurie stated, pleading with her eyes for Rich to understand where she was coming from.

He said nothing.

For a few moments all was silent. What was he thinking? He was certainly giving nothing away, that was for sure.

"Rich, can't you see where I'm coming from?" she pleaded.

Still, he said nothing.

"I'm totally shattered ALL the time, I have NO downtime, I just have this endless list of stuff to be done, it NEVER stops. I just feel you don't give me enough support and..."

"STOP," Rich shouted. "That's ENOUGH!" He jumped out of his chair and stood menacingly over her. "I've said this before and I'll say it again, one last time...do you hear me?"

"Yes," whispered Laurie.

"YOU chose to return to work. I was quite happy as we were. YOU said you needed a change and I've agreed to that but don't now try to get me to do more just because YOU wanted to work! Oh no, no way!" Rich shouted, getting louder and louder as he got into his stride. "I work really hard, Laurie, my work is really tough and all I want when I get home from work is some peace and quiet, tea on the table, you know? Is that too much to ask? Well, is it?"

Rich was getting almost demented now and slammed the palm of his hand on the table, causing Laurie to jump. "Christ, I can't *believe* you're having a go at me! I do everything for my family. Do you ever go without? Well...do you?" he ranted, his spittle landing on her face.

"No Rich, no, of course we don't. This isn't what this is about though. All I want is the odd bit of help and support," she pleaded, grabbing at Rich's hands.

"All I want...all I want...that's all I ever hear from you Laurie. Goddammit!" he screamed, shoving her hands away violently and grabbing his car keys from the kitchen worksurface. "I'm off out," he added as he snatched his coat down from the coat peg and slammed the front door behind him.

19

Laurie sat, pensively, at the kitchen table and took a deep breath to try to stop the tears from falling. Shit, she thought. That went really badly, her tears refusing to be stemmed and beginning to pour down her cheeks onto her lap. Just as she was giving in to them she heard a cry from upstairs.

"I'm coming Marie," cried Laurie softly, taking the stairs two at a time as she didn't want the others waking up.

"I'm here darling, what's the matter?"

"Wet bed, mummy, wet bed," cried Marie, totally distraught.

Great...fabulous...fanfuckintastic!

"It's okay, Sweetheart, no worries," placated Laurie, placing Marie gently on the floor and pulling her clothes over her head. "Let's get you washed and comfy again, change your bed and you can fall nicely back to sleep again eh?" she encouraged, hoping fervently that Marie would do just that but suspecting otherwise.

Chapter 4

Wednesday 4th August 1996.

One week later.

"Park?" smiled Laurie to Frankie.

"Can't today, sorry. Got some stuff to do in town."

"Oh, okay. See you later then. I'm going anyway - the weather's too nice not to, so if you change your mind you know where I'll be," said Laurie, picking up her bag and cardie from the back of her chair.

"Okay, thanks. Not likely though, to be honest. I have LOADS of errands to get done."

"No worries, I've got a good book I'm into anyway. See you later."

Striding down the corridor as quickly as possible, her head down, Laurie almost collided with Mike as he came out of one of the conference rooms.

"Hello," said Laurie shyly.

"Hello again," smiled Mike, looking as sexy as she had remembered, his tie slightly loosened and his shirt a little crumpled.

Feeling the same stirring in her lower regions again, Laurie smiled some more.

"Lunchtime?" questioned Mike. "Stupid question, yes of course it is!" he added.

"Yep," she answered, laughing. "Off to the park again. Too nice to be sat inside," she gabbled.

"Good idea...I might join you later...could do with some fresh air myself...that's if you wouldn't mind of course?"

Not wanting to sound too keen, but equally, not wanting to put him off, Laurie started to saunter away from him as she looked over her shoulder and quipped, "Well, you know

21

where to find me!" in a sing-along voice, whilst smiling broadly.

Sitting on her favourite bench, looking upwards towards the sunshine, Laurie felt an excitement she hadn't felt in a long time. And a slight nervous fluttering in her stomach. Crikey, how one man can make you feel! She didn't know Mike at all but it was strange because she felt like she DID. She LOVED how he smiled at her...LOVED how he made her feel...like she was the only girl in the world. How is that possible? She had literally spent no more than ten minutes in his company! How on earth could she feel she knew him so well?

She didn't know and wondered whether it may have something to do with the fact that she felt so starved of attention at the moment. Maybe she would be susceptible to anyone who gave her the time of day?! No, that's not true, she told herself. She felt a tremendous attraction to Mike and she realised she needed to tread very carefully. She would simply enjoy his company for what it was and try not to over analyse, she decided emphatically, feeling better as a result.

Life at home had got no better since last week. Rich had come home really late the night of their argument, stinking of booze and fallen into bed beside her, snoring almost as soon as his head had hit the pillow.

There then followed two days of the 'silent treatment'.

He had said absolutely nothing to her...not a word. He was clearly extremely angry with her and just ignored her completely, the kids too. He simply got up, went to work, came home, ate tea, then went to bed. After two days, Laurie could take it no more.

"I'm sorry," Laurie had said, finally, on Saturday morning. "I know you do your best and I obviously made you feel really bad Rich. Please..."Laurie had pleaded.

"Please...let's forget I ever said anything...I can't *bear* a weekend like this."

Rich had simply shrugged his shoulders before delivering his bombshell. "I'm not happy," he had stated. "When you weren't working, everything was fine. Now you are and it's NOT fine, so, as far as I can see, the answer's simple Laurie. Give up work!"

Just like that!...So simple...So typically blokelike, she thought angrily. All was not well in Rich's world so Laurie had to change HER life in order to improve HIS!

Since the weekend, no more had been said on the subject. Laurie knew Rich was expecting her to do as he had asked...well...not even asked...demanded, more like!

Laurie was really frustrated. She felt angry...sad also. Rich seemed to refuse to see anything from her perspective. It wasn't as though Laurie hadn't already tried being a 'stay at home' mum. She HAD, but had found it quite stifling. She had done it for just over three years, having left 'kays' when pregnant with Sarah.

That had been a lovely time, she mused. They had a lovely home, Rich was doing well at work and Laurie had found herself looking forward to her maternity leave with excitement. She had been working at 'Kays' since leaving school at sixteen and felt ready for a change. The romantic in her was looking forward to being a 'proper' family and she could hardly wait for her first born to arrive. The fact that her maternity leave had begun just before Christmas made it all the more magical.

All was looking really rosy for them. And life HAD been good. Laurie was a good mum...she loved Sarah *so much*...she loved the feeling of being the most important person in her child's life. She felt an enormous satisfaction in all the monotonous daily routines and knowing Sarah was well looked after, but...but...it simply hadn't been enough for her.

Laurie had struggled on, trying to make it work, accepting Rich's decision that she need not return to work after her maternity leave ended. Falling pregnant with Marie had also helped. Laurie was aware her decision to have another baby so soon had been as much about boredom as anything else. At home all day with just one child to care for had driven for batty, she had literally felt like screaming some days, especially in those long afternoons. Sarah had been a good sleeper and could sleep for hours in the afternoon, sometimes three, and Laurie would be climbing the walls, waiting for her to wake up.

She had met the odd mum at 'baby and toddler' group, but the conversation!... Well...it was all about kids and housework! God, some of them had been worse than the 'stepford wives'! She hadn't had a real 'adult' conversation since leaving work, and, whilst she loved Sarah, one baby had simply not been enough to keep her fully occupied, hence, the decision to have another...keep her busier...two to lavish her attention and love on...less time to feel so goddamm lonely. And for a while it had kept her more content. Pregnancy seemed to do that, she thought wryly, must be the hormones. She always felt satisfied with life when pregnant, smug almost, with her obviously pregnant belly on show to the world.

Marie had arrived February 13th 1993, just over two years after Sarah and life had suddenly become a whole lot busier. One child was only one child. Two, however, was suddenly a family, with all the resultant chaos.

And it HAD been chaotic, very busy all the time, very little time for Laurie to reflect at all for the first nine months or so.

Rich had been happy too. He had taken to the role of fatherhood very naturally, always happy to take the girls out to the park on Saturday mornings to give Laurie time to do the housework in peace. Thinking about that now, Laurie believed he may only have offered so that the house was tidy for him over the weekend! He hated it when the girls' toys and books were strewn all over the living room carpet. She noticed he couldn't seem to sit amongst the mess and used to get very tetchy some weekends. The evenings were never a problem as Laurie always managed a quick tidy around after putting her girls to bed and prior to Rich returning home at around 6ish. So, really, in the week, Rich's life hadn't changed that much at all, she reflected. It was only weekends when suddenly family life appeared before his eyes!

The decision to return to work after Marie had been Laurie's. Marie had just turned one and Laurie couldn't bear it any longer. She had started feeling very lonely again, feeling herself getting increasingly depressed. Sarah, now three, was attending playschool three mornings a week and Laurie felt the same acute desperation she had experienced previously.

"I want to go back to work," she had blurted out one evening, after having prepared Rich his favourite meal of gammon, egg and chips. "I know you don't want me to Rich, but I need to. I really miss it, you know," she had pleaded.

Rich had eventually relented, although it had taken two whole weeks. "If you must," he had sighed. "But I do not want my life to have to change. I want my tea on the table every night, I'm NOT doing any more at home," he had grumbled. "No way. If you go back to work, that's fine, but I don't want my home life to be any different."

"No, it won't, I promise. You won't even know I work. Nothing will change Rich."

And she had meant it. Lizzie, her childminder, who she had met at the 'baby and toddler' group had been great right from the start and going back to work had felt wonderful! Laurie had negotiated hours to suit at 'Kays' ensuring she left home later than Rich and got back earlier. Tea was always prepared, the house tidy and Rich saw little difference.

Laurie was happy too. She relished the adult conversation again and enjoyed the sense of purpose working provided.

And all would have continued to go well, she reflected, had Laurie not fallen pregnant again by accident. She had had two weeks off from work at Christmas, ten months after returning to work and was feeling the, oh, so familiar sickness. Oh no...please no, she had thought. She had not wanted another child. Two had been just right, but there was no way she could even entertain an abortion. She wasn't anti-abortion as such, she just knew she wouldn't have been able to live with herself if she had one...especially when there was no justification for it...after all, they were a solid couple and enjoyed a comfortable lifestyle. An abortion would have been for purely selfish reasons.

And so, along came Cara. Laurie had dug her heels in regarding work this time. She was taking the stipulated maternity leave and then she was returning to work. Nothing Rich said could deter her otherwise.

And it had been hard, harder than Laurie could have imagined. The last six months had really taken their toll and Laurie knew it was unsustainable. She barely managed really. She felt as though she was continually spinning ten plates in the air, not being able to take her eye off the plates for a second, otherwise they would all come crashing down. She was absolutely exhausted and the thought of hitting thirty in a few weeks' time wasn't making her feel any better about things either!

Still...she decided she would just enjoy the sunshine on her face for now, worry about everything tomorrow. Maybe she would feel a little brighter by then.

Laurie was certainly an optimist, she always tried to look on the bright side of life.

Maybe, tomorrow, she would be able to do so again!

"Hello," said Mike, seeming slightly out of breath. "Is it *really* okay if I join you? I rather railroaded you earlier."

"Yes, of course it is," smiled Laurie.

Mike took a seat beside her.

"No lunch?" she asked.

"No. Never have any."

Men could do that, she marvelled. They seemed to be able to go all day with just coffee and the odd bit of cake if offered and still sound human in the afternoon!

She said as much to him. "I couldn't do it. God...I have to eat every four hours at least, otherwise I turn into a monster," laughed Laurie.

Mike looked over at her, looking at her for a second too long to feel comfortable. "I don't believe that for a minute," he laughed. "Look at you, there's no way you could ever be a monster as far as I can see," he said softly.

"You wait," she laughed. "Spend any time with me at all and you will soon see!" she said playfully, looking straight back at him.

Mike's expression changed. "I'd really like that chance," he said quietly.

Feeling more than a little disconcerted, Laurie abruptly changed the subject. "Anyway, how are you finding things at work now? Any more settled?"

Taking his cue from her, Mike launched into a full tirade, sharing with Laurie some of the complaints he had been dealing with over the last week and causing her to laugh out loud as he began to imitate one old lady who had been complaining about the way we always answered the phone. The complaint had been simply that we were always too cheerful! Mike, then, had Laurie in stitches, describing the many ways we could remedy the situation. "Hello. Kays.

Catalogue. How. Can. I. Help. You?" he groaned in a slow, monotone, slightly grumpy manner. "There...that would do, don't you think?"

And so, the lunchtime passed, superfast, with Laurie realising as she walked back to the office, that she hadn't had such a laugh in a long time. He is gorgeous, she thought...and he doesn't seem to be even slightly aware of the fact, which, of course, made him even *more* attractive.

Smiling broadly, she took her headpiece and answered her first afternoon call.

Chapter 5

Saturday 7th August 1996.

"Well," demanded Rich, cup of tea in hand, leaning against the kitchen worksurface.

"Well what?" asked Laurie in a slightly confrontational manner.

She knew exactly what Rich was getting at. It had been a week now since he had effectively told Laurie that she had to leave work, and, knowing Rich as she did, she knew he would be feeling very frustrated by her apparent reluctance.

Part of Laurie understood where Rich was coming from. All he wanted was a quiet family life. He had been brought up in a very traditional family, his mum, Mavis, having been a housewife all her life. Even now, she didn't work! And she seemed perfectly content with her lot too...she actually often stated that she didn't have enough hours in the day, there was always so much to do! In fact, she had confided one day that on some occasions she had to neglect herself as she was so busy!

Laurie had always been bewildered by this comment. What did she mean? Everytime Laurie saw her, she was pristine, hair always immaculate, make-up on etc...clearly there were days when this wasn't so...why? Just because the windows needed yet another clean! Laurie didn't get it, not at all. Her mother-in-law had no friends, dedicating all her time to her perfect family home, seeming to have no needs of her own.

Well...that may have been *her* way...but it certainly wasn't Laurie's! Laurie had always been very aware of their differences, knowing full well that Mavis disapproved wholeheartedly of Laurie's decision to work. "If you choose to have children, then you should choose to look after them too, not palm them off," had been her mantra following Sarah's birth.

This statement continually amused Laurie. Her beloved son had chosen to have children too, so why didn't he choose to stay at home with them? Oh yes, of course, she thought sarcastically, don't be silly...Rich was a MAN. Mavis's son was allowed his own life as well as a family, it was just Laurie who had to sacrifice hers!

So, Laurie understood why Rich thought as he did; he knew no different and, to be fair to him, had never previously been challenged about his deep seated beliefs.

However, whilst Laurie could appreciate where Rich was coming from, it still didn't make it right. This was the 90's not the 50's for God's sake and Laurie had finally had enough. She was developing a back-bone, she thought...Finally! All those years of keeping everyone else happy, believing she could just go along with things, finally, her wishes and needs were coming to the fore.

Maybe this is what happened as you hit your thirties, she pondered. A realisation that life was not a dress rehearsal. This was it! This was Laurie's life and if she didn't like it, then it was up to her to change it.

Piling a load of clothes into the washing machine, cramming as much in as she possibly could, she turned it on. Taking a deep breath she turned to face her husband. "Well, what?" she demanded again.

"You know what," Rich answered in a very slow, deliberate way. "Your work," he spat out, with a nasty sneer. "I assume you've given in your notice but decided not to tell me," he continued pompously.

"Are you for real Rich...Really?...Come on, have you listened to yourself? Who the fuck do you think you are?" Laurie was angry now, very angry. She was aware that losing her temper was not the best way to handle him, she generally placated him, pleaded with him, pandered to his feelings. However, not this time. Why should she? He never pandered to her feelings did he? In fact he seemed totally oblivious to any feelings she may have. He must surely realise what a big decision this would be for her. Couldn't he see how much she enjoyed her work? He also knew how low she had got when not working. Did he really care so little for her? It seemed that way and Laurie was feeling deeply hurt. It hurt her sufficiently to really lash out at him. "Well, come on?" she urged. "Answer me! Who the FUCK do you think you are?" she screamed. "Oh...my keeper?...my boss?...No...no, just my husband, that's all. My PARTNER actually Rich! Yes, my partner. That means my EQUAL the last time I checked!"

Laurie had totally lost it with him. She had gone further than she ever had dared before and was now shouting at him hysterically. It had gone way too far as far as Rich was concerned. He slammed his half full cup of tea down on the work surface, Laurie watching, fascinated, as it smashed into hundreds of little pieces, tea spilling all down the front of their kitchen cupboards and making a large puddle on the floor.

"Oh, you can throw your tea can you? Very clever," screamed Laurie, striding over to her own drink. Grabbing the cup with both hands, she hurled it against the wall. "Well... guess what...so can I, Rich, so can I," she added for good measure. She picked up her car keys from the side as Rich gawped at her, too astonished to react. "And whilst we're at it, I can also drive off just like you do! Enjoy the kids Rich. See you later."

Grabbing her coat and handbag, she ran to her car, placing her keys in the ignition and driving off at speed.

Tears streaming down her face, Laurie drove; she had no idea where she was going, nor did she care right now. She drove out of town and onto the M5, heading north. She needed to get away to think. Seeing the sign for

Bromsgrove, Laurie exited and found herself driving towards Frankie's.

Pulling up outside, Laurie sat for a couple of minutes trying to pull herself together. Her anger had dissipated now, her tears had dried and she was feeling quite empty. Should she go into Frankie's? Would it help her or would she be better just going right back home?

Rich would be frantic probably. She had never driven off like this before, (that had always been Rich's trick), and she knew he would be worried. Or would he? She was not really sure of anything anymore. Things seemed to be changing. Rich was getting colder towards her and she couldn't seem to reach him like she used to. His rigid stance about work was becoming a serious issue, driving a massive wedge between them. Unbuckling her seat belt and sighing deeply, she exited her car and walked along the path towards Frankie's front door.

She knocked gently, Laurie wondering whether Frankie would even be in. It *was* a Saturday morning, she may be out shopping for all Laurie knew.

Laurie realised how little she knew about Frankie and felt slightly guilty. Theirs was a relationship very much erring towards Laurie's needs, she thought. Frankie was always asking after Laurie's weekend, what she had done etc. Laurie rarely asked after Frankie. She resolved to be a better friend going forward. She knocked again, louder this time. Yes, she was going to make more of an effort...ask Frankie about *her* life more often. She acknowledged that she didn't tend to because Frankie always seemed totally 'together', not seeming to need anyone else to be honest- but that was no excuse, she told herself firmly.

"Laurie!" exclaimed Frankie in surprise as she opened the door. Seeing Laurie's blotched face, Frankie pulled her into a firm embrace. "Oh goodness, Laurie, whatever's the matter? Come in, come and sit down. Let me make you a cup of tea."

Sitting Laurie down on her settee, Frankie rushed out into the kitchen to switch on the kettle, giving Laurie a couple of minutes to reflect.

Oh God, why had she come here? This was going to make everything too real; she was going to have to explain why she was so upset, bringing all her shit out into the open, something Laurie was always reluctant to do. "Airing your dirty linen in public" was her mum's regular saying and was something her mum would *never* do.

Laurie's parents lived in Turkey, having taken the decision to give up work, sell their house in the UK and buy a plot of land there three years ago. At the time Laurie had been distraught.

She had been hoping that they might have stayed close, give her a helping hand with her girls, but clearly not. She couldn't blame them really. They were in their late fifties now and a couple of health scares had made them realise how precious the rest of their time was. They seemed truly happy there too, Laurie having managed to visit them for a week on her last maternity leave and she was genuinely pleased to see how happy and healthy they both looked.

It had obviously been the right decision for them, but still...she really missed them, her mum in particular, especially at times like this, she thought miserably.

"Here you go," said Frankie softly as she passed the mug of tea over. "I've put two sugars in it. I know you don't normally have any but you need it, I think. Now is not the time to be looking after your figure!" she admonished, sitting down beside her. "I'd offer you a biscuit too, but I suspect that would be going too far!" she joked.

Laurie bit her lip, smiling wanly. "You know, Frankie, today I don't really care. I *will* have a biscuit if you don't mind – in fact, Fuck it, bring in the whole packet!"

"Wow! Things *must* be bad," laughed Frankie, getting up to fetch them.

Bringing them in and handing them over, she looked at Laurie quizzically. "Come on," she urged. "Tell me all about it, you'll feel a whole lot better getting it off your chest," she added, dunking a chocolate biscuit into her scalding tea.

And Frankie was right.

For an hour Laurie talked and Frankie listened. She didn't hold back and Frankie learned all about Laurie's difficulties when she had been a 'stay at home' mum. She explained how she loved the girls but equally, wanted a life of her own too.

She also explained where Rich was coming from, trying to be fair and not too critical. She finished with the row they had this morning.

"Oh dear Laurie, I really don't know what to say. I can certainly understand your predicament. I mean, I only really know you from work but you seem to love it there and you're very good too – an absolute natural with the customers. To be honest with you, I often feel quite jealous of you, listening to how well you interact. I can see you struggle sometimes, what with juggling all the family stuff an' all, but I hadn't realised it was this bad! Not being funny Laurie, but Rich sounds like a right dick, like someone from the dark ages!" remarked Frankie indignantly.

Laurie smiled. "He's not that bad really, it's just his way, it's actually what he believes and he can't understand why I am not just fitting in. He has been brought up to be the provider and..."

"Don't, don't, don't, *please*" interrupted Frankie, putting her hands up to stop Laurie continuing. "Don't try and justify his behaviour. Listen...you are not his chattel, you are a person in your own right. Never forget that. You have your own needs too and it's about time you made sure they were met. I'm being serious," she added, seeing Laurie's bemused expression. "If you're not careful he will gradually beat you down. You have talent Laurie, you have potential to go far at work if you want to. Don't...please don't just give in to him. My mum did that, you know. I saw it for myself when I was a teenager. She was a brilliant seamstress and used to have all her friends and neighbours paying her to make them dresses. She used to love it, you should have heard all the laughter that went on every evening, material strewn all over the living room carpet! But dad complained, he said he wanted his living room back. I remember him saying it so often that eventually she relented. She stopped sewing altogether after that and, do you know, it was as though all her lights had gone out, she never seemed to sparkle again. Dad had effectively beaten her down...not physically no, but mentally? Absolutely! Anyway, sorry Laurie, I'm going on too much, I just get so mad when I see this happening, I really do!"

Frankie picked up her tea, taking a big slug and sat back in her chair, grimacing a little as her tea had gone cold.

Having Frankie divulge as much as she had, so freely, shocked Laurie and she could see how upset she was. "I'm sorry Frankie, that must have been horrible for you to witness," she said, taking her hand.

"Yes, it was. Anyway that's all in the past now. This is about you, not me! So...the question is, what are you going to do?"

Leaning back into the settee, Laurie put her hands over her face. "I don't know, Frankie, I REALLY DO NOT KNOW. But I know this much...I have so much to do this weekend...God, I've only just *started* the washing, I have three more loads to do yet, plus all the ironing. Food shopping too! I've no idea what we're having for tea and God knows what Rich will have fed them for dinner!"

Laurie stood up decisively, placing her empty mug on the coffee table. "I've got to go. I'm really sorry for bothering you, you don't need me moaning to you at the weekend as well as during the week!" she added, attempting a smile.

"You're welcome here anytime, Laurie, you know that. Just take care driving home will you? And promise me you won't just roll over and give in," implored Frankie, standing up and taking Laurie into her arms again.

"Promise," whispered Laurie, fighting back a fresh deluge of tears. "And thank you Frankie, you're a real good friend to me, I don't deserve you. And don't worry, I'll be fine...right as rain by Monday," she added, attempting to reassure herself as much as her friend.

Driving home, Laurie reflected on what Frankie had just said. Whilst she felt that Frankie was being a little melodramatic, comparing Laurie to her mum, Laurie could also see she had a point, which helped strengthen her resolve.

She was going to go home and attempt to talk to Rich again, calmly this time! She was not going to leave work, definitely not. So, they would simply have to make it work! And it could, of course it could, there was always a way, she thought. Yes, always a way. They just had to find it!

Chapter 6

Lunchtime at the park, midweek, seemed to have become a given now, Laurie always having lunch at twelve and Mike catching up with her around twelve fifteen. Laurie still invited Frankie and wouldn't dream of stopping doing so, and, if Frankie came, then Mike would probably just stroll by, she thought. Anyway, nothing was going on, she told herself, defensively, so why shouldn't she be friends with him?

Yes, indeed, who was she kidding? She fancied him to bits and if she was being really honest with herself, Mike was all she could think about these days.

Wednesdays were the only day of the week that Laurie felt free, just to be herself, away from the demands of family and work. It actually took her back to how she used to feel in her teenage years. She did indeed feel like a teenager again when she was with him. He was very attentive, caring and so funny. Always funny and oh...it was so nice to smile again. With Mike, life seemed full of possibilities, adventure...Love.

Yes...and that was the problem!

She realised she had fallen for him in a big way. She knew it and didn't know how to stop it. In fact, she didn't want it to stop, she couldn't imagine going back to life pre Mike. How strange that was; she had only met Mike on Cara's birthday, little less than a month ago.

Shit...shit...shit. She was getting in way too deep!

And what of Mike's feelings? Truth be told, she had no idea. He always seemed happy when he was with her, he nattered on about anything and everything really, but he had not exactly given much away. She knew he was divorced and had no kids. Where he lived, she had no idea, how long divorced, any brothers or sisters?...No, she didn't know. In many ways they seemed to have skipped all the banal stuff, moving very swiftly into a very comfortable way with each other. Laurie felt she knew all she needed to know about him. The main thing being, they just 'clicked'.

She recalled reading books as a teenager about the 'meeting of souls' and she used to scoff, believing it to be utter rubbish. Her pragmatic self told her it was a ridiculous theory. How, in a world of six billion people, could there be just ONE person who was your soulmate? Romantic drivel, she used to think. As long as you got on with someone sufficiently, liked roughly the same things and felt a special connection to that person, then that was sufficient wasn't it?

Well, maybe before, yes. Not now though. Oh no, now she knew the difference. Mike was her soulmate. She would do anything for him, she knew that already. She LOVED him, she realised.

This was REAL love...And it frightened Laurie to death!

Realising the seriousness of the situation, Laurie took a mental step back, trying to analyse her feelings as she always had a tendency to do.

She was hormonal, her period due any day now and she had started suffering quite badly with PMT over the last six months or so. Sometimes she felt like two people – the sensible, pragmatic one three weeks of the month, and then this wilder, more sensitive creature for a week. They were totally different too, seemingly wanting, even needing, opposite things from life. She was therefore very aware that this was a bad week for her and her feelings may be completely different in a week's time.

Maybe she was over-egging the pudding?

She decided that she would simply wait it out, see how she felt in a couple of weeks. She would probably laugh at herself then for how dramatic she was being.

Yes...that's what she would do. Enjoy her lunchtime, NOT analyse, just give it time. Having decided, she immediately felt so much better.

Home life had been 'interesting' since their argument. She smiled as she thought back to their fight.

Laurie had shocked herself in the way she had reacted to Rich that day.

Ever since they had got together, over eight years ago, Rich had always had the upper hand. He was three years older, which, in itself had naturally given him the upper hand at the beginning of their relationship and then, Rich's coldness and temper had ensured it had remained that way. It was always Rich who shouted...always Rich who gave out the ultimatums. Always Laurie who would back down. Laurie, who would sidle up to Rich, put her arms around him, nuzzle into his neck and whisper "sorry" into his ear.

She hated conflict of any sort which is exactly why he always had the upper hand, she supposed, because Rich didn't seem to be adversely affected by conflict at all.

It was probably why he did so well at work, she thought cynically.

He was a solicitor and already talking about being made a partner next year. Whenever he used to talk about work, Laurie used to cringe. His arrogance was unbelievable as far as she was concerned and Laurie disliked how he used to speak about his work colleagues in such a derogatory manner. He certainly didn't view them as friends! It was as though they were always in battle with each other, one big competition seemingly. Everything he did or said, there had to be a hidden agenda. He attended work events, just as Laurie did, but not to enjoy himself, oh no...he would sidle up to his boss, making casual conversation before dropping hints regarding his career. God, Laurie used to get so embarrassed whenever she heard him. It was certainly a different world to hers...she went to a work's event simply to enjoy herself, have a laugh with her colleagues, a great chance to catch up with all the gossip!

So...in all their years together, not once had Laurie done anything like throw a cup of tea against the wall. She had shocked HERSELF that day, let alone Rich!

She recalled Rich's face when she had returned home from Frankie's.

Gone was the pompous look from earlier. He had actually looked a little lost, Laurie reflected. Perplexed almost, at this turn-around from his wife. Crikey, he had even cleared up the mess in the kitchen. Laurie had fully expected to find the kitchen in the same state she had left it!

Even the girls had been fed and watered!

Heaving a sigh of relief, Laurie had walked over to Rich and put her arms around him, holding him tightly for a long time. "We *do* need to talk Rich," she had whispered softly into his ear.

"I know," he had whispered back, his voice breaking slightly with emotion.

And talk they had! Laurie had put the girls to bed by seven o'clock and they had then talked late into the night. It was probably the most honest conversation they had ever had. Rich had opened up fully. He had actually apologised!...That was a first! His stance was still the same, Laurie expecting nothing different. In Rich's *ideal* world, Laurie would be a 'stay at home' mum and would love it just like his own mother had. He acknowledged, however, that whilst Laurie *could* leave work and stay at home, she would never love it, and therein lay their problem.

Laurie took her time, explaining all this to him as clearly as she could and, for once, he listened.

She could see that she was actually getting through to him a little.

It was finally dawning on Rich that Laurie was not the woman he thought he had married, and whilst he acknowledged her feelings at long last, she could see he felt deeply saddened as he witnessed his idyllic family life coming crashing down around him.

So...he had relented...eventually, and Laurie, always looking for compromises, suggested a six month trial.

Laurie would continue to work full time but she would get some more help in, in the way of a cleaner twice a week. Rich had always been against cleaners. "Not having anyone messing with my personal belongings!" would always have been his sentiment. And his *mum*...well, she would be absolutely outraged when she found out. Again, Laurie found herself smiling at that thought. She had never failed to disappoint her mother in law so far, so why start now!

Lesley, the cleaner, she had found through Lizzie, and she had started last week. And OMG...what a difference. Tuesday and Friday it was...and it was lovely, such a treat!

On those days Laurie would come through the front door with a huge smile on her face. All was neat, ordered and smelled fresh. She was able to get straight on with tea, rather than having a mad half hour tidy up.

No dirty nappies, babygros, half drunk bottles, dirty breakfast bowls to clear away. No beds to make either! It was bliss, definitely worth the twenty pounds Laurie was paying.

She had also agreed that Rich's life would stay as it was, she wouldn't pester him to do anything more. All she asked is that he continue to take the girls out on Saturday mornings, for an hour, no more, just so that Laurie could get on with other chores still needing to be done. Although, Laurie thought smugly, having agreed with Lesley that she would do an hour's ironing every week too, Laurie's 'to do' list was an awful lot smaller.

She had even grabbed half an hour's peace and quiet with a cup of coffee last Saturday morning...an unheard of event. Not that she mentioned that to Rich, when he returned from the park looking slightly worse for wear! Even the park wasn't as calming as it used to be. Trying to keep an eye on a five and a three year old, running off in different directions, whilst pushing Cara on a baby swing was not exactly a relaxing pastime!

It used to be, thought Laurie fondly, when there were just the two of them. Laurie and Rich had spent many a pleasant hour, sat watching them, smiling indulgently as they played in the sandpit.

"Hello again," smiled Mike as he sat down beside her. How are things?" he asked, looking pointedly at her.

"Not so bad," answered Laurie, looking down at her feet.

"No...I mean, how are things REALLY? You seemed down last week and I don't like to pry but to be honest with you, I've been quite concerned. Something's up I know?"

Laurie hadn't really spoken to Mike about Rich and the problems they were having. She had obviously mentioned him from time to time, but only in passing. She had talked endlessly, last week, about her girls, so much so, she wouldn't have been surprised had he not turned up today!

Looking over at Mike, his face full of care and concern, she was so, so tempted to tell him about the argument they had had over her working.

She felt he would really care and she could do with someone else to talk to, other than Frankie.

But she mustn't. With such a massive dose of PMT, nothing she said would come out right and when...or if...she talked to Mike about Rich, it needed to be thought through, a balance given.

She didn't want him to get the wrong impression of Rich.

No. Far better to choose her timing.

So, she simply smiled up at him, "No, no, really Mike, I'm absolutely fine, honestly," thinking how lovely it was that he had been so concerned about her.

Her unhappiness last week had clearly been obvious and as Laurie had not alluded to anything in particular, he was obviously quite perceptive, having seen right through her continual non-stop chatter about her girls. Yes...really perceptive...she would have to watch her step!

'Fine,' she mused. She knew exactly what that meant.

Fucked up, insecure, neurotic and emotional!

And that was about right, that's exactly how she felt. She needed to change the subject as she could feel her eyes watering and that was the last thing she wanted Mike to notice.

"Fine huh?" said Mike gently, giving her a sideways look with half a smile. "I know exactly what that means!" He placed the palm of his hand ever so gently onto her knee. "Anyway, are you going to the work's "do" next week?" he enquired, his hand having lingered on her knee for just a few seconds.

"Are you going?" she asked, throwing the question right back at him.

"Well, that depends."

"Oh, really?" she asked, quite innocently.

Mike turned to look at her, holding eye contact and placing his hand gently back onto her knee again. "That depends totally on whether you will be there or not."

Holding his gaze, Laurie's heart lurched into her mouth. Smiling delightedly, "Yes, I'll be there," she whispered.

At that, Mike stood up, stretched and then, so quickly, Laurie wondered whether she might have been mistaken, he leant over and gently kissed the top of her head. "Got to go," he said quietly, "More complaints than ever, you know," he joked, lightening the atmosphere a little.

Laurie looked up at him and gave him a small smile and wave as he walked away.

Well! Had he actually come on to her then? Oh yes, he definitely had! That kiss...such a small thing but WOW! Yes, Laurie decided, he really did like her, that was crystal clear.

A warmth enveloped her from head to toe... a wonderful, warm feeling that stayed with her for the rest of the day.

Chapter 7

Friday 20th August 1996.

It was Laurie's thirtieth birthday today. She had the day off from work, booked a while ago, as had Rich. Woken up in the morning at 6 am, her two eldest came bounding into their bedroom.

"Mummy, mummy," shouted Sarah excitedly. "Happy birthday mummy!" she exclaimed jumping onto her parents bed.

"Oh God, Sarah, do you have to be so loud?" moaned Rich from under his covers

Ignoring her daddy's comment, Sarah threw her arms around her mummy and gave her a big sloppy kiss. "Happy birthday mummy," she cried, even louder if anything.

"Oh, thank you sweetheart, that's a lovely kiss Sarah, you remembered too, well done!" encouraged Laurie.

"Happy birthday mummy," whispered Marie, who had eventually managed to climb up and make herself comfortable in between her parents. She also planted a sloppy kiss on her mummy's lips.

Groaning, Rich surfaced from underneath the covers. He peered at the clock. "Christ, girls, it's only 6am. What are you playing at?"

"Leave them Rich, they're excited, that's all," placated Laurie. "Anyway they're right, it IS my birthday, thirty at that!" she exclaimed. "So, do I get a cup of tea in bed then, girls? Do you think Daddy could manage that eh?" she asked the girls playfully.

Taking the hint, Rich climbed out of bed. He always wore pyjamas in bed, even in the height of summer. Laurie found this highly amusing and used to tease him about it.

"You never used to," she had queried one evening after Cara had been born.

"No, I didn't, did I," he had acknowledged, "but there's nothing more disturbing to a bloke than having your two daughters jumping into bed with you whilst you are doing your utmost to conceal a 'hard on', don't you think?" he had retorted dryly.

She had had to agree with him on that one and the pyjamas had been a regular item ever since.

The girls followed Rich downstairs, presumably to retrieve her presents. She stayed still a moment, listening out for Cara. No, she couldn't hear a thing. Excellent, she thought, snuggling back down under the duvet.

She was looking forward to her birthday. Her parents had flown over, staying with her nan in Leeds overnight, making their way over to Laurie's today. With Laurie living on the outskirts of Worcester, they had quite a journey really, especially as they had only flown in yesterday. It was a shame she couldn't put them up...she *had* offered but she supposed there was little attraction to a blow up bed on Sarah and Marie's bedroom floor. Still, they said they would be here by lunchtime.

Mavis and Jim were coming too, of course. Oh joy! She couldn't wait...NOT! No, that wasn't fair, Jim was alright, it was just Mavis who got on her nerves.

Still...her mum and dad would be there too, so that would soften things. At least there would be a buffer. Laurie's mum, Jackie, was well aware of Laurie's relationship with Mavis, having listened countless times to her daughters' moans and groans. Jackie always did her best to put Mavis's point of view across, attempting to get Laurie to see things from a mother's perspective, especially taking into account the fact that Rich was an only child. "She only wants what's best for you, you know," Jackie would say. "She's only interfering with the best of intentions, Laurie. Stop taking everything she says to heart, love. She's Rich's mum and as such, she's going to be around for a long time. Just let her words go over your head."

Laurie had lost count of the times she had heard this advice over the years and she knew her mum was right. However it wasn't always as simple as that was it? Laurie felt that the more she let things go over her head, the more Mavis would interfere! On the odd occasion Laurie HAD put her foot down over something, Mavis would give in, not only that, she would back off for a few weeks at a time too! However Laurie would then start to feel guilty, realising she had offended her and always threw the olive branch. And then the whole merry go round would start up again! Sighing, she brought herself back to the day before her. She was going to have a nice day, she decided. She just had to be positive and, if it all got too much, then she would just have to turn to the wine!

Thirty...God...yes, she probably needed the wine regardless. She couldn't get away from the fact that she was a fully fledged adult now! NO excuses! Thirty, she repeated again to herself, married, three children...crikey...and in love with someone else...she thought soberly. No, not today, she wouldn't think about it all today.

Mike had sent her a card, she had found it placed, half hidden, under her in-tray yesterday morning. How had he known it was her birthday? She hadn't said anything. Of course, he had access to all the staff records didn't he, and if that wasn't enough, he knew she was off on the Friday from the staff duty list plastered all over the office, not to mention the '30' banner Frankie had organised, strewn all over her computer! Still, the card had to have been bought and written so he had obviously gone out to do that and the banner had only gone up yesterday. The card had been lovely, nothing mushy or too jokey. A simple card, saying 'happy 30th.' All Mike had added was a comment about putting her feet up and telling her she deserved it, oh, yes, and two kisses! Yes, very nice and thoughtful. She hadn't

47

brought the card home with her though...oh no...that would have been asking for trouble and so she had left it in her in-tray last night, feeling incredibly guilty about it. Mmm, they weren't involved as such, but the fact that Laurie was hiding her friendship with Mike from Rich spoke volumes.

"Happy birthday to you," sang Sarah as she came walking in very slowly, holding lots of cards and presents under her arms. She looked so sweet! Oh, what Laurie would give to be Sarah's age again! Everything in life so simple. Kids were always able to focus on the 'here and now' and that was something that continually fascinated her. What a skill! We must all have possessed it at one time, she reflected, but somehow the skill diminishes over the years.

She was going to dig deep today, attempt to hone this lost skill, live only for the moment, nothing else. No OVER-THINKING! She took the cards and presents from Sarah, beaming at her as she did so, and began the task of reading every line of every card out loud...a process that always drove Rich crazy!

"Hello Laurie, oh it's so good to see you love. How are you? How do you feel reaching thirty? No...better not say I suppose," joked Jackie as she threw her ample arms around her daughter."Oh, it's SO lovely to see you again," she repeated enthusiastically.

"Hello mum, dad," smiled Laurie, hugging her mum tightly and throwing her dad a beaming smile.

"Hello love," answered Phil, "Do I get a turn?" he chuckled as he gently pushed his wife away from Laurie to grab a hug for himself.

Sitting outside at the top of their garden on their 'less than comfy but looked neat' chairs, Laurie chatted to them both. The sun was shining, the two girls happily playing on their swings, Cara sitting contentedly on her nan's lap. Rich was being kept very busy preparing their barbecue. Give him his due, he was going all out for Laurie today. "Tomorrow you won't have to lift a finger Laurie," he had promised.

"Really?" she had replied, laughing at his enthusiasm. She had popped into Tesco on her way home from work last night and bought all sorts of 'easy to do' barbecue food. Lots of nice pre-prepared salads together with sausage rolls, nuts, crisps and three puddings!...All stuff that literally needed to be unwrapped and placed out. All Rich had to do was to cook the sausages and burgers. Laurie had even bought him a twelve pack of 'Carling' to keep him happy.

"You look a little tired love," said her mum. Trust *you* mum, Laurie thought wryly. She couldn't hide anything from her, never had been able to and whilst, in many ways that felt very comforting, it could also be very wearing, especially when Laurie was *trying* to hide things from her.

"I am a bit, to be fair," acknowledged Laurie. There was a moment of awkward silence as her mum was clearly waiting for Laurie to elaborate and Laurie was deciding quite what to say. She never liked the idea of her parents worrying about her so she didn't want to say too much. "I'm just finding work a lot harder now that we have Cara too, you know?" she admitted.

"God, I can imagine," agreed Jackie, a little too eagerly for Laurie's liking. "To be honest love, I don't know how you do it!" She paused before she continued. "Do you really HAVE to work full time, Laurie?"

"No, no I don't...I don't really have to work at all...Rich would be perfectly content for me to stay at home full time like I used to, but God, mum, we've had this conversation before!" said Laurie, her voice rising in exasperation. "You know how I feel about work mum, I love it there!"

Laurie was now quite irritated, she felt as though she was going round and round in circles with all her family and this was her own side! "You obviously don't understand mum,

49

so there's really no point in saying much more about it is there?" she challenged.

Jackie stood up, rocking Cara in her arms as she had started to whine a little. "No Laurie, no I don't. I loved being at home with you so I really can't see why you don't. They were the best days of my life actually. But clearly you need more, I DO see that. It's just that I worry about you. I don't know how you work like you do and have any quality time with the girls, and they grow up so fast. Before you know it, they'll be flying the nest. You might regret your decision then you know. Once they're gone, they're gone, trust me..."

"Jackie," Phil interrupted. "Jackie, that's enough love. Laurie has heard all of this before. She has her own life to live...her own decisions to make and she's thirty now!" he joked in an attempt to lighten the atmosphere.

"I am, aren't I," Laurie acknowledged smiling over at her dad, grateful for his backing. Shrugging, she continued. "I'm okay really mum, don't worry, just a few bad weeks that's all and, guess what, I now have a cleaner so that should help!"

"Well, that's good. At least that's some help for you isn't it?" enthused Jackie. "I bet that went down well with you know who?" she chuckled.

Speaking of the devil, Jackie waved enthusiastically over at Mavis and Jim, who were walking up the garden path. "Hello, you two, it's SO nice to see you again Mavis, you too Jim. How are you both?" asked Jackie, passing Cara over to Mavis. "Here you go, Mave. Have a cuddle with Cara."

Laughing, Mavis took Cara from Jackie's arms. "Ooh, isn't she lovely?" cooed Mavis. "I do love them at this age, don't you Jackie? Aren't we lucky?"

"Aren't we just," agreed Jackie, organising seating for Jim. "Here you go, Jim, sit here," she bossed. "I'll go and get two dining chairs if that's okay Laurie? So Mave and I can sit down too."

"Yes, that's fine mum," smiled Laurie.

This was nice, she really appreciated how all the in-laws got on so well together, thought Laurie, taking a sip of the wine Rich had thoughtfully brought out to her only a few moments ago. "Sit back, relax and enjoy," he had whispered.

Yes, she would do exactly that, she thought, smiling to herself...and what bliss! A few hours whereby all was being done for her and grandparents to entertain the girls too! Wow...she was going to milk this for all it was worth!

Everyone had a wonderful day. The food was delicious, the weather couldn't have been better, warm enough without being blistering hot and Rich had been really attentive. Having so much attention, the girls had really enjoyed themselves. Watching Sarah, Laurie had had to smile. Sarah moved from one grandparent to another, depending on her need. A cuddle required and it was nanny or grandma...playing...certainly the granddads. She had even cottoned on to the type of play. Quiet play, cards, dominoes, snakes and ladders, she always collared Jim; boisterous play, then it was Phil she went to.

Wow...Go, Sarah, thought Laurie. Already at such an early age Sarah was learning who to go to for what, Laurie marvelled.

And so the day went on, Laurie feeling quite sad when her parents took their leave just after the girls' bedtime. They were flying back the following day which was a shame, but being the animal lovers they were, Turkey had proved to be an impossible place to live animal free. Every time they saw a stray on the roadside, they had not been able to resist getting involved. They had taken in four dogs and three cats so far, not to mention the countless animals they fed whenever they could. They never left home without a bag of dried cat and dog food in the car with them and a journey that supposedly took ten minutes invariably took them thirty, involving many impromptu stops along the way.

This curtailed their freedom somewhat, hence their very short stay.

Mavis and Jim went shortly after, leaving Rich and Laurie some 'quality time' which Laurie had to concede was very thoughtful of them.

"That was nice, wasn't it?" said Rich as he closed the front door after waving his parents goodbye.

"Yes, it was, I had a lovely time. Thank you Rich," she said, giving him a big hug.

"Well, you know me, always happy to oblige," he joked, with a twinkle in his eye.

Laurie laughed with him, knowing full well Rich was taking the mickey out of himself.

"I love you Laurie," he said, solemn all of a sudden. "I do, honestly," he reiterated. "I know I'm not always easy to live with and I don't tell you that often enough."

"You don't tell me what?" Laurie teased. "That you love me or that you're not easy to live with?"

Smiling, Rich reached for her and gave her a long, lingering kiss on her lips. "Both," he said quietly as he took her hand and led her upstairs to their bedroom. "And now...I'm going to show you exactly *how* much I love you," he whispered, taking Laurie's face in between his hands and looking into her eyes.

Having had at least a bottle and a half of wine, Laurie was well relaxed and immediately surrendered to his insistent kisses.

Their lovemaking had been very gentle, not their normal style at all. Strange, reflected Laurie as Rich fell asleep, snuggling into her, it's as though he knows, she thought. She shuddered and then told herself not to be so silly as she snuggled down herself, breathing in Rich's familiar musky smell and fell into a deep, relaxing sleep.

Chapter 8

"Which have you picked?" Frankie asked Laurie, studying the board on the wall.

"No. 2, 'Cara's Delight' obviously!" Laurie smiled, glancing over Frankie's shoulder. "I'd never forgive myself if that one won and I hadn't put money on it."

"Yes, of course, I hadn't made the connection. Oh, well that's me decided then, I'm going for it too."

They were at the 'dogs' on a work's 'do' and Laurie couldn't help feeling a frisson of excitement in the pit of her stomach. She hadn't seen Mike this past week, he having been on a course and she had found she was missing him dreadfully.

"Who are you looking out for?" asked Frankie, a playful twinkle in her eye.

"Nobody," replied Laurie defensively.

"Really? Come on Laurie, I'm not daft. He'll be here, don't you worry."

How did Frankie know? Were they talking at cross purposes? Not knowing quite how to continue the conversation, Laurie said nothing. But Frankie, as forthright as ever, was not to be put off. "Mike," Frankie stated simply. "He's carrying a torch for you my girl, you'd better watch out and it seems so are you for him if that blush on your face is anything to go by?" she exclaimed.

Puzzled as to how Frankie had come to this conclusion and not wanting to confirm her feelings for Mike, she simply asked Frankie what on earth possessed her to think Mike was carrying a torch for her, as Frankie put it.

"Well, it's not rocket science," Frankie answered sarcastically. "I first saw you at the park the other week and decided not to come over...I couldn't tell you why really...call it instinct...but I certainly didn't want to play 'gooseberry' all lunchtime! Then Mike wouldn't stop pestering me as to why you had booked the Friday off either. So, taking into account your issues at home, I've rather put two and two together and I don't think I'm wrong either, judging by the look on your face," she announced proudly.

Shaking her head, Laurie gave in. "Aye, you're not that far off really," although she was very eager to point out that nothing had actually happened.

"So far!" warned Frankie .

"I know, I know, you don't have to warn me, I'm well aware. I do really like him though," she admitted. "If I'm being honest, it's more than that too, but that doesn't mean I'm going to act on it though does it?"

"You be careful, you're playing with fire my girl," warned Frankie, a solemn look on her face.

"Yes, yes, okay, enough." Laurie was feeling quite irritable by this point. "Come on, let's put some money on this dog anyway, that's what we're here for." As they walked down the stairs out into the open air, Laurie willed herself to concentrate on the task in hand, looking at all of the bookies odds to see who had the best.

"YES!" shouted Frankie euphorically. "Brilliant," she added jumping up and down with glee.

"Crikey, we only put a pound on, I wouldn't get that excited!" laughed Laurie.

"I should've put more on," moaned Frankie. "Still...that's a fiver back isn't it?"

"Six, actually, you get your pound back too," commented a voice from behind them. Recognising Mike's voice, Laurie turned around, her face beaming.

"Hello, fancy seeing you here," she exclaimed jokingly.

Laughing, he turned his face towards Frankie too. "Well, seeing as you two are on a winning streak, I think I'll be sticking around. So, who's it to be in the next race then?" "God, I've no idea," answered Laurie, looking down at her booklet. "I haven't looked yet." Laurie began perusing all the names, Mike leaning over her shoulder. "Now, that's a good one," he said. "Moaning Minnie. That's perfect," he added, laughing. "I deal with them every day. Definitely a sign, don't you think?" "Absolutely," agreed Laurie. "Come on then, let's see the odds. Maybe I'll put more than a pound on this time!" Walking over together, Laurie realised that Frankie had slipped away and she hadn't noticed. Neither, it seemed, had Mike.

They had a fabulous evening, with two more of their chosen dogs coming first. Not 'Moaning Minnie' it had to be said and they both became very competitive with each other after that.

"Go on then, you choose the next one, you have more luck than me," urged Mike.

"Luck!" exclaimed Laurie indignantly. "You think it's just luck! Oh no...talent this is, Mike, pure talent. You stick with me and you'll never regret it," she laughed.

"Oh, I intend to, don't worry," he answered casually, putting an arm around her waist as he began studying the form for the next race.

They seemed to fit together so well, nothing was forced at all, she thought, smiling happily as she watched him go in search of a drink for them both.

Frankie came over to tell her she was off.

"Already?" Laurie asked in surprise.

"Yes," she answered. "I'm tired, big weekend on too, so see you Monday, yes? Be careful girl," she whispered in her ear as she gave Laurie a big hug. "People are beginning to talk, you know," she warned as she walked away.

This brought Laurie down to earth in a big way and when Mike passed her drink over with a huge grin all over his face, he suddenly looked serious. "What's up?" he asked. "Oh, nothing really Mike, just something Frankie said." "What?" asked Mike looking completely perplexed. "Oh, you know," answered Laurie quietly, not elaborating further.

"No, I don't actually Laurie. What on earth did Frankie say to you? We've been having such a great time, such a laugh and the next thing I know you look as though someone close to you has died!" Mike joked.

She smiled, he always made her smile. "Do you really want to know?" she challenged.

"Er, yes I do, otherwise I wouldn't have asked would I?" he remarked sarcastically.

"Do you know sarcasm is the lowest form of wit?" she quipped, laughing up at him. "Okay, if you really want to know, here goes, but you might not like it!" she warned. "Frankie came to tell me she was leaving, but she also warned me to be careful, her exacts words being "People are starting to talk".

Looking directly at Mike, she waited.

Mike smiled ruefully. "About what?"

"Us."

"Is there an us?" asked Mike quietly.

A full minute elapsed before Laurie answered. "Yes, Mike, yes, I think there is, don't you?"

Letting out a deep breath Mike beamed at her. "Really. Wow. Yes, absolutely there is, Laurie. You know, I think I'm falling for you."

"Me too," acknowledged Laurie. "Me too," she stated again and then, ominously, "And therein lies the problem!"

Chapter 9

Wednesday 1st September 1996.

"Laurie, have you got a minute?" asked Louise, her team leader, smiling over at her.

"Yes, of course," said Laurie easily, taking off her headset. "Let me just finish with this order and I'll be right with you, okay?"

"Yes, that's fine," Louise answered, already walking away.

What's this about? wondered Laurie. Louise didn't normally seek her out for anything more than her regular 'one to one' and she wasn't due another of those until next week. Could it be about Mike? she asked herself fearfully. Surely not! she thought a little indignantly.

It had been obvious, on Monday, that people HAD noticed and a few vibed comments had been thrown her way, but nothing outright at all. Women could be bitchy like that when they wanted to be and Laurie regretted playing into their hands. She liked to get on with people and hated to cause waves of any kind.

"I told you," Frankie had said simply, coming over and giving her shoulders a quick squeeze. Sandra, an older woman in her fifties, had been particularly unpleasant, alluding to the fact that mothers should be at home with their babies, not 'cavorting around the world with other men.' She had been talking about Princess Diana and seemed to completely miss the point that she wasn't with her children half the time anyway due to her divorce. But, whilst making the comment, she had also looked over nastily at Laurie.

"Ignore them love, you'll be yesterday's news soon enough," comforted Frankie wisely.

So, it was with a certain trepidation that Laurie walked over to Louise's desk. Seeing her walking over, Louise stood up and grabbed some keys from behind her, hanging on the wall. "Conference room 2 seems to be free," she said, smiling over at Laurie. "Shall we grab a coffee to go in with?"

"Okay," answered Laurie. "What do you take?"

"Coffee, black, no sugar."

Smiling wryly to herself Laurie went to fetch their drinks. She would, she thought, Black, No sugar... Bloody typical...It will be de-caff soon too, no doubt! Choosing white coffee with two sugars for herself, (she had managed to drop sugar from tea already but had not managed so far with her coffee) Laurie followed Louise into the room. Seated opposite Louise, a desk in between them, Laurie took in a deep breath in an attempt to steady her nerves.

Louise gave Laurie a big smile. "You look nervous," she said. "There's no need to be, it's good news. How do you fancy becoming a team leader?"

"What...seriously?"

Louise laughed "Yes, seriously Laurie. A position is becoming vacant, Tom's leaving. You know Tom I assume? It's a different team but that's a positive. It's easier to lead a team whereby people haven't become pally with you already."

Seeing Laurie's look of excitement, seemingly tinged with worry, Louise continued. "You'd be really good at it," she encouraged. And it would mean more pay too!"

"Yes, yes, I realise that," said Laurie and then joked. "I mean more pay! Not that I'd be really good at it!" she laughed. "I'm not sure I *would* actually, you're always moaning that I spend too much time with the customers!"

"Yes, I know and that's EXACTLY why you would be so good," Louise smiled. "You have the customers' interests at heart and you are confident enough to bend the rules whenever you feel it's required. Plus you have bags of initiative and that's never a bad thing. You get on well with people too, you'd be brilliant Laurie, trust me."

"Okay," Laurie said slowly. "I probably need time to think about this Louise. I'm really flattered you've thought about me, I have a lot going on at home, though, three children too! I don't want to go for it unless I feel I can do it. I really wouldn't want to let you down."

"No, of course not. I tell you what, how about you think it over tonight and we can chat some more tomorrow?" stated Louise, standing up and walking over to the door.

"Yes, I will do and thanks again, you've gob-smacked me!" she added, laughing as she followed Louise out.

Looking up from her desk, Frankie raised her eyebrows. "Well?"

"She's only gone and offered me Tom's position!" she whispered, a beam spreading across her face.

"Really!" cried Frankie. "That's brilliant, hey, well done girl," she added enthusiastically.

That was what she loved about Frankie, she always had her back! It was a nice feeling, she thought, not something to be taken for granted, she told herself, picking up her next call. "Good morning, Kays catalogue, how can I help you?" she sang.

Lunchtime came all too soon and Laurie found herself on her normal seat at the park. The weather was still nice, a balmy summer's day with little breeze. She had no lunch with her, having fully intended to buy a sandwich from 'Gregg's' but hadn't as she didn't feel she could eat a thing.

Life was spiralling out of her control, she thought, as she drank in the sun's beautiful warmth. She veered from excitement to trepidation as she thought through all the recent events, Friday, in particular.

The weekend had been particularly harrowing for her and she had felt immense guilt that she had allowed things to go so far with Mike. Not in the physical sense, no, not really, but emotionally...absolutely.

They had now opened up to how each other was feeling, a long kiss on their way back to the carpark being the extent of any physical contact, but what worried Laurie more was that by acknowledging their true feelings, they had effectively opened up a 'hornet's nest' and, imagining thousands of hornets flying off in all different directions, she knew there was no way in the world all those little buggers would come flying back!

So... there WAS no way back...only forward.

What DID Laurie want? she asked herself. If she was being totally honest, it was Mike, every minute of every day for the rest of her life.

She smiled to herself. Yes, she could actually see a future for them and she knew they would be very happy together.

Friday evening had simply confirmed to Laurie what she already suspected. It felt as though Laurie was home when she was with Mike. She felt so happy, so safe, so ALIVE...and yes...so 'at home'. An odd description. Home is normally associated with the totally familiar but that's exactly how she felt with Mike, which was strange considering they still had a lot to learn about each other, not to mention the physical aspect of their relationship! Two kisses! That was the extent of it so far. And, whilst those kisses had felt wonderful, it didn't necessarily mean that they would gel physically did it? He may be crap in bed, she thought, smiling to herself to lighten her mood. She knew he wouldn't be, though. No, definitely not. And if Laurie allowed a full physical relationship to develop, who on earth knew where it would lead!

Arriving quietly, sitting beside her, Mike smiled uncertainly. An unusual smile, not his normal easy-going confident smile at all. Instead it was full of uncertainty and questions, thought Laurie.

"Hello," he said. "How are you?" he asked immediately.

"I'm okay," she answered carefully. For a few seconds Laurie entertained the idea that Mike might want to back off. Friday might have frightened him, she thought. This thought terrified her and she started feeling a little breathless panic, until he started to speak.

"Okay," he repeated. "Just *okay*," he joked. "Right, here goes then Laurie. You are clearly playing safe but I think we've gone past that don't you? Well, I have anyway. I'm more than okay, Laurie. I loved being with you on Friday and I was 'cock-a-hoop' all weekend! I had a fabulous time and I know you did too, however cool you want to be about it now," he said, turning towards her and taking her hands in his own.

An immense feeling of happiness and wellbeing flooded through Laurie's veins. She was amazed at how open and honest he was being, and Mike, seeing the reaction on Laurie's face, continued.

"Laurie, I've been married, as you know and I've had a couple of other serious relationships since but NOTHING has felt like this," he said emphatically. "I love you, I always will," he said, solemnly. "It's easy for me, I suppose, I'm single, no complications. You're not, I'm well aware."

Laurie sighed. "No, I'm not," she said, feeling particularly anguished. "How could we work Mike...really? How can I disentangle my life so much? I have three girls Mike...three girls!! That's massive, not to mention a husband!"

Holding Laurie's hands tightly, Mike replied. "I know you do and I love kids Laurie. I could tell you now, I would love your kids too. How could I not? They're a part of you," he continued, smiling. "If we want to make this work, then it can. Yes, okay, it will be shitty to begin with, but look longer term Laurie," he pleaded. "We can have the rest of our lives together, have more children if you wanted, no pressure though!" he then went on to say, seeing the look of horror in her eyes. Laughing, he back-tracked. "Sorry," holding his hands up. "I'm going too fast for you aren't I?" "Just a bit," she laughed. "You are serious though? You could take on three children that weren't yours?" "Absolutely. Without a doubt Laurie. In the blink of an eye," he joked. "I want you Laurie and I would take on your girls as if they were my own, have no doubt about that," he said seriously. Minutes elapsed. Mike continued to hold one of her hands as he turned away from her slightly and began to gaze at his feet. He was waiting, thought Laurie, waiting for her response.

So many thoughts were going through her head. On a practical level, this conversation seemed ridiculous. How could she just dismantle a life built over the last six years really? How could she take her three girls away from everything they knew, a life where they felt secure and take them from their daddy too? Have a new person entering their lives, what would happen practically? Who would live where? And that's before she started to think about the impact on Rich. He would not take it well, she knew that for a fact. "Shitty for a short while!" Mike had said. Laurie felt that to be the understatement of the century!

If Laurie had any sense at all, she would tell Mike they needed to finish this before it got started. Just go back to being colleagues at work. Mind you, if she became team leader that would be extremely difficult as she would have far more to do with Mike then, management having meetings with the team leaders all the time, seemingly.

Frankie always used to joke about it. "God, what on earth do you think they have to talk about?" she would invariably ask. "They've been in that room two hours already!" she would exclaim.

"God knows," Laurie would answer, shrugging her shoulders. Not being a particularly nosy person, she had little interest.

Realising her mind was wondering, Laurie shook her head, forcing herself back to the present. Yes, she thought, with sudden clarity, she SHOULD tell him it was over...absolutely...but she couldn't. There was no way on God's earth she could walk away from him now.

Brilliant!

She couldn't see a way to move on with him and she couldn't walk away either!

Fuck...what a mess! Placing her head in her hands she took a deep, calming breath. Seeing the worry etched on Mike's face, she attempted a watery smile. "I don't know what to say, Mike," she whispered. "As crazy as it sounds, I *so* want to be with you and I *know* you'd be good with the girls. That's mega important to me as you know. But HOW Mike?" Laurie felt immense anguish. "How is it possible? You don't know Rich, he will go crazy, he certainly won't make it easy for us and I don't know how I could do that to him, I really don't."

Mike could see how upset Laurie was getting and he took her in his arms as she began to cry.

"Hey, hey, shush," he whispered softly into her ear. "We'll just take it one day at a time shall we? Let's just see where it all goes Laurie. No need to make decisions today is there?"

He spoke as though he was speaking to a distraught child and Laurie felt comforted.

"Okay," she mumbled into his shoulder.

Mike kissed her, deeply, with a passion Laurie responded to in an instant and for a few moments nothing else seemed to matter at all.

Walking back together, Laurie told Mike about the job offer. He wasn't surprised and Laurie realised he was probably already aware. He was very positive about it and encouraged her to go for it. "You'd be great at it."

63

"I need to think about it, I'd love to say yes but it means working Saturdays too and that might be a step too far for Rich!"

Mike said nothing more. As they were walking into work though, he placed his left hand gently onto Laurie's lower back. "Can we see each other again, do you think, you know, more of a date?" he added smiling. "My backside can't take much more of those park benches!"

"Yes, Mike, I'd like that, I really would," she laughed. "We'll sort something out eh?" she promised, squeezing his hand slightly. "Meanwhile, how about tomorrow lunchtime again?"

Raising his eyebrows , a look of sheer delight on his face, Mike beamed. "Two days on the trot!" he exclaimed. "That's worth putting up with a numb bum for," he added, laughing.

She smiled. "Absolutely. See you tomorrow," she said quietly, moving away from him slightly just in case of prying eyes.

Chapter 10

That evening.

"NO. No fucking way Laurie," shouted Rich. "No fucking way. And I damn well bloody mean it!"

"Shhh...You'll wake the girls up," hissed Laurie.

"I don't give a flying fuck right now Laurie. Anyway, you seem unable to hear me unless I shout. "NO WAY," he shouted again. "You are NOT working Saturdays too. God, it's bad enough as it is," he continued. "I'm *sick* of all this," he exploded, slamming his fist into the kitchen door. "I'm sick and tired of it all, I don't want you working at all as you well know. Not even part time! I've agreed to full time but NOT Saturdays. No, they are sacrosanct. I'm not having the girls all of Saturday by myself. It's NOT happening," he said churlishly.

"First of all Rich, it's not every Saturday, its normally just one in every three and it's only till three, not five. I get a day off too, in lieu, so I'm not actually working any more hours." Laurie didn't know why she was saying this. It would make no difference to Rich would it? She got a day off in the week, a day when Rich was working so he wouldn't even notice, but he would certainly notice the Saturdays!

Lizzie, her childminder, was unable to have the girls at weekends so it would be down to Rich and she knew how difficult he would find it. He never had them on his own for more than a couple of hours at a time. It would do him some good though, she thought ruefully, help build up his relationship with them and show Rich how much work was involved in looking after them!

But this was not the way to persuade him, she needed to show him how he could benefit, and, to be quite honest, she didn't know how she could do that.

65

More money? Well, yes, there would be that, but that would not do anything for him, she knew that. More satisfaction for Laurie? A chance for her to build a career of her own? Well, she thought, getting a little annoyed, that *should* be a way to talk Rich around. If he loved her, he would want what she wanted, he would be happy she was fulfilling her dreams, wouldn't he? But no...oh no...here we go again. Rich's way or the highway! He had no concern for Laurie, he was selfish, she thought angrily. He could only see it from HIS perspective, how HE would be affected, the extra work HE would have to do.

"You've obviously decided already though," she said quietly, giving up.

"Yes I have. You're NOT taking it," he shouted again. "Saturdays...till three!" he said incredulously. "You must be fucking joking!" He then stormed out of the kitchen into their living room.

Laurie took herself straight off to bed. She lay stretched out on top of the bed sheets...still being very muggy...and tried to think clearly, but found it impossible. She was furious with him and for once she found herself unwilling to try to see things from his point of view. She didn't care right at this moment. Tomorrow, she was going to say yes to the role and to hell with him! Decided, she turned onto her stomach, her head facing the wall.

AND she would see Mike too...arrange a night out with him. She had had enough, she realised as tears began to trickle onto her pillow.

Chapter 11

Thursday 2nd September 1996.

"Yes," she agreed readily. Laurie and Mike had met as normal in the park and Mike had immediately asked Laurie to meet him for the day on Saturday. He had proposed a day out in Stratford, some lunch somewhere, a stroll around the town. Laurie didn't know how on earth she would get away but she knew she would. She'd work something out, she decided, somehow!

"Really?" he said, excitedly. "Are you sure? How about Rich? I don't want to cause any trouble for you," he added, concern written all over his face.

Laurie had to laugh at this remark. "You don't want to cause any trouble," she repeated, mocking him. "You've done that already!" she teased. "And yes Mike, I am absolutely sure. I can't wait," she said seriously.

"No, me either," he answered softly.

The rest of their lunchtime sped past, talking of anything and everything but nothing of any importance. Mike seemed to be acutely aware of Laurie's fragile state and he spent an hour trying to cheer her up, regaling her with many tales from his childhood.

He was one of those people that couldn't really say where they were from, his parents moving around every few years. He had been born in Scotland, so in theory he was Scottish but as his parents had moved there for work only and moved on again when he was only one, he couldn't really say he was Scottish, he would have felt a fraud, he mused. A series of moves then took place every two or three years and Laurie had to laugh when he took an age trying to count how many houses he had lived in during his life. "Eight," he said, counting on his fingers. "Eight, until I went to Uni and then 1,2,3,4,5,6...six 'till now, so fourteen altogether," he said, laughing. His Mum and Dad were teachers, he went on to explain. "They could work anywhere as a result, and so they did! House prices dictated at first, my mum once said that when they left college, they looked at all the cheapest areas to live and looked for jobs accordingly. That's how we ended up where we did. Mablethorpe was their first house, I believe, before I was born though, Scotland next...Kirkcaldy," he stated. "It's Just outside Edinburgh. Couldn't take you there even if I wanted to, I wouldn't have a clue, can't remember it at all."

He then proceeded to list the other towns, cities and villages he had lived in over the years.

"How did you get on moving schools all the while?" she asked, feeling a little sorry for him always being the new boy at school.

"Fine," he said, "didn't know any different did I? I never questioned it, neither did my brothers, it was normal for us. It's helped me in many ways I think. As lovely as a place or my home might be, I could move again tomorrow if need be, it wouldn't bother me. Saying that, though, I do like it here," he reflected. "Worcester's lovely and I really like the surrounding countryside too."

Sitting in the warmth, one of her hands touching his slightly, Laurie felt an immense peace flood over her. Listening to Mike had taken Laurie away from all her troubles for a while and had helped her immensely.

Her anger towards Rich had not receded and she hadn't spoken a word to him this morning. She had barely acknowledged his shout of "bye" as he left for work. Her decision to see Mike on Saturday had been partially as a result of Rich's attitude last night, she thought. She had had enough of pandering to Rich's needs. She wanted her needs fulfilled for a change and Mike was certainly doing that!

She felt fearful about Saturday. She really hadn't a clue how she was going to get away for the day. It was impossible! How was she going to pull it off?

Another work's 'do'? No, that would never wash, not with just a few day's notice. Anything like that would have been planned weeks in advance.

A day shopping? Normally they all went shopping together, Laurie never took off by herself. Shopping was something both Rich and Laurie enjoyed and they often made a day out of it, well, prior to Cara being born anyway! Laurie had always loved clothes shopping and Rich took a pride in his appearance too so they had always enjoyed those days out together. Worcester was such a lovely place to shop as well, plenty of small boutique shops around as well as all the bigger department stores to wile away their time in.

A sudden day out shopping in Stratford by herself? Mmm, wouldn't really add up would it? Sighing, she wondered what other excuse she could come up with. Her friends had all slipped by the wayside over the years, some having gone to Uni and never returned home, others moving away over time. One or two were still in town but she didn't really see them. Yes, she would have a quick catch-up if ever she bumped into them, but nothing more.

Family life and work took all her time now. The friends they did see had evolved from couples they both knew who had children of a similar age to their own. So...to suddenly announce a day out with a friend wouldn't work either.

Frankie?...That was a possibility...Rich heard about Frankie all the time but they had not really moved their friendship on outside of work.

But Frankie WAS a possibility. The only problem being, she would have to tell her what she was planning and she didn't think Frankie would like that. Laurie didn't either, she didn't want Frankie to feel she was being used and it wasn't fair of Laurie to ask her. She *could* just tell Rich she was going out with Frankie, they never socialised together, so he would be none the wiser.

As that was the best she could come up with, then it may have to do but she knew Rich would find it all very odd! In all their years together Laurie had never taken off for the day without Rich and certainly not without the girls in tow!

"Time to get back to the grind," Mike groaned.

They walked back into work together again, Laurie acknowledging to herself that they were being less and less careful about being seen together. Let them talk, she thought.

Chapter 12

Same day.

"Yes, Louise, I'd love Tom's job."

"Really?...Right, that's excellent then. Here you go," she said, taking an application form out of her top drawer. "You'll have to apply obviously but, don't worry, it's only a formality," she whispered, seeing Laurie's look of concern. "Fill it in as soon as you can and give it back to me, next Friday latest, okay?"

In Laurie's excitement, she hadn't given a thought to the whole process and felt a little deflated. "Stupid idiot," she chided herself walking back to her desk. Of course she would have to go through a process, it was obvious.

Looking at the application form, she groaned. She didn't mind the process as such, it was just the *detail* these forms went into! She felt put off just looking at it! And when on earth would she have the time to complete it? Despondently she folded it carefully and placed it in her handbag, thankful she had picked one of her bigger bags for work this morning.

"Is that what I think it is?" asked Frankie.

"Yep...a bloody application form," muttered Laurie. "God knows when I'll have the time to fill it in."

"You've got the job already by the sounds of it, don't let a form throw you. Just get on with it," smiled Frankie.

She was right, of course. She would find an hour sometime in the next week, she decided emphatically. And actually, if she couldn't find an hour, then how on earth did she think she could take on a more responsible job? she thought, picking up her headset again and getting lost in her customers.

71

Chapter 13

Friday 3rd September 1996.

As it transpired there had been no need to use Frankie as an excuse.

Friday evening had been awful, Rich having spotted Laurie's application form on the kitchen table. He had picked it up and thrust it in her face. "What's this?" he demanded. "I've told you. You're not going for it, so you don't need a fucking application form do you?" he had bellowed, tearing the form into little pieces, his spittle flying in all directions.

Cara had just been put into her cot but Sarah and Marie were still up, having their bedtime milk and biscuits, sitting at the kitchen table. They both stared wide eyed at their Daddy, Sarah's lower lip beginning to tremble.

Laurie was absolutely furious. "Shut up Rich," she hissed in his face. "You're scaring the girls," she whispered angrily.

"No, Laurie. YOU'RE upsetting the girls," he muttered in a dangerously quiet voice. "It's You," he spat, jabbing his fingers into her chest. Throwing the shreds of her application form into her face, he stormed upstairs.

Picking up the pieces from the kitchen floor, Laurie sighed and she could feel her tears dangerously close to falling. It's only a form, she comforted herself. She would pick up another on Monday, she decided, a determined stubborn streak flooding through her bones. She wouldn't be put off that easily!

Shutting the lid on their kitchen bin, she turned to the girls. "Come on girls, drink up," she urged, giving them both a big bright smile in an attempt to reassure them all was well.

"Mummy, Daddy fighting," whispered Sarah, tears starting to fall down her cheeks.

"Hey, sweetheart, come here," comforted Laurie, walking over to where Sarah was seated. She bent down so she could look into Sarah's face, wiping her tears away with her thumb. "It's alright. Really Darling, come here," she said again as she hauled Sarah out of her chair and into her arms.

Hugging her tightly, Laurie continued. "Mummy's and Daddy's do argue sometimes. It's perfectly okay, Look at how you argue with Lisa at school and you still like her don't you? She's still your best friend isn't she?" asked Laurie.

"Mmm, I Suppose," Sarah mumbled, clearly unconvinced.

"Well then. Daddy's still my best friend too," she said automatically.

That hit Laurie hard. It was something she had always said. "He's not only my husband but my best friend too." That wasn't true anymore, she realised. Not at all. Oh God, she thought. How have we come to this? How had her marriage crumbled so quickly? She couldn't pinpoint the exact day all had begun to go downhill but she knew it was, and at a race of knots too!

AND she was playing with fire, as Frankie so eloquently put it. God, she was feeling so confused as well as extraordinarily guilty.

"Come on you two, let's get you into bed eh?"

Taking Marie's chubby hand as well, she struggled upstairs. Sarah was getting too heavy for this, she thought, but on the basis Sarah was holding onto Laurie as though her life depended on it, Laurie was not about to make her walk. Marie was also looking down in the dumps so Laurie suggested they both sleep together in Sarah's bed. Marie loved to do that and she would often come in to wake them in a morning to find them both cuddled up together.

Sitting on Sarah's bed, one child each side of her, Laurie read to them until she could see their eyes dropping with tiredness. Only then did she come away, leaving them both curled together, Marie clutching tightly to her slightly grubby silky blanket and Sarah's arms wrapped around both Marie and her favourite pink teddy.

Closing the door gently, Laurie sat on the top of the stairs. Rich was clearly in their bedroom. She couldn't hear anything but didn't believe he would be asleep...it was only 8 o'clock for goodness sake.

So now, what did she do? She could go into him but she felt emotionally exhausted already. He had probably calmed down by now, she reflected. That's what he did. He blew up very quickly but then, normally, he came down as quickly too.

Laurie was much slower to react therefore didn't lose her temper often, but she took longer to get over things and could find herself stewing for days over an argument. She liked to talk things through in a calm manner, coming up with a solution when there were issues to be resolved but that was not Rich's way at all. He shouted, said his piece, seemingly expecting her to just fall in with his commands.

This had been how their relationship had *always* been though, so Laurie understood why Rich was feeling so angry right now.

Laurie was beginning to voice her own needs and their marriage felt a lot more fragile. Cracks were beginning to appear in their relationship and Laurie felt at a complete loss as to how to repair them, not withstanding the whole mess with Mike!

Laurie could see these cracks vividly but it was as though Rich was completely unaware. He was being as dogmatic as ever! The day Laurie had gone over to Frankie's *had* given him a 'wake up' call and they had had a really good discussion following that day. She thought they were making progress then. Rich had actually listened to her for once. Agreeing to a cleaner had been a massive step for him and she knew he found it hard. He always seemed to 'go into battle' when they argued, wanting to win at all costs and acquiescence to Laurie's needs was not his normal way at all. She felt a mixture of anger, despondency and immense sadness as she sat whilst the darkness crept all around her.

Creeping downstairs she lay on the settee, curled up into a ball and wept. She wept until she felt there could be no more tears to fall and then, feeling strangely calm, she fell into a deep sleep.

Chapter 14

Saturday 4th September 1996.

She woke with a start.

Sitting up, she looked at her watch. 5am and all was quiet. She had slept remarkably well considering. Not being a deep sleeper any longer, this surprised her. She didn't believe it was possible for any mum of young kids to be a good sleeper, they got used, very quickly, to having half an ear listening out for any crying. Funny, that was. There were normally two parents, but it always seemed to be the mums who heard the kids at night, never the dads.

This was an ongoing conversation they had with their friends, all of whom said the same thing. Laurie looked back over her years pre children with envy, marvelling at how she used to sleep, waking up totally refreshed every morning...not even a loo break! If only she had known! She wouldn't have taken it for granted so.

Laurie had butterflies in her stomach, she was feeling all sorts of different emotions this morning. Should she go, or not? SHOULD she go? No, most certainly not. Any responsible adult would stay home and attempt to sort out this mess, she told herself. Did she WANT to go though? Absolutely. She felt a desperate need to see Mike, a need that somehow seemed to override everything else, even her girls right now! She couldn't bear the idea of a weekend full of hurtful, barbed comments and accusations. No, she couldn't do it, she thought.

Grabbing her car keys from the kitchen, she scribbled a quick note to Rich. "Gone out Rich. Need time to think. Don't worry about me, will probably be out for the day."

Looking at the scribbled note, she re-read it. What would he think? He would be livid, she knew that. Before she had chance to change her mind she walked out of the front door.

5am! She had to laugh, she thought as she drove out of the close. No one was about obviously. Taking a look at herself in the rear view mirror, she gasped. She had panda eyes, her hair was all over the place and she still had yesterday's work clothes on! What was she going to do? She wasn't meeting Mike until eleven! That was six hours away.

So, she found herself driving up the M5 again towards Bromsgrove. She stopped on route at McDonald's to grab herself some breakfast and a coffee. She wasn't hungry and didn't touch the muffin that she had bought but she drank the large coffee gratefully, taking her time.

She was going to call in at Frankie's...she had no other choice. She needed a shower, that was for sure. And her clothes? Could she turn up in these, she asked herself, looking down at her crumpled trousers. What would Mike think? That she was a madwoman probably, she thought wryly.

Smiling to herself at the prospect of seeing his face, which she knew would look concerned and amused, all in one, she also knew it would make no difference to Mike how she looked. He was a decent man, all he would care about was her wellbeing. That was why she loved him so much.

Draining the last dregs from her cup of coffee and feeling so much more awake now, she strode back to her car and drove on.

It was still only 7.30 when Laurie knocked on Frankie's door, feeling very relieved when Frankie opened it almost immediately. She was in her pyjamas with a cup of tea in her hands. "Hello," said Frankie questioningly.

Laurie smiled sheepishly. "Thank God you're up, I'm really sorry Frankie, barging in here at this time in the morning."

"Don't be daft Laurie, come on in," she interrupted. Making light of it, Frankie ushered her into the living room and went to get her a cup of tea.

"No, don't bother Frankie," said Laurie sheepishly, stopping Frankie in her tracks. "I've only just had a coffee at McDonald's," she said by way of explanation.

Raising her eyebrows, Frankie sat beside Laurie. She said nothing but she was obviously perplexed. She would be, Laurie thought wryly. She had turned up at the crack of dawn with yesterday's clothes still on and had just let out that she had been sitting in a McDonald's at God knows what time in the morning. Not to mention the fact that this was the second time that she had turned up unannounced in less than a month!

She put her head in her hands. "God, what a mess," she said. "What a bloody mess," she repeated, slower this time as her tears began to fall.

Over the next half hour, Laurie brought Frankie up to date.

Being aware of much of Laurie's situation, there were no surprises and Frankie simply listened, whilst Laurie poured her heart out, finishing with the fact that she was planning on seeing Mike today.

And Frankie was brilliant, not at all judgmental. Allowing Laurie to finish, she then went into the kitchen, bringing them both some tea and hot buttered toast. "Right, okay Laurie. Yes...it's a mess," she confirmed, smiling slightly, "but firstly let's talk about today. Do you still want to see Mike?"

"Yes," Laurie said definitively. "Yes, I'm going."

"Okay," said Frankie, looking at her watch. "Well, you'd best go and have a shower, I'll fetch you a towel. It's 9.30 already, you need to be leaving by 10.15 latest I would say," nattered Frankie as she led Laurie upstairs and into her bathroom.

Frankie handed her a fresh towel and then looked her up and down. "What size are you? A twelve?"

"I'm not sure now, should be a twelve to fourteen but I've not been eating much lately. Why?" she asked, slipping out of her trousers.

"Just asking," Frankie quipped chirpily, leaving Laurie to it.

Laurie was standing in Frankie's bedroom, drying her hair as best she could.

"Here you go," said Frankie. "Try these on, they may fit you I think. Maybe not to your taste but got to be better than those work clothes."

She handed Laurie a pair of faded blue Jeans and a pink T shirt. "Yes, I know, don't look like that. They're a size twelve and yes, they are mine. Believe it or not, I was your size a few years ago and I've kept them just in case. You know...wishful thinking I suppose," she said wistfully. The Jeans fitted perfectly. Well, she thought, there had to be some advantages to going through this shit. She had at least dropped a clothes size, although, she thought, she would much prefer doing it the traditional way! The T-shirt fit nicely too, the colour almost matching the mules she had slipped on this morning and as the weather was still very warm there would be no need for a jacket either.

Laurie couldn't thank Frankie enough as she gave her a goodbye hug at the front door. "You're a lifesaver," she said smiling brightly.

"Go," urged Frankie. "Go and have a nice time, I'll be thinking about you all day," she smiled, gently pushing Laurie out of the door. "And no guilt," she added bossily. "Mike's a lovely man, and from what you've told me, Rich doesn't deserve you, so go and enjoy," said Frankie, her eyes twinkling as she waved her goodbye.

79

Chapter 15

She spotted Mike standing outside 'Ann Hathaway's cottage'. He was looking around anxiously, peering through the droves of visitors, a great mob of Japanese excitedly chattering around him, their cameras working overtime.

He didn't spot her until she was a few feet away and when he did, he gave her the brightest of smiles. "Hey," he said, coming up to her and enveloping her in a big hug. "You came!" he exclaimed.

"I did," she replied softly.

"I thought you might have chickened out," he said, relief clearly evident in his voice.

Laurie was clinging onto Mike, taking in his scent in deep calming breaths. She didn't want to let go and it was Mike who moved away first.

He was looking closely at her and could see that she had been crying. Taking her face in his hands, he kissed her very gently on her forehead. "It's alright, it will be okay, I promise," he mouthed into her hair.

Those words were heaven to hear and, coming from Mike, she truly believed this to be true.

"I know," she said quietly.

"Right," said Mike decisively. "You have choices to make. Ann Hathaway's cottage or we can take a boat out onto the river, that's assuming you know how to row, of course," he added jokingly.

"Of course I can row!" answered Laurie, laughing, although she had never rowed in her life. "I don't know, what do you want to do?" she asked. She didn't really care herself. Simply being with Mike was enough for her.

"Well, I've never been into Ann Hathaway's cottage," he said, turning to look at it. "Five hundred years old," he added. "May be interesting."

Yes, it might be, she thought, if it wasn't for the crowds milling around. "How about the river?" she asked. "It will be less busy," she added.

"That's true," answered Mike, looking around him.

Taking her hand in his, they strolled together through the market town. Even the feel of Mike's hand in hers felt amazing...so natural. As though they had always been together.

Taking a breather from the rowing, they sat back enjoying the sunshine. They had been on the river for about fifteen minutes and hadn't stopped laughing. Mike wasn't exactly a good rower himself, she had teased, but he had eventually gotten into a nice rhythm and found a slightly quieter spot in which to slow down a little.

Looking at Mike quizzically, Laurie smiled. "I've told you a lot about me but I don't know much about you at all."

"You've not really told ME too much either," Mike came back at her. "Your girls, yes lots, but nothing else," he challenged.

There was silence for a moment, Mike staring intently at her as he had a tendency to do. His face was a mixture of inquisitiveness and love as he continued to stare.

"Okay," Laurie said slowly. "You first though," she added, laughing. "Then I'll tell you everything too."

Mike took a deep breath and rolled his eyes. "I don't much like talking about myself, there's not really a lot to say. I've told you about my parents, you know I've moved around a lot. You're after my love life aren't you?" he asked, a twinkle in his eye as he wagged his index finger in her direction.

"I might be," she answered coyly.

"Well, okay," he conceded. "I'm not surprised really, only that you've waited so long! As a divorcee you get used to women wanting all the gossip. God, *anyone* asks! I had the cleaner at work grilling me the other evening, wanting to know all the gory details and it was only the second time I'd ever met the woman!"

"Really?" asked Laurie, a note of genuine concern in her voice.

"Oh yes, you'd be amazed at how little people need to know you to come right out with direct questions about your love life. Not men, generally, but women do it all the time!"

"You don't *have* to tell me," Laurie said, beginning to wish she hadn't started the conversation.

"No, it's fine, honestly. Anyway, you're different," he said smiling over at her.

Mike looked into the distance as he began to speak. "I got married just after leaving Uni where we had met. She's called Fiona, I met her in our final year. We were together for ten years, the first few of which, we were very happy." He went quiet then, still looking out over the river.

"And..." she prompted as the silence grew.

"Then...well, we just grew apart....simple," he sighed, with a hurt expression all over his face.

"Right," said Laurie, dragging out the word. Mike was obviously not going to open up without a push. "So what happened then? Something must have?" she probed.

Taking a deep breath, Mike exhaled slowly. "We fell apart due to our problem having kids," he said. "We'd been married five years when Fiona got pregnant and we had both been ecstatic as we had been trying for a very long time, almost since we got married! We both knew we wanted children. Fiona used to talk about having a brood, she wanted at least four, she used to say," he said, smiling at the memory. "It hadn't occurred to either of us that it might not happen. Anyway, she got pregnant at last, which was such a huge relief. You cannot imagine how difficult life had become, Fiona convincing herself that this month would be it, only to be devastated every month when her period arrived. It took over our life and took a lot of our happiness too. We only ever talked about pregnancy...how to get pregnant, what to eat, what to drink, how to avoid stress. The irony being," he continued bitterly, "we were piling on the stress, blaming each other a lot of the time. Anyway, just as we had started the whole process of having tests done, she got caught. Truth be told, Laurie, I was in my element, and so was she. We threw ourselves into the planning and after finding out it was going to be a boy, we'd decorated his bedroom, bought loads of baby stuff, I'd even made up his cot! Stupid really," he chided himself. "It was all way too early. Fiona had shown no signs of having any problems at all, all her ante-natals had gone fine, no sickness, nothing." He went quiet for a few seconds, clearly reliving his past. "Then, just after five months pregnant, she miscarried," he said quietly, his voice breaking. "No particular reason, they said...'Keep trying' were their exact words." He laughed bitterly. "Keep *fucking* trying! We were both devastated. After trying for nigh on five years and getting so close to our dreams, we both went into shock, I think. Fiona closed up, didn't speak about him much at all. She's not really a talker you see. Deals with everything internally, whereas me...I needed to talk. I'd *named* him, Laurie!" he whispered, tears streaming down his face. "Thomas, that was his name. I'd envisaged playing football with him, showing him the world, you know? I really couldn't wait to be a dad," his voice breaking as he continued. "So, we carried on trying but I don't think our hearts were really in it. I used to cry a lot over Thomas but Fiona seemed to go deeper and deeper into her shell. I came home from work one day to find his room had been stripped, all his baby clothes removed, cot taken away. That *killed* me," he said. "It's where I used to go to think about him and she just stripped the room as though he was NOTHING...as though he never existed!"

The anguish on Mike's face was apparent and Laurie found herself crying too. "God, Mike, I'm so sorry, I can't imagine how you must have felt," she said gently.

Seeing the effect his words had had on Laurie, Mike pulled himself together a little. "It's okay now," he said. "It was five years ago, I've got used to it, well, normally anyway!" He smiled. "But it broke our marriage up, definitely. She never did conceive again, as much to do with the fact that we rarely had sex as anything else," he said, a sad smile on his face. "And we never really talked...you know...we didn't grieve together at all. I couldn't understand Fiona, to be honest and she turned so cold towards me. She wouldn't speak of him and seemed to lose all enthusiasm for anything. I think, on reflection, she was probably seriously depressed but I just didn't know how to get through to her. Anyway," he added shrugging, "she eventually told me she wanted a trial separation. It coincided with a new job I'd been offered and we were having to move. She just told me she wasn't coming with me. I was GUTTED. I knew things weren't good but I hadn't expected that! She filed for divorce within a year and so, here I am," he finished. Looking up at Laurie, he wiped a tear away. "I bet you wished you'd never asked?" he said, smiling, in an attempt to lighten the mood.

Laurie crawled over to him, gently, trying not to rock the boat too much and put her arms around him, kissing him softly on his lips. "I'm SO sorry," she repeated. "I love you Mike...so much. I hate to see you so sad," she added, kissing him again a little more insistently

"Mmm," said Mike, in between kisses. "I'm glad I told you now. You can feel sorry for me as much as you like if it gets this result from you," he added, moving his hands under her 'T' shirt and gently stroking her breasts.

84

Laurie laughed as she reluctantly pulled herself away from him.

Mike stared at her for a moment, a long, thoughtful look. "I love you, Laurie, more than I've loved anyone. You know that, don't you?" he said seriously.

Smiling, Laurie looked up into his face. "Let's go and book ourselves a room somewhere," she said impulsively, surprising herself as much as him.

"Not going to refuse that offer!" he laughed, a wicked grin spreading all over his face as he began to row back as quickly as possible before either of them could change their minds.

Chapter 16

Their lovemaking had been everything Laurie could have possibly dreamt of. A mixture of gentle, combined with an urgency, both aware of how precious their time was together, too aware of Laurie's responsibilities which would separate them both later in the day.

Lying together, fully satiated, Mike lay on his back with Laurie cuddled into him as much as she could.

"Wow," he whispered. "That was worth waiting all these weeks for," he added, chuckling to himself. "I'm bloody starving though aren't you?"

Laurie looked at her watch. 3.30 already! They had skipped lunch, too desperate to get into a room, food being the last thing on either of their minds! Laurie was not really hungry now either but she asked Mike if he wanted some food.

"Well," he said. "Therein lies the problem. Yes, I want food but I also want you. And, as I can't have you all the time but I can eat whenever, then No, I'm fine," he answered, laughing as he turned to her again. Stroking her inner thigh, the thought of food having long gone, he whispered all the things he would like to do to her. "I'm going to eat you instead," he said, sliding down the bedsheets and parting her legs enough so that he could probe her deeply with his tongue. She was so wet already, it didn't take long until Laurie was completely lost, coming loudly enough for Mike to attempt to quieten her, Laurie waving away his hands from over her mouth, crying out over and over again.

"What are we going to do?" Mike asked into the silence of the room.

Laurie was half dozing. "I don't know," she whispered. The light was beginning to fade and Laurie was starting to feel worried. As beautiful as the day had been, Laurie knew she was going to have to set off home soon. She should have done so already, she told herself.

She wanted to stay. Couldn't bear the thought of them parting. It seemed so wrong, she thought. She didn't want to leave him, she wanted to stay here forever. Stop the clock, right at this moment in time. Oh, how wonderful that would be!

Sighing, Laurie sat up and looked over at Mike. "I don't know," she repeated. "But it's been wonderful today Mike," she said. "I don't want to leave you...ever...truth be told, but I've got to go. I'll be in enough trouble as it is," she added, sounding quite worried.

"Does he know where you are?"

"No, no he doesn't. We had a huge row last night and I just left him a note this morning before he got up. He has no idea about us, but, still, he will be fuming. I've never done anything like this before, I can't imagine how angry he will be," she said, almost to herself.

"You sound scared of him," stated Mike, looking increasingly concerned.

"No," she said instantly, trying to put Mike's mind at rest. "Not like that," she added. "He's not violent or anything, I'll be fine, really, he just has a temper, that's all."

"What are you going to tell him?"

"I've got no idea," she said. "I'll come up with something though," she added, walking over to where her clothes were strewn all over the floor.

"Tell him the truth," said Mike, decisively. "Tell him about me," he continued. "Don't mess him around Laurie, it's not right."

"I know," Laurie answered despondently. "And I will, you are right. It's not fair to string him along. Our marriage is unhappy...it has been for a while...I need to face it."

"Come and live with me," Mike said, jumping out of bed and taking her in his arms.

Laurie started to cry, the enormity of their situation hitting home. "If only it was that simple Mike," she cried, tears cascading over her cheeks.

Mike lifted her face to his. "It can be, Laurie. I love you, I will love your girls too as if they were my own, I promise you. I will always take care of you, Laurie, till death us do part. It CAN be that simple," he urged, desperation causing his voice to break slightly.

Wanting so desperately to believe this, Laurie nodded. "Okay," she said after a long pause "Okay, I'll tell him," she confirmed. "Now, I've *really* got to go," she said, glancing at her watch again.

Mike walked Laurie back to her car, holding her hand tightly all the way. "Are you sure you're going to be okay?" he asked as she put the keys in the ignition.

"I'll be fine," she sighed, turning to give him as much of a reassuring smile as she could muster. "See you Monday," she shouted as she pulled out of the car park, only allowing her tears to fall again when Mike was well out of sight.

Laurie drove slowly. She was trying to give herself time to assimilate her feelings. The day she had experienced had been one of the best days of her life. She had not experienced love like this before and she wanted more of it. When Mike had asked her to live with him, her heart had danced with delight for a moment. He made it all sound so simple and in those moments she could see a future for them. She would have no worries with regards how he would be with her girls and she could easily picture many wonderful, happy carefree days as a family, not to mention how they would grow together as a couple. She felt an incredible warmth as she pictured them both growing old together...it would be idyllic.

"Till death us do part," he had quoted. Being faithful to one another, honouring each other through sickness and in health, she mused. Yes, Laurie had heard those words many a time, had said them herself, but they had just been words, repeated most of the time with fingers crossed, she thought cynically.

But with Mike...every one of those words, every promise...she would be delighted and honoured to make and she would absolutely mean it. Finally, she understood the seriousness of marriage vows and, whilst she hadn't known Mike for long, she knew she could say those words tomorrow and she would never deviate. She would never *look* at another man as long as she lived.

Her emotions were running deep as she realised she finally understood 'real' love.

She couldn't keep the smile off her face either as she thought back to their afternoon together and felt a powerful tugging between her legs. She was still throbbing gently, a feeling of immense physical satisfaction causing her to feel both very alive and very calm. Satiated. Putting a finger between her legs, she only had to rub slightly to bring back a flood of sensation, enough for her to have to pull over at the next lay by to satisfy herself again, so desperate was the feeling she stirred. Satiated? She queried. Okay, maybe not, she thought delightedly as she laughed out loud. She wasn't sure she would ever feel as though she had had enough. They could do it morning, noon and night and still not be sufficient as far as she was concerned.

Her feelings were so powerful, she was refusing to think of Rich right now. She didn't want to go there and she knew it would bring her crashing down. Equally though, she knew she couldn't avoid it. She was going to tell him tonight, she decided. Mike was right. It *wasn't* fair to string him along. On a purely selfish level too, Laurie was desperate to move things forward and that was going to be with Mike! She wanted all this mess to be over and she was going to have to be very strong. 'Cruel to be kind' she decided. How was he going go take it? she pondered. She knew he wouldn't let her go without a fight and she felt very uneasy about it all. Firm and strong, she kept repeating.

Keep thinking of today, keep positive and all will be okay she told herself as she pulled up outside the house.

Chapter 17

It was 10.30pm. Rich was sitting in the kitchen, no lights on anywhere in the house and Laurie could just make out a whisky glass sitting on the kitchen table close to where Rich was seated. "DON'T," he bellowed as Laurie went to switch the lights on. Her hand stopped in mid air. "Don't. I don't want the light on."

Placing her hand back by her side, Laurie stood stock still. She didn't know what to do or say at that moment so said nothing and waited for what seemed an interminable amount of time.

"Where have you been?" he whispered. Although his voice was a mere whisper, there was no warmth in it at all and Laurie felt a chill creep through her bones. He'd been drinking, that much was obvious, she could smell the alcohol fumes from here. He had also been smoking, something he never did in the house anymore.

"Stratford," she answered, still staying put, not daring to move an inch, hardly daring to breathe! She felt scared...scared of her own husband, she realised.

"Stratford!" he spat out in fury. "Fucking STRATFORD! What the fuck were you doing there all day?" he shouted, rising from his chair. "You've been out fucking shopping whilst I've been worried sick?" he stated incredulously. "You could have at least phoned!" he added, placing his hands behind his head and pacing the kitchen floor in exasperation.

Feeling a huge sense of relief for an instant Laurie gave herself a few seconds to think. He had no idea, clearly, not even a thought that she might have been seeing someone, he just assumed she had gone shopping! Mind you, he would work it out pretty quickly when he realised there were no shopping bags in sight. Even so...she could tell him she had just been sightseeing, she didn't have to tell him the truth, did she?

As tempting as this was to Laurie, Mike's words came back to her as though he was standing right beside her. "Tell him." She could almost hear his voice in her ears and she knew what she had to do. She had to be strong, she had to do the right thing.

Laurie went to sit down and Rich followed suit. "I'm not happy anymore Rich," Laurie began. Rich said nothing. How could she word this?, she thought desperately. How do you just come out with something so earth shattering? Her next words would rock his world as he knew it. She was feeling decidedly queasy too as a result of not having eaten anything all day which certainly wasn't helping matters. So, she said nothing, wanting Rich to take control.

"What are you saying Laurie?"

Laurie sighed deeply as she looked over at him, grateful she couldn't see his face in the dark. She didn't want to see his expression as she began to tear his world apart. "I'm *really* unhappy Rich and I think we should maybe separate for a while."

Her voice broke at that point and she could not get any more words out as she began to cry. The words were out there and could not be retrieved. Okay, she reflected, not *exactly* telling him everything...in fact, not really being honest at all

Thinking we need to *separate* for a *while?*

This was not true in any sense! She didn't *think,* she KNEW! She didn't want to *separate, she wanted a* DIVORCE! And she didn't mean for a while, obviously!

So, whilst she felt relief she had voiced her desires, she was well aware her words were woefully inadequate. Why was she doing this? She knew why. She was trying to soften the blow, deluding herself into thinking that once he had agreed to a separation then Laurie could take things forward, minimising his hurt, also his anger.

It wasn't right though and it wasn't fair. Either she needed to tell him the truth or not. No half measures.

"*Separate!*" Rich exclaimed in disbelief. He was shocked, he had not been expecting this at all and it hit him hard. "*Separate?*" he said again in a much quieter, calmer voice. "Why? What on earth's going on?" he asked, completely perplexed. "I know things haven't been easy lately but CHRIST, Laurie, they're not *that* bad are they?"

"Yes, Rich, they are. I'm so sorry," she blurted, tears streaming down her face. Putting her face in her hands, she mumbled to the floor. "I've met someone Rich. I can't tell you how sorry I am it's come to this. I didn't go looking Rich, believe me please," she pleaded. "But I *have* met someone else and I want to be with him."

Her heart was going ten to the dozen and she was sweating profusely.

She'd said it! There was no more to say. It really was *that* simple, it's out there and...shit... there was no going back, she thought, full of trepidation. She was grateful to be seated, she didn't feel her legs could possibly hold her weight as she awaited Rich's response.

The silence grew as Rich was clearly trying to make sense of the words he had just been dealt.

"Have you slept with him?" asked Rich incredulously.

"Yes," she whispered, holding her breath not daring to make a single movement.

"You slag," he said quietly, picking up his whisky glass and draining it in one large gulp. Banging the glass back on the table, he stood up. "You fucking SLAG," he shouted, moving over to where she was seated in one quick movement. He was towering above her, his arms raised to strike out as Laurie looked up at him.

"I'm sorry," she cried out. "I *never* meant for this to happen Rich, you have to believe me," she pleaded again, fear taking hold. He's going to hit me, she thought, shrinking into her chair as much as she could in an attempt to make herself as small as possible.

Seeing her shrink away from him brought Rich to his senses. He *wanted* to hit her, that was evident and Laurie could see the internal battle he was having.

As quickly as his fury had risen though, it also deflated and he sat back down in his chair. "Who?" he demanded. "Who is this bastard?" he asked, disgust and anger evident in his voice as he spoke.

It didn't really matter who it was, she thought, what good was it going to serve by telling him?

"Just someone from work," she replied softly. "You don't know him," she added.

"Well, he must have a fucking name Laurie! What the fuck is it?" his voice beginning to rise again in anger.

"Mike," she answered. "His name is Mike," she said, feeling anger rise within herself too. "Feel better?" she shouted. "You feel better now you know his name?" she screeched. "No, I didn't think you would," she continued, seeing the distraught look on his face. She let out a deep sigh as she looked over at Rich, sitting dejectedly, hunched over his empty whisky glass. "I'm going to bed" she said simply, standing up, walking over to the kitchen door. She felt absolutely drained, an exhaustion coming over her she had never felt before.

Showering quickly, she climbed into the bed they shared, tears soaking her pillow as she wondered how much more she could take.

Chapter 18

Sunday 5th September 1996.

Laurie woke early, just after 6am. For a few blissful seconds she felt normal and then everything came flooding back to her. Loving memories from yesterday made her want to hug herself in delight whilst their ugly fight last night made her feel extremely anxious. Rich had not come to bed last night and she assumed he had slept on the settee. She'd told him!! Her heart felt heavy, her stomach churned. She had no idea how she would get through today, let alone the next few weeks and months!

Mike telling her to be honest was all well and good but it was her dealing with the fallout and she wondered, once again, whether she was capable of handling it. She certainly didn't feel strong enough today. She *must* keep thinking about Mike. That was the only possible way she could cope, she told herself. The trouble was, she felt so sorry for Rich. She didn't want to hurt him, she still had feelings for him, still loved him in a way. Was that possible? She hadn't believed you could love two men at the same time before, but of course you could, she mused. Rich had been her life for so long. She loved him when they first married and she loved him now. Not quite in the same blind way, it was a softer love now, grown out of knowing all his weaknesses too and she felt protective towards him. She was aware that some of his ways...his temper, his attitude towards her working... were because he felt threatened and he was acting in the only way he knew to protect himself.

"Mummy, mummy," exclaimed Sarah as she came bounding into the bedroom and dived onto her.

She hugged Laurie so tightly that Laurie felt her tears beginning to return again.

"Morning Sweetie," Laurie said into Sarah's mass of tangled, slightly sweaty smelling hair, hugging her so tightly, not wanting to let her go.

Sarah moved away a little and looked at her mummy. "I missed you yesterday, mummy. Daddy said you went to work but it was a Saturday. You don't work Saturdays," she said reproachfully.

"I know Sweetie, I'm sorry, I had to go in. We have been very busy lately and there was lots to do," she answered, grateful for Rich's cover up.

Christ, if she took this new role she'd be working some Saturdays anyway, she thought, feeling the same familiar guilt she always felt about her girls, beginning to understand the impact it would have on her girls as well as Rich. Kids *did* get used to things though, they could be very resilient when they needed to be, she told herself. "So, what did you do yesterday then? Did you have fun?" she asked Sarah in an attempt to move the conversation on.

"Yup," said Sarah, nodding enthusiastically. "We went to Grandma and Grandpa's," she announced.

Oh God. Laurie wasn't surprised. What else would Rich do all day with three kids? It was obvious he would land on his parents. But Laurie's stomach took a dive as she thought of Mavis. Rich wouldn't have lied to his parents, they would know therefore that Laurie had taken herself off for the day and she could only imagine Mavis's disapproval!

Oh well. Tough, she thought as she realised it was going to get a whole lot worse when Mavis discovered exactly what was going on. Taking off for the day was nothing in comparison!

"Oh, how lovely, Sarah," she said, attempting a smile.

"You look sad mummy," observed Sarah, putting her little hands either side of her mummy's face and peering into her eyes.

Always observant, doesn't miss a thing, bless her, she thought.

God, she loved her girls so much. She wanted them wrapped up in cotton wool forever not allowing life to penetrate. She knew this was impossible and she felt an incredible sense of foreboding as she attempted a brighter smile. "No, Sweetheart, not sad, no. Just tired, that's all," she placated. "How about you lie next to me and give me a big cuddle whilst I tell you a story eh?"

"Ooh, yes please," she answered enthusiastically. "I like your stories." Jumping up suddenly, "Shall I get Marie in?" she asked. "She likes your stories too."

So typical of Sarah, she was always so considerate and Laurie had a huge lump in her throat as she answered her daughter. "No, let's just have 'you and me' time for a while eh? Marie's obviously still asleep, so let's make the most of it."

Sarah listened for a second. All was quiet. "Ok Mummy," she said as she snuggled into her mummy's side, getting as close to her as was humanly possible.

Laughing, Laurie began making up a story. "Once upon a time..."

When Marie crawled into her bed too, thirty minutes later, Laurie was feeling a little calmer. Sarah was reading to Marie and Laurie took a little time to reflect.

"Tell him," Mike had urged. And so she had. So, now what? What should she do today? How were they going to sort everything out?

Start from the beginning, she told herself, in an attempt to stem the feeling of panic flooding through her. Laurie wanted...No, not wanted...*needed* Mike. She needed him so badly, it actually hurt. She couldn't *wait* to see him tomorrow and she had absolutely no doubt that he felt the same way towards her. He had asked her to go and live with him! Could she *practically* do that? It would mean such an enormous change for her girls. Surely, from their perspective it was better for them to stay here? The only home they knew. Yes, it would be far better for Rich to move out, that was for sure and then maybe Mike could move in over time. Take things slowly so as not to upset the girls any more than was necessary. They could *date,* thought Laurie, laughing at the thought. Who was she kidding? She didn't see the girls enough as it was anyway without swanning off some evenings too! So...dating was out. He could come here though. They could have cosy nights in when the girls were in bed. Yes, that could work, she thought dreamily, imagining the two of them curled up on the settee unable to keep their hands off each other.

A sudden cry from Cara's bedroom broke her reverie and she was brought back to earth with a bump. "I'm coming Cara," she said softly, as she ran in to fetch her. "I'm here Sweetie, hey, hello," she smiled, picking Cara up and taking her back into her bedroom, lying her besides her two sisters. Cara grinned and chuckled as her two sisters began lavishing her with attention. Looking over at them, Laurie's heart almost burst with love, followed immediately by an incredible wave of sadness. She didn't want their world to have to change. She wanted them to feel safe and secure and she realised that by fulfilling *her* needs, their world would change for good. It would not be one of a happy family, mummy and daddy together. Could she do that to them? She didn't have the answer right at this moment. She only knew what *she* wanted. She was painting a new picture in her mind, her girls, together with her and Mike. She felt it could be rosy for them, she really did and she had no doubt about Mike's parenting skills. In many ways he would be better than Rich. Far more involved, she imagined. But, was that enough? she asked herself. He would never be their father. How would that affect them going forward? "You can never have a happy divorce as far as children are concerned." She had heard that comment only yesterday on the radio, a comment that was stuck in her mind and kept replaying, time and time again.

"Daddy, daddy," she heard both Sarah and Marie exclaiming in unison as they jumped all over Rich. The TV was on but it was clearly only background noise as Rich was sitting with his head in his hands. "You're crying daddy. Why are you crying?" asked Sarah, a look of concern immediately wiping away the smile from her face.

"I've just got something in my eye," he answered. "I'm not crying Sarah," he whispered croakily. Standing up quickly to avoid further interrogation from his daughter, he suggested they go and get some breakfast.

Taking his cue, Laurie chivvied the two girls out of the living room into the kitchen, sitting them at the table. "Right then," she said, in as chirpy a voice as she could find. "How about a treat for breakfast? How do you both fancy pancakes?"

"Yaaaay, yummy,yummy," shouted Sarah, getting off her seat to jump up and down with glee.

"Okay then, right. Sit back down then and I'll get them on the go eh?"

Whilst Sarah and Marie happily tucked into their pancakes, Laurie gave Cara her bottle and once all was quiet, she went in to Rich. He was sat back down again, head back in his hands, yesterday's clothes all crumpled on him after a restless night, Laurie assumed.

She sat in the armchair facing him.

"Do you love him?" he asked.

Wow! Talk about straight in at the deep end! "Yes," she whispered.

Rich jumped up, clearly agitated, worry etched across his face as he began to understand the seriousness of their situation. "Oh God, no," he cried out. "No, no, no, no, no" he kept repeating in such a desperate tone Laurie could not fail to be affected.

She cried...really cried as she witnessed the devastation her actions were causing. "I'm so sorry Rich. So sorry," she kept repeating.

Rich was crying now too, tears streaming down his face and his continued cry of 'no, no, no' worried her. She desperately wanted to go over to him and put her arms around him in an attempt to calm him, but she didn't dare. She didn't know what his reaction would be so she sat stock still as he cried. GONE was Rich's temper, GONE were his hurtful words. In fact all of his fight seemed to have left him and Laurie had never seen him in this state before. She'd never seen anyone in this state before in fact! He looked and sounded so vulnerable, so desperate and she felt sick to her stomach. She was responsible for this, she thought. Her actions had caused this and she *hated* herself at that moment in time. If she could turn back the clock right now, she would do so in an instant.

Rich took one last look at her and fled up the stairs, taking two at a time. Following him into their bedroom, she watched as he shoved some of his clothes into a small suitcase they kept under their bed. "I've got to get away," he kept saying as though he was talking to himself. He seemed barely aware of Laurie's presence as he manically threw his stuff into the case and zipped it up. "I can't even bear to *look* at you, you're not my *wife!*" he spat out as he barged past her, suitcase in hand.

"Where are you going?" asked Laurie, running after him, panic rising within her. He was not in a state to be going anywhere! "You can't go like this," she cried, reaching him just as he got to the bottom of the stairs. Touching his arm, she said again, softly this time "You can't go like this Rich. You're in no state to go anywhere. Please...come and sit down a minute. I'll do you a cup of tea and..."

"Get off me!" he shouted, moving away from her as though he had been burned. "Get off me," he said again, a look of pure hatred and disgust in his eyes. "You worry about me now?" he sneered "Huh, fucking laughable, Laurie, don't you think? You weren't worrying about me yesterday were you?!"

His temper dissipating, tears taking over, he opened the front door and all she heard as he ran to his car was his agonized cries.

Laurie sank to the floor after shutting the front door. She felt absolutely wretched and she was extremely worried about Rich. What if he had an accident? How would she ever forgive herself? Where was he thinking of going? Taking a few deep breaths she forced herself to calm down and think more rationally. Yes, it was true he was in a state, but it was highly unlikely he would have an accident, he was an excellent driver, so she wouldn't allow herself to worry about things that hadn't actually happened. It was bad enough dealing with the facts at the moment without piling on more worry! He would be fine, she told herself. He would be fine, she repeated. She must believe this otherwise she would drive herself crazy.

"Mummy, Cara's being sick mummy," Sarah cried out in panic.

"I'm coming," she answered, picking herself up and walking back into the kitchen.

Chapter 19

Monday 6th September 1996.

They met up as usual at lunchtime, both of them clinging to the other as though their lives depended on it.

The weather had changed, it was no longer warm, the coldness having a certain 'back to school' feel about it.

"Let's go to the pub," she suggested as they released each other.

"Good idea," he answered. "I think you could use a drink....I certainly could!" he added, taking her hand and guiding her away from the park. "How about the 'Prince Albert?'"

Laurie nodded. She didn't care where they went, she was just so grateful to be with him. God, she had *needed* that hug! So much.

She had felt wretched all of yesterday, the feeling growing worse, if anything, throughout the day. Rich had not come home and he hadn't called either. She had kept herself busy enough, the girls always being a huge distraction. She couldn't really wallow too much when there were three girls to keep fed and entertained and she had thrown herself into all that needed doing, cooking a proper Sunday roast too.

Sarah was back at school on Wednesday and Laurie spent much of the afternoon sorting out her school clothes, seeing what still fit her and what she needed to buy. It was supposed to have been sorted on Saturday, she thought. Now she would have to go by herself in her lunchtime tomorrow. Hopefully there would still be some left in the shops!

Last year, being Sarah's first year at 'proper' school as Sarah referred to it, Laurie had bought all of her uniform at the beginning of August and Sarah had repeatedly tried it on, so excited she was at the prospect of being a big girl now. Laurie had had to take it from her eventually in order to keep it looking new for her first day. Smiling at the memory, she berated herself again for having left it so late this year. Even today, she had put *her* needs first!

"Do you want something to eat?" asked Mike as he sat her down at the quietest corner of the room.

"I couldn't eat a thing," said Laurie. "No, just a white wine please," she added, smiling up at him.

"Right...coming up," he said, striding over to the bar. God, he was gorgeous to look at, she thought. And he looked after himself. No mean feat when he was on his own. Both his trousers and shirt were neatly pressed and he looked like a man in control. Always an attractive trait, she thought, smiling over at him.

"Here you go...a large wine...I thought you might need it," he said, gently placing the glass on the table in front of her.

She took one large gulp from it immediately in an effort to calm her emotions somewhat. "Wow, you *did* need that didn't you?" he said, staring at her intently.

"Oh YES!" she replied vehemently. "Not the best day yesterday, you could say!"

Raising his eyebrows questioningly, she continued. "I told him about you."

"O...kay" he replied slowly. "And?"

"Well, he wasn't best pleased!" she answered, smiling sadly, thinking *that* was the understatement of the century!

Mike said nothing, looking at her over the table, concern evident in his eyes, willing her to continue.

"He asked who you were, whether we had slept together and I told him the truth."

"What exactly did you tell him then?"

103

"I remembered what you said on Saturday about being honest so I told him your name, that you were from work and that, yes, we had slept together and that I love you."

Mike sat back in his chair and took a large gulp of his beer. "Right," he said, a look of shock on his face. "No holding back then!" he joked.

"Well, you *did* say, didn't you?" she challenged Mike

"Well, yes I did. And it's the right thing to do. You've just taken me by surprise, that's all. Crikey...it makes it all feel very real all of a sudden doesn't it?"

Feeling a little defensive now, Laurie's anger rose. "Fuck's sake Mike! I did what you told me to do, that's all. You're not having second thoughts are you?" she dared to ask, holding her breath as she waited for his response.

Mike moved over to sit by Laurie's side and took both her hands in his. He could see how upset she was and could see she was desperately trying not to burst into tears and he was anxious to calm her as soon as possible. "No, Laurie, no, not at all, don't think that please, not even for a minute. I'm sorry. You took me by surprise that's all. I don't suppose I'd understood the enormity of the situation until now, if I'm being completely honest. You, telling him who I was, you know? And *of course* he would ask about me, it's obvious really and it doesn't matter. It's all going to come out eventually, anyway, isn't it? We both have to be prepared, it's not going to be pleasant, that's obvious. So..." he asked, seeing she had calmed down a little, "how did he take it?"

"As you would expect," she muttered sadly. "No. That's not true actually Mike, he took it really badly, I mean REALLY badly. He broke down. I've never seen him as bad, it was horrible," she said, her tears coming again.

He put his arms around her and waited for her tears to subside a little. "I'm really worried about him Mike...he took off yesterday and I haven't heard from him since!"

"Where do you think he might have gone?"

104

"I can only think he's gone to his parents; either that or he's stayed in a hotel somewhere. I don't know, to be honest, but you should have seen the state he was in!" Laurie's voice rising in panic as she took herself back to yesterday morning. "God, he shouldn't even have been driving, he was in such a bad way!"

"Shhh, he'll be okay Laurie," said Mike in a reassuring manner. "It's bound to have been a shock for him, of course it is, but he will be fine. He probably just needed some time to think, you know?"

"Probably," she acknowledged, nodding her head in agreement. "But you don't know him, he's always so in control, he has never broken down like this before. It was like seeing a stranger. He was a broken man, Mike, and I feel so bad, I really do. He took a suitcase too, so I don't think he's coming back anytime soon...not that I want him back," she added quickly, worried Mike would get the wrong idea. "I just want to know he's okay, that's all."

"You could phone his parents?"

"I could," she agreed slowly. "But, if he's not there it's going to get pretty awkward," she said, feeling mortified at his suggestion. "God, I can't *imagine* speaking to his mum! God, no, I'm not *that* strong!" she said, laughing as she took another gulp of her wine.

"Like that is it?" he asked, smiling at her. "Look Laurie," he said, suddenly serious again. "Life's going to get a lot shittier before it gets better but you've done the worst part. Rich is bound to be upset, angry too as it all sinks in. You need to be prepared, but if we want to be together, we are going to have to plough on. I'm with you all the way, I'll protect you as much as I can. I hate to see you so upset. Try to look forward Laurie," Mike urged. "Try to look into our future because it will be fantastic. I know it will."

Mike spoke with such emotion and it was everything she needed to hear right now. "You're right," she said, sinking back into her seat and taking a few deep breaths. "I've just got to be strong, I know that."

They were silent for a few moments, both seemingly lost in their own thoughts. "Don't worry Mike. I want you *so* much. We will be together, I promise you we will. We just need to work out how!" she said, smiling at him. "I was thinking about that yesterday and I want to have as little upheaval as is possible for the girls. It will be bad enough having me and their dad living separately so the *last* thing I want to do is take them away from their home too!"

"Yes, I can see that," nodded Mike. "I wasn't really thinking when I asked you to move in with me. So, what are you saying, Laurie?"

"I think we need to take it day by day. I can introduce you to the girls slowly...get you to know *them* a little too...you can always come over in the evenings as well?" she said, smiling coquettishly at him.

"I could, couldn't I?" he laughed. "That would be nice," he added, a twinkle in his eye.

They laughed together, Laurie holding Mike's hand tightly. God, she loved this man, she thought. She loved him so much she couldn't imagine ever having had a life without him by her side.

Chapter 20

"Pub again?" Mike gasped as he caught up with Laurie just outside of their workplace.

"I can't today Mike, I'm sorry. Sarah's back at school tomorrow and I have to get her uniform. I can't believe I haven't got it yet!" she said, sounding flustered.

"That's okay," he said, genially. "I'll come with you."

Taking her hand in his, they walked towards the high street. Laurie had to smile, he seemed to take everything in his stride. "Okay," she laughed. "It will be boring though, so don't go moaning," she warned, wagging her finger at him.

"Nothing can be boring with you," he quipped. "So, where do we get these uniforms from then? I've never bought any before, haven't a clue where to even start!"

"Well, follow me then," laughed Laurie playfully as they headed towards Marks and Spencers.

Fortunately for Laurie, there was still uniform left on the shelves...probably because she'd come to Marks' she thought wryly. One of the most expensive shops to get it so there *would* be some left.

And thank God, she thought, picking up some white shirts, aged 5-6. Would they be the right size? There was age 4-5 too. Would they be a better fit? Sarah was not exactly big for her age and Marks' were normally very generous with their sizing. Putting down the age 5-6, she picked up the smaller pack instead. No, don't be daft, she told herself. They were only shirts, it wouldn't matter if they were slightly too big anyway, she thought, putting down the pack she was holding and picking up her first choice again.

"Crikey," laughed Mike. "I didn't realise you were so decisive!"

"Shut up," she said, laughing herself. "It's serious stuff this is, and we haven't got around to the skirts yet! That's far more difficult to get right. It's not even as though I have time to bring them back either," she added anxiously.

Holding his hands up in surrender, he couldn't help chuckling. "Okay, okay, I'll be quiet. This is obviously more serious than I had realised. I'll just watch from the sidelines... No, maybe from your rear...a far better view!"

Laurie smacked him playfully before turning her attention to the task in hand.

Walking back to work, a bag bulging with Sarah's uniform, Mike asked how things were. "You mean, have I heard from him?" Laurie asked.

"Well, that too... but more to the point, has he come back? That's *my* concern."

"No, he hasn't and I haven't heard from him either. He *must* be at his mum's," she added, worry evident in her voice.

"How are *you* feeling?" Mike asked, putting an arm around her waist.

"Worried, to be honest. It's like I am just *waiting*. I don't know what's going to happen next! The girls are asking about him and I don't know what to say. Thank God they are so young, at least I can fob them off a little. I've told them he's away with work but Sarah keeps asking when he's coming home and I don't know what to tell her. Do I tell her the truth? Is it too soon?"

"Mmm, I get that. Difficult to tell her things until you know what's going on. Maybe best to keep fobbing her off for a while. It's not really as though you can tell her much, not knowing where Rich is even! Take it day by day," he suggested. "Just like *you* said yesterday."

"Yes, I think you're right," she said, her anxiety building.

"I'm worried about you though Laurie. I mean, he may come back anytime and God knows what he may do! Truth be told, whilst I appreciate you are worried about *him*, I really couldn't care too much, it's *you* I'm bothered about." he said, solemnly. "I couldn't settle yesterday evening at all, imagining all sorts of stuff going on. Its killing me, too, just seeing you for a few minutes each day. So...I was wondering.." He broke off at that point and Laurie could see the worry and anxiety etched on his face. "I was wondering whether I should come round tonight...not until the girls were in bed of course, but afterwards maybe?"

"I don't know Mike. GOD...Can you imagine if he comes back?! There'll be hell to pay!"

"And that's what *I'm* worried about too. Not for me though Laurie, but for you. You said he'd taken it really badly and the longer he remains quiet, the more worried I'm getting for you. I *can't* stay away another evening. I simply *can't* have another evening like yesterday! One piddling phone call from you was just not enough. The worry eased for five minutes and then came back again! I just can't bear it! Anyway," he added, "If he *does* come back, tell me honestly what difference it would make, me being there. He knows about us already, it's nothing new!"

Laurie scoffed. "Well...no Mike. It may be 'nothing new' to him as you put it, but even so!" she commented, her voice rising. "Its a massive slap in the face for him, don't you think? Come on!" she said sarcastically, "You, with your feet up in his house with his kids?! It's not exactly going to keep him calm is it?"

"Well," he sighed "When you put it like that...I just can't bear to think of him coming back and me not being there to protect you. It makes me feel so helpless."

"I can understand that Mike," she conceded. "I tell you what...how about I keep in touch with you through the evening. We'll talk *all* evening if that will make you feel better. What do you think?"

Feeling slightly appeased and realising he was not going to get any further, he nodded as they continued walking slowly back into work.

Chapter 21

Same day.

"Are you okay?" Frankie asked. "You look really stressed, I'm getting worried about you."

God, two people in the last few hours, she thought. Sighing as she picked up her coat, Laurie answered quietly so as not to attract unwanted attention from the other girls. "Well, things could be an awful lot better if I'm being honest with you. Do you fancy a quick drink? I can spare half an hour before I have to pick up the girls."

"Go on then, I could murder a coffee."

Smiling to herself, Laurie walked out with Frankie. Coffee was not exactly what Laurie had had in mind! A stiff *drink* was required, but that was typical of Frankie and actually a coffee would be better for Laurie anyway.

As they had such little time, Laurie filled Frankie in quickly and Frankie just listened, not interrupting, allowing Laurie to let out all her anger and frustration. "So," Laurie said when she had finished. "That's where I am at the moment. Desperate to be with Mike and worried sick about Rich!"

"Worried in what way?"

"Well...worried about *him* first of all, but then also getting more worried about his reaction as I don't know when or if he's going to try to come home, I mean it's *his* house. He left so abruptly and we've discussed nothing properly Frankie. He just knows the bare facts...God...they were enough! So, he just packed and went, but he was in such a state."

"He will be at his mum's, Laurie, licking his wounds I expect."

"Yes, I think you're right. It's his reaction *once* he's licked his wounds I'm worried about! Its making me ill just thinking of it!"

"He's only been away two nights, Laurie. You need to stop worrying about him so much. He's a big boy now and if he *is* at his mum's then he will be being looked after. *You* need to start thinking though, having a plan for yourself. You don't want him coming back do you?"

"God, no...no, I don't, but it's his house too. How can I stop him?"

"Laurie, if you're serious about this, and I think you are, then you have to see a solicitor and find out your rights. I also think you need to consider changing the locks as quickly as possible...stop him just waltzing back in."

Seeing the look of shock and horror on Laurie's face, Frankie softened her tone as she continued. "Surely the first thing you need to do is protect your position. You need the girls as settled as possible and you want custody I presume?"

Seeing Laurie nod profusely, Frankie continued. "Therefore, for now, it's *you* that wants to remain in the house until all the financial stuff is settled. Rich made a big mistake leaving and you need to capitalise on that. Changing the locks stops him coming back.Then, go and see a solicitor and take his advice. This is serious shit Laurie and you can't look after everyone. Whether you like it or not you are going to have to develop a backbone! This is going to be tough and you need to get your priorities right. All you can do at the moment is protect your position," she reiterated. "Look after yourself, look after your girls, hopefully bring Mike into the scenario too, over time, but none of this will be easy. And if you try to take on Rich's worries and anxieties too, then it *will* make you ill! And that's *before* you start telling the world, you know, your mum, dad, in-laws? They will all have an opinion and you need to face facts, they won't all be on your side!"

"God Frankie, you make it sound like a battle!"

"That's exactly what divorce *is* Laurie. Rich will be looking after himself and you need to do the same. Didn't you tell me Rich is a solicitor? I can *guarantee* you he will be getting advice." Seeing Laurie's face beginning to crumble, Frankie put her arms around her. "Its going to be tough, yes, but it will all work out, it always does. And if you love Mike like you say you do, then this will all be worth it, honestly. You'll be fine Laurie...and I'll be here, anytime you need me, just call me, promise?" she urged as they got up to pay the bill.

Driving to Lizzie's, Laurie tried to take stock. Frankie's words had shocked her but she could see the sense in them. She needed to take control and she wasn't doing that at the moment. She was not doing that at all! She would make an appointment to see a solicitor tomorrow.

As for the locks, she wasn't so sure about that. It seemed a little extreme! Cruel too, she thought. But yes...seeing a solicitor and taking it from there was a good idea. 'Develop that backbone' as Frankie had so aptly put it. Crikey, she thought, Frankie was a great friend but she certainly wouldn't want her as an enemy. Talk about formidable!

Not for the first time Laurie found herself wondering about her friend. She always seemed so together, very rational, but hard too, and she wondered what may have happened in Frankie's past to make her like that. Maybe in the future as life calmed down, Laurie could get Frankie to open up a little. It would certainly make a change, Laurie listening to Frankie as opposed to the other way around! Yes, she would make it up to her in the years to come, definitely, she decided.

Feeling slightly more positive now she had a plan, Laurie plastered as bright a smile as she could muster on her face whilst knocking on Lizzie's back door.

Chapter 22

That evening.

"Daddy, daddy!" exclaimed Sarah and Marie in unison. "Daddy's back mummy," shouted Sarah excitedly as she scrambled out of the car as fast as her little legs would allow and ran to the front door.

SHIT, she thought. Shit, shit, shit, she thought again, panic flooding through her body. Rich *was* indeed back, his car parked on the drive. Oh God, she thought as she helped Marie who was struggling to get out of her seatbelt as quickly as possible in order to follow Sarah in search for her daddy.

Picking up Cara from her seat, grabbing her handbag in one hand, Cara's baby bag and Sarah's uniform in the other, she struggled up the path.

"You're back daddy! You're back!" shouted Sarah from inside the hall. Laurie smiled. Whenever Sarah was excited she always repeated herself, it was so sweet. She loved how excited she could get. It hit her hard too, though. It was clear how much Sarah had missed her daddy and it hit her again how difficult the split up was going to become.

Rich was hugging both Sarah and Marie tightly and did not look up to acknowledge Laurie. Dropping the bags in the hallway, she went into the kitchen. She felt grateful for all the mundane tasks that had to be done over the next half hour as she got on with preparing some tea for the girls and a bottle for Cara. She didn't feel hungry herself and couldn't face going in to Rich to see if he wanted anything. Rich was pointedly ignoring her, spending time with the girls in the living room. They were ensconced on the settee together watching some children's cartoons and Laurie could hear giggles every so often as she began peeling some potatoes.

"Come on then girls, time for bed," said Laurie. The girls had eaten their tea and gone back into their daddy whilst Laurie sorted Cara out. She had taken as long as she could with Cara, talking to her...Crikey...even giving her a bottle whilst sitting Cara on her lap in the rocking chair she had used for all the girls. This used to be Laurie's favourite task, sitting, rocking, a lamp on in the corner and just her and her babies. She would sit for hours, feeding them and then gently rocking them to sleep, the rocking motion soothing her as much as them!

And it worked a little this evening. Cara fed happily and Laurie watched as Cara's eyelids grew heavier and heavier until, finally, she was fast asleep. Laurie's panic had subsided sufficiently for her to think a little more rationally. She would get the girls into bed and then they would talk...not fight...but talk like two responsible adults. It was essential they sorted things and the girls *must* come first. Therefore *surely* Rich would see how important it was that Laurie stayed and Rich moved out, wouldn't he? God, she was getting anxious again, her stomach doing somersaults. She needed to eat too though, otherwise she wouldn't be able to think straight, she told herself. Lowering Cara gently into her cot, Laurie walked downstairs.

It was 7.30pm and she knew she should be getting the girls into bed but she decided to eat first. It wouldn't hurt as a one off to leave them enjoying some 'daddy time.' Opening the fridge door, she peered in to see what there was. Not seeing anything she fancied, she settled on beans on toast, which she warmed up in no time.

"There's beans on toast here if you want it," she said, walking into the living room carrying Rich's plate. Rich shrugged, staring at the TV as though his life depended on it. The girls were sat either side of him but were quieter now, the channel having been changed for Rich to watch the news. "I'll put it here then," Laurie sighed, placing his plate on the coffee table.

Sighing again, Laurie walked back into the kitchen to eat hers at the table. Her first mouthful got stuck in her throat, such was the level of her anxiety but she forced herself to plough on, managing at least half before it defeated her.

"Come on then girls," she said as brightly as she could, bending down to pick up Marie who looked fit to drop. "Come on sleepyhead," she whispered, smiling towards Sarah as she watched her stretch out and yawn.

She took her time again putting them both to bed, but as they were so tired already, it didn't take long for them to be dead to the world.

Laurie then took her time getting Sarah's new uniform out of the bags, hanging it all up and then laying out a shirt, skirt, knickers and new white socks at the bottom of Sarah's bed, ready for her to wear in the morning. There was something about a new school uniform, smiled Laurie, especially in September when it was usually a little too big for them. She loved seeing Sarah all smart and clean, her little stick legs looking so sweet against bright white socks and black clumpy shoes. Thank God she'd bathed them *last* night, she thought to herself. At least Sarah would *be reasonably* clean tomorrow morning! Hopefully all her new uniform would fit her okay too, she thought, crossing her fingers, berating herself again for having left it till the last minute. Stop fretting Laurie, she could almost hear her mum's voice in her ears. 'Stop *fretting* the small stuff' was one of her mum's favourite sayings and right at this moment it couldn't have been more apt!

Laurie walked into her bedroom and lay down on her side. It was starting to darken now and all was quiet. She watched the shadows moving quite quickly over the wall as darkness fell all too soon and tried to empty her mind but found it an impossibility. Her mind was racing. She knew Mike was expecting a call from her and he would be getting very anxious by now. He might have been okay earlier on, reasoning that she had the girls to sort but now he would quite likely be getting frantic. How could she alert him? She couldn't. They had a phone in the hall and one in the bedroom but she couldn't risk phoning him now could she? What if Rich picked up from downstairs? God, she couldn't imagine! Maybe later then when Rich was asleep. Or she could nip out to do it. There was a phone box on the corner. Yes...maybe nip out for some milk and call him then. She would have to find a way, so desperate was she, not only to put his mind at rest, but also simply to hear his voice. God, what she would give for him to be with her right now! She wrapped her arms around herself and drew strength from his words earlier today.

Thank GOD she'd stopped him from coming round though!

"Are you coming downstairs?" asked Rich, standing in their bedroom doorway, his arms folded and a coldness in his voice Laurie hadn't heard before. "I think we need to talk, don't you? he added, his tone still the same.

"Yes, okay," she whispered, getting up from the bed and following him downstairs into the living room.

Laurie perched herself on the edge of one of the armchairs and looked over at her husband. He looked haggard, she thought. He was wearing a suit so at least he had been to work, that was a relief. His suitcase was in the hall, he had not taken it upstairs. Maybe he was not staying? she questioned, hope fluttering slightly in her heart.

"I've been talking to Simon," he said, again in the same cold tone.

FUCK, thought Laurie. Simon was the senior partner at Rich's office and he dealt in family law from what Laurie could remember. She also knew he was good from how highly Rich always spoke of him. You idiot! She said to herself. Idiot, idiot, idiot. *Of course* Rich would have taken advice. He had it on tap! What on earth had she been *thinking*! She waited with bated breath to see what he was going to say next and she had a feeling she wasn't going to like it...not one bit! Feeling on the back foot, she stood up suddenly. I'm going to make a cup of tea, do you want one?"

"Sit the fuck down!" shouted Rich as he stood up and towered over her. "Sit the fuck down and listen to what I've got to say."

Laurie was trembling as she sat back down and did not meet his eyes as he began to talk.

"As I've already said, I've taken advice and this is how it's going to be," he stated calmly. "I'm not going anywhere. I was stupid to leave but I'm back and I'm staying. So are the girls. If you want to leave, then I won't stop you."

A chill flooded through Laurie's veins.

"But you won't have the girls, Laurie. OH NO! I will put in for full custody and I will make it *so* awkward every time you get visitation rights that eventually you will give in. MY girls, Laurie. They are MY girls and I will NEVER give them up. I will also tell them what you've done. They will *hate* you, Laurie. I will make sure of that!"

Such a panic rose within Laurie and she was physically sick, the beans on toast coming up so violently, she couldn't keep it all in her hands as she ran into the downstairs loo. She retched and retched until there was nothing to come up, only a vile tasting bile.

Exhausted, she sat beside the loo, her back against the wall. He couldn't do that could he? *Surely,* he couldn't get custody of the girls? Who would look after them? He was always at work! She had not, in her worst nightmares imagined this scenario. All kids went to the mums didn't they? Dads generally had them at weekends as far as she was aware, although she knew the tide had been turning lately. A lot more dads were coming to the fore, complaining about the injustices of the system. She was vaguely aware of 'shared care' too, where parents literally divided the week. But Laurie had given none of this too much thought and she realised how foolish she had been.

118

Walking back into the living room, she looked at Rich and felt an immense hatred. "You can't do that," she said as firmly as she could. "That would be *so* cruel to the girls, you *know* that. They need me, I do *all* their looking after. I am their MUM! You wouldn't even *want* them Rich. You work all the time! How could you *possibly* look after them?" she shouted, her voice rising incredulously.

Rich shrugged, looking over at her with contempt. "I'd get help," he said simply. "And you're right. I wouldn't want them, not really. But I'm *certainly* not letting *you* have them," he shouted angrily.

Laurie couldn't believe what she was hearing. "How can you say this?" she asked in disbelief. "How can you use our kids in this way? I can't *believe* it!" She was struggling to think clearly as she continued. "Anyway...why would *you* get them and not me?"

"Well, I fight better than you do and I will play dirty. Anyway *it's you* having a sordid affair, not me! You can go to any solicitor Laurie and get them to order me to give you visitation rights whilst we sort out their ongoing care but I *guarantee* Laurie, you will not see them," he warned coldly.

"How?...What do you mean?" she asked, perplexed.

He scoffed. "It's simple. When you come to fetch them, we won't be in! Oh, I'll always have excuses that sound plausible and, knowing the legal system as I do, they will believe my excuses to begin with. The system is slow, it will take months before they cotton on. And months in children's lives are a long time. Certainly long enough for me to turn them against you. I will tell the kids what you have done and I will tell them you don't care for them any more. IF," he shouted. "IF you get custody, then I will move away with them, start again somewhere, don't think I wouldn't! I would go abroad somewhere you'd never find us."

Laurie could not take in any more. Rich made it all sound so convincing and she had no doubt he would do as he said.

Yes...even to the point of moving away and starting over. Rich was bitter and angry and saw this as a battle...a battle he had no intention of losing.

Just at that moment there was a soft knock on the door. Looking at his watch, Rich looked over at Laurie. It was 10 o'clock. No-one knocked on their door at this time of night so Laurie knew it could only be one person and her heart went into her mouth.

Rich obviously came to the same conclusion at the same time and he jumped up, yanking the front door open violently. "Ahh. Mike, I presume. The man himself!" he boomed. "What the fuck do you want?"

Mike put his hands up in a gesture of surrender, doing all he could to calm the situation down. "Hey, I'm not looking for trouble, I just need to see if Laurie is okay, that's all."

"You want to see if Laurie is okay? Is that what you said?" demanded Rich, his voice, manic, rising with anger. "You mean MY WIFE!" he spat. "My wife...yes...here she is."

Grabbing Laurie hard around her upper arm, he pulled her to the front door. "Yes, here she is," he repeated coldly. "So...now you've seen her, do us a favour mate...fuck off!"

Rich's voice was ranging from a quiet, sinister coldness to a bitter, angry, manic tone and Laurie was frightened. Mike looked over at her and his eyes conveyed so much love and tenderness, she couldn't bear it. She needed Mike's arms around her so much, she burst into tears.

"Oh, for God's sake, don't turn on the waterworks!" Rich said, with derision.

"Hey, Laurie," Mike whispered softly.

"Don't 'hey Laurie' *my* wife. As I've *already* said, you've seen her now, so fuck off." Rich went to shut the door in his face but Mike was too quick and put his right foot inside. "Move your foot, you bastard!" shouted Rich.

"No," Mike said as calmly as he could. "No" he repeated. "I'm not going anywhere until I know Laurie is okay," he said, staring challengingly at Rich.

Moments went by as Rich stared at Mike and then he shrugged. "Okay," he said easily. "Okay, talk to her then," he added, pushing Laurie in front of him.

Laurie looked pleadingly at Rich. "Can you give us a minute?" she asked softly.

"I'm not going anywhere Laurie. Anything you have to say to lover boy here, you can say in front of me," he remarked, folding his arms defiantly.

Seeing he was not about to give them any privacy, Laurie sighed as she looked over at Mike. "I'm okay Mike, honestly. It's probably best you went. I'll see you at work tomorrow," she whispered as quietly as she could.

Laughing cruelly, Rich interrupted. "Oh no you won't Laurie. No way," he said vehemently. "You needn't think you're going back there again."

Laurie looked at him, further disbelief on her face. "What do you mean?"

"I don't think I've made myself clear enough," he sneered. "You have a choice to make and you can make it now. Choose *Mike*," he spat, "and you can go now. Or choose to stay and you can have your kids. But if you choose to stay then *obviously* you are not going back to work. You will never see *him* again," he said, looking over at Mike, a triumphant look plastered over his face.

"Come with me Laurie," urged Mike desperately. "Come on love. We'll sort the girls out, I promise. You won't lose them. I can't leave you here like this Laurie," he pleaded softly.

"You don't understand Mike," she whispered quietly. "I can't," she said, beginning to sob uncontrollably.

"Why?" asked Mike, a look of desperation mingled with bewilderment on his face.

"I won't get the girls," she answered. "He said he won't let me have the girls. I'll lose them Mike! I couldn't *bear* that." She was gabbling now and her panic was rising. What she wanted more than anything in the world was to walk away with Mike. She wanted it so badly, it hurt. But she also needed her girls and Rich was telling her in no uncertain terms that she couldn't have both.

"You won't lose them Laurie, I promise. They're your kids and we'll fight for them," he urged. "You're their *mum*. No court will give them to their dad!" he added, in as convincing a voice as he could muster.

"Mike, I'd *so* like to believe you, I really would," she said in an anguished tone, torn between going or staying.

"I meant what I said," said Rich in a dangerously quiet tone. "Walk now and you can kiss goodbye to those girls forever, I *promise* you."

Laurie's world fell apart at that moment, her heart breaking into a million little pieces. She knew what Rich was capable of and she knew he meant *every* word. She had no choice.

She would have to stay.

Backing away from the front door, her sobs turned into agonized cries as she mumbled to Mike, "I can't do it, Mike. I can't do it. I'm so sorry."

As her legs gave way beneath her and she sank to the floor, she was vaguely aware of Mike's tormented cries as the door was slammed in his face.

Part 2

Chapter 23

Twenty years later.

It was Cara's 21st birthday and Laurie was watching her as she danced around the living room, so excited she was, in coming of age.

Being the youngest, she knew what to expect and hadn't been disappointed. Rich had always made a big thing of their 21sts and he had bought both the elder girls brand new cars, so Cara was jumping up and down in delight having spotted a new car on the drive.

It was a brand new shiny BMW 1 series, the car she had repeatedly mentioned. She could now sell her 'banger' that her parents had bought her after passing her test. Laurie had at least won *that* fight, she thought. Rich had wanted to buy them all new cars at seventeen which Laurie thought to be a ludicrous idea.

"Yes," she had argued, "they might have passed their tests but *come on* Rich, you know as well as I do that the learning goes on *after* that!" They would have all sorts of bumps and scrapes to contend with, no doubt. More importantly Laurie didn't want them to have a car in which they could so easily speed. She had witnessed too many of her friends' children in hospital as a result of car accidents and new cars were so powerful, it was too easy not to realise the speed you were going.

So NO, she had put her foot down regarding this and insisted on an older car, less umph. And on this battle, she had won, much to her girls' disgust. To be honest, Laurie thought that buying them a BMW at twenty one was ridiculous but at least they had all had plenty of practice by then, therefore more likely to be sensible, she reasoned, crossing both her fingers behind her back.

Money was no issue now. Rich had been made a partner in the business years back and continually earned what Laurie thought to be an excessive amount. They had moved twice in the ensuing years and now lived in a large six bedrooms house, very grand looking, imposing even, which again, Laurie thought, suited Rich down to the ground. There was a large kitchen diner, separate imposing dining room, a massive living room, study, conservatory and last, but not least, an enormous games room. Upstairs consisted of the six bedrooms, three with en-suite. It was absolutely beautiful and, together with large landscaped gardens and electric gates, was a perfect statement for Rich. It screamed of success in every which way.

The girls loved it too of course. Why wouldn't they? They were continually pestering their parents to put in a pool. There was plenty of room for this and Rich was seriously considering it. Laurie could not see the point. It wasn't as though the girls would benefit from it for long now as they were all grown up. Maybe it would have been worthwhile when they had first moved in, five years ago, but not now.

Only Cara and Marie were still at home. Sarah had gone to Uni and never really returned. She had gone to UCE in Birmingham and then continued living in the city afterwards, finding work with various companies and house sharing along the way with old uni friends.

She seemed to be enjoying her life, her social life being far more important to her than work and, at twenty five, Sarah was showing no inclination to settle down. Laurie had lost count of the amount of boyfriends she had brought home over the years but Laurie could see that none of them had bowled her over as yet. Money was not an issue to Sarah *either* as Rich had paid all her fees and given her ample money whilst she studied, so Sarah had been able to fully immerse herself in the uni way of life unlike most of her friends who all had part time jobs to contend with.

Not that it seemed to be doing Sarah too much good, thought Laurie sadly. She wasn't sure Sarah was learning how to manage money that well. But why would she? Laurie asked herself. As long as her dad was there to bale her out all the time, then what was the need?

Sighing, Laurie picked up her empty cup of tea and walked through to the kitchen. Laurie's head was banging, she couldn't seem to handle much noise anymore. Marie's music was blaring upstairs, Sarah was shouting excitedly into her phone, gabbling away about the weekend she had just had at a festival and Smokey was barking like mad as the postman attempted to post envelopes through their letter box. "Come away Smokey," she shouted, dragging him away by his collar. "Just calm down," she said quietly, feeling exasperated. "It's not as though the postman comes only once in a blue moon is it?" she muttered, bending down and looking into Smokey's eyes as she patted him on his back. "No, he doesn't," she added, giving the dog another affectionate hug.

She loved Smokey, she sometimes felt he was the only member of the family on her side and she thoroughly enjoyed their time together in the week when everyone else was at work. Yes, she sometimes couldn't wait until Monday morning when the last one shut the front door. Laurie would feel a huge sense of relief. This was *her* time. She could do anything she wanted! There was no-one to consider but herself and she *revelled* in it. It was the only thing keeping her sane right now, she thought, sighing again at the thought of the day ahead.

They were all going out to a fancy restaurant later on. Rich, Laurie, the three girls, accompanied by Cara's latest boyfriend, Tom, who Laurie thought was a complete arse, and Adam, Marie's boyfriend who Laurie liked a lot...a lovely quiet man. Mind you, with Rich he would be quiet! He must frighten all their boyfriends to death! Rich had become more controlling as he had climbed the corporate ladder, very arrogant too and his manner was very bombastic. He had an ability to put people down and he was not afraid to do so at any given opportunity.

He had grown to love his girls though, with a passion. Too much, as far as Laurie was concerned and all three had become very spoilt over the years. At the beginning, Laurie had fought this. She loved the girls too, but also felt a responsibility towards bringing them up to become caring, loving, responsible adults and she was feeling that she had failed miserably. She knew how it had happened. Rich had simply worn her down. Well... that and her own difficulties dealing with the menopause! Her parenting had been excellent prior to the girls hitting their teens. She had total control over them and Rich had been so barely around, he had had little day to day influence. However as they hit their teens they soon worked out how to get their own way and would always wait for their daddy to come home before asking for anything of significance.

And Daddy gave them everything! He undermined Laurie at every turn and it wasn't long before the girls seemed to lose all respect for her. They *loved* her, she knew that, but they knew who wore the trousers and, as with any girls of that age, they manipulated the situation to their own advantage.

Walking over to the medicine cabinet, Laurie grabbed two paracetamol as well as a Sertraline, which she gulped down quickly with some cold water. Laurie had been prescribed Sertraline three years ago after having gone to the doctors in tears one day. She had described how she was feeling as best she could; vulnerable, helpless, old, and her doctor had been *so* kind. He had alluded to her being depressed as well as talking of the perimenopause which he said would be affecting the balance of her hormones. She had resisted the anti-depressants at first as she didn't want to feel a failure as she saw it and had spent the following six months throwing herself into all sorts of self help, taking plenty of walks with Smokey, joining a gym, eating healthier, and, whilst all of this had no doubt helped, a particularly low period had led to her giving in.

And she had to admit, she *did* feel a lot better. The sertraline seemed to numb her feelings. She noticed much of what had previously annoyed or upset her would now go over her head, so to speak. If she could describe it to anyone it was as though she had a bubble around her no-one was able to penetrate. And that suited Laurie perfectly!

Chapter 24

"Are you ready?" asked Rich, walking into their bedroom.

"I'll be two minutes," Laurie replied, desperately trying to find something suitable to wear.

"It doesn't look like that to me," Rich remarked, grabbing his jacket as he left the room. God...what was she going to wear? She had loads of appropriate clothes due to the numerous business dinners she had been forced to attend over the years but she had to admit that her figure was getting a little thicker around the middle and therefore many of her more fitted clothes were not as comfortable as she would like.

She picked out a more stretchy brightly coloured dress that she could wear, throwing it on quickly and looking at herself in the mirror. God...What a *state*. Her stomach...whilst not big... *did* show. And the dress was knee length too! No-one wore tights these days so her bare legs would be on show and she hadn't thought to use any self tan early enough. Stick thin white legs did not look attractive, she decided as she pulled the dress back over her head. And God...she was getting *so* hot again! *Fucking* menopause, she thought to herself as she wiped the back of her hand over her damp forehead.

It would be so much easier had she been going out in the winter. At least then she could have got away with some tights! Okay, trousers or jeans then, thought Laurie, looking longingly at her stretch Jeans. Jeans had come on leaps and bounds over the years and the stretch in them made them so comfy, she found she lived in them during the week. Maybe she could get away with some if she put on a sparkly top? She had a few that dropped low enough to conceal her stomach and were really pretty. Rich wouldn't approve though, not of Jeans, she thought despondently, settling for a boring pair of black trousers instead which she had had for years, together with a lacy top and some low kitten heels.

That would do, she thought as she looked in the mirror. It was comfy but still managed to look quite elegant. No 'wow' statement though, in fact, pretty boring really, but a safe choice.

No-one would notice her anyway, she realised as she picked up her black clutch bag. Going out with three grown up daughters soon put you in your place, Laurie thought, smiling a little sadly to herself. They all looked so fresh and vital, their skin so perfect! Why hadn't Laurie realised when she had been that age? She had always concentrated on the little things she didn't actually like about herself, not appreciating that her youthful beauty was so short lived. It seemed ridiculous to Laurie now as she remembered a time on holiday when the weather had been beautiful but Laurie hadn't *dared* wear the shorts she had packed. She had only been twenty one for God's sake! Her legs had been perfect and yet she had been too shy to show them off. If *only* she had known!

"Come on then!" shouted Rich from the bottom of the stairs.

"I'm coming!" Christ, he was impatient! He had gotten more so, over the years, especially towards her. They had been married twenty six years now, she reflected, as she walked down the stairs. What a waste of her life! She had never forgiven him for his actions all those years ago and she never would. Rich had been willing to use their girls as a weapon and she still had *no* doubt he would have carried out all that he had threatened, willing to sacrifice their girls' happiness as long as he won! This was something Laurie could never come to terms with.

He clearly didn't love Laurie anymore, he showed no concern towards her feelings. Everything was about him and keeping up appearances.

Not for the first time, Laurie felt a tremendous sadness sweep over her. She had experienced 'real' love with Mike and it hurt her deeply to know the difference. Rich and Laurie had never had love like that, not even in their early years. Is it better to have loved and lost or never to have loved at all? How many times had she heard that saying over the years? She still didn't have the answer either. Maybe ignorance *is* bliss after all!

"You're wearing those *trousers?*" Rich asked, contempt in his voice.

Used to his barbed comments, Laurie ignored him. There was little point trying to explain to him, and, quite frankly, she didn't think he cared that much. Thanks to her sertraline, neither did she, so she just shrugged her shoulders as she continued down the stairs.

"Christ! It's only your daughter's 21st after all," he sneered, climbing into their car. Nothing to dress up for!"

Ignoring him, Laurie turned on the radio to 'smooth' and immersed herself in the soft dreamy music as they sped into town. Sarah was travelling with them and she was sat in the back, texting away on her mobile. Both Cara and Marie were joining them at the restaurant. Cara was picking up Tom...he had no car of his own ...and Marie and Adam were also coming into town under their own steam, although Laurie believed Adam would be driving so that Marie could enjoy a drink.

Adam was very caring like that and it pleased Laurie immensely to see what a lovely couple they made. Adam got on well with Laurie, he would often seek her out to talk to, showing an interest in her life, however boring her life must seem to a youngster! He was extremely gentle too, a trait she loved. Yes, she would love to see them make a proper go of it, she would be delighted to have him as a son-in-law one day. Not Tom though! God, no way. She was rather hoping their relationship would fizzle out over time. She didn't like how Tom spoke to Cara. He would often talk down to her and Cara didn't seem to think there was anything wrong with that. Too many years of hearing mum and dad communicate, she thought wryly. Why would Cara see it as wrong when her own mum allowed it to happen all the time? Hmmm, she needed to stop analysing.

She would listen to the music and allow herself to drift off. In fact, that's how she would get through the whole evening, be there in body only, allow her mind to be elsewhere, she told herself, as she heard the constant tap, tap, tapping from Sarah in the back.

It was a lovely meal and there was plenty of good quality red wine to go around, so everyone was feeling merry as Laurie looked around the table. She, too, was feeling mellow; mixing alcohol with anti-depressants certainly did the trick, she thought.

God, her youngest daughter was now twenty one!! She hadn't *really* thought about this fact until now but actually they were all *adults!*...well...in theory anyway.

Her job was done! They did not need her anymore, they were old enough to go out on their own and make their own place in the world. How did that make her feel? She wasn't sure really. The last twenty years had been all about her girls. Everything she did had been for them and she dreaded to think how many hours a day she used to drive them around prior to them learning to drive! Cara had taken an *age* learning and even when she finally passed, Laurie would take her and pick her up anytime drinking was involved. Would she still ask now she had a new car? Probably not for a while until the novelty had worn off. That would make a nice change for her. Sitting up on her own most Friday and Saturday nights, often until the early hours of the morning, waiting for Cara to call had not been fun. No, not at all! Very lonely in fact. So...she would welcome a reprieve.

Equally, though, Laurie felt a certain trepidation. Her girls' lives were all moving forward and, whilst the girls and Rich all still had roles to play in life, Laurie was not sure she had.

She had nothing to do all day except clean, cook and be a general skivvy. She *did* enjoy going to the gym but that was it, the rest of her days were pretty empty. It wasn't even as though she had her evenings to look forward to! Rich would come home late, more often than not, which suited Laurie anyway. She would always have a meal prepared for him which he would tuck into and then promptly fall asleep on the sofa afterwards. They spoke very little to each other, literally communicating when necessary. Gone were the days when they would just talk for talking's sake and Laurie missed having a 'proper' partner. She missed it tremendously.

Thank God for Frankie, Laurie thought, not for the first time. She didn't know how she would have gotten through all these loveless years without her.

Rich didn't like Frankie, but that was no surprise. Frankie was very sure of herself and way too outspoken as far as Rich was concerned. Add to that the fact that Frankie was an old work colleague and Rich had done his best to stop their friendship over the years. However, he had little ammunition to use, thought Laurie. He had tried forbidding their friendship, but, as Laurie used to say to Frankie, "What's he going to do about it? He has no leverage. I will always see you. He will not know half the time, he's too busy at work."

And, so, their friendship had continued to grow. In recent years Frankie had been included in many of their family events and had become a good friend to her three girls. This had softened Rich a little and he had finally stopped giving Laurie a hard time over her. Yes, thought Laurie, cynically, a battle he wouldn't have won and therefore he had retreated, not wanting to lose face.

It was a shame Frankie hadn't managed to come tonight. Cara had invited her, but her dad was quite ill and she was spending a lot of her spare time looking after him. He had been diagnosed with cancer nine months ago and Frankie was devastated. Terminal too, so she was naturally spending as much time as she could with him.

Laurie had tragically lost her parents four years ago. They had been involved in a car accident in Turkey in which they had both been killed instantly, or so she had been told. It had been such a shock to Laurie at the time and she still *really* missed them, her mum especially. She had never told her mum exactly what had gone on and her mum had never pried, however they had regular contact and her mum had always been such a positive character, she always made Laurie feel a lot happier about things. That she loved and cared for Laurie was obvious in everything she said and did and Laurie missed her support so much.

Jim had also died, a sudden heart attack ten years ago, which had left Mavis widowed in her early seventies. A rich widow, though, and she now spent the majority of her time on cruises. Thank God, thought Laurie. Mavis had known everything that had gone on and had never let Laurie forget it. Her disapproval was always most apparent and she seemed to revel in putting Laurie down at every opportunity in much the same way as Rich did. Laurie had put up with it, but invited her round as little as she could get away with. After Jim's death, Laurie had been concerned that Mavis would become a permanent fixture and had been pleasantly surprised when she realised that Mavis had no such intention. Her initial booking of an 'around the world' cruise in the January following Jim's death had been such a shock to everyone and Rich had been very concerned. However she had returned, raving about it and, seemingly, was away all the time now. Laurie actually felt quite envious.

Taking another large gulp of her wine, Laurie looked around again. Cara and Tom were nattering away, Marie and Adam were busy looking on Facebook and Sarah was chatting to her dad, asking him if he would help pay for a holiday to Costa Rica she was desperately wanting to go on.

Laurie didn't really need to be here, certainly not required and maybe not even nice to have around, she thought sadly as she drained her glass and hastily refilled it.

Chapter 25

4th August 2016.

"So, how did Cara's birthday go then?" asked Frankie, sitting down opposite Laurie, simultaneously waving a waitress over. "Small white wine please," she said, smiling brightly at the young girl. "Have you ordered Laurie?"

"Yes," Laurie answered. "It's coming, I think."

"Okay, that's great. Are you eating?"

"No, just a drink for me."

"Right. I'll have the quiche and salad I think," said Frankie, passing the menu back to the waitress.

"Can't we tempt you?" asked the young girl, smiling over at Laurie. She was only about seventeen, such a sweet smile and her simple caring comment nearly brought tears to Laurie's eyes. Laurie was never hungry these days but she knew she needed to eat. "Go on then," she answered, a sad smile on her face. "I'll have the same, thank you."

As the waitress walked away Frankie looked at Laurie expectantly. "Oh, yes, Cara's birthday," laughed Laurie. "Sorry, I'm in another world. Yes, it was fine," she answered with little enthusiasm.

"Did she get what she wanted?"

"Yes, of course she did," answered Laurie bitterly. "They always do, don't they and it's not doing them any good at all, but he won't listen to me. It worries me to be honest. Well, you know that anyway. God, I've gone on about it often enough. They're all spoilt rotten!"

"He *does* spoil them, yes, but they're good kids underneath, Laurie. Don't forget that."

"I know," conceded Laurie. "It's just I love them all so much, but right now, the stages they are all at, I don't have much in common with any of them and, truth be told, I don't always like them very much either!"

"Well that's perfectly natural Laurie. They're still kids in many ways, finding their own way in life. As they all get older they'll come back to you, I bet," soothed Frankie.

"Do you think?" asked Laurie desperately.

"Yes, I do," answered Frankie firmly. "Anyway, how are *you*? You don't look very happy," she commented, reaching over the table and touching one of Laurie's hands gently.

The tears arrived immediately. Oh God, she thought. "I'm just a mess, I can't seem to stop crying especially when someone is being nice to me," said Laurie, lightly, whilst dabbing at her eyes with her napkin.

"Hey, whatever's the matter?"

"Oh, nothing ...And everything," she then went on to add, laughing a little. She looked around the restaurant. They always met here and it was a lovely quiet place. Fortunately there were no people close enough to witness her upset. Not that it would bother Frankie, she thought, but Laurie didn't want to embarrass herself either! "Oh, I don't know," she sighed. "I suppose having Cara reach twenty one has hit me hard. Add to that my fiftieth in a couple of weeks and I just feel old and a bit useless. Surplus to requirements, you could say," she said jokingly. Frankie took a sip of her wine and waited for Laurie to continue. "I mean, what is life for Frankie?" she asked, a desperate tone in her voice. "God, I feel I'm just living a life of quiet desperation and its killing me. I'm wasting my life, *that* I know."

Laurie knew Frankie was not going to protest as she had voiced this opinion many times over the years.

Frankie felt that Laurie had made the wrong choice twenty years ago, and at the beginning, had done everything in her power to make Laurie change her mind. She had tried to reason with her, telling her that a good solicitor would get Laurie custody of her girls, telling her that men like

Mike were not 'two a penny'. She had been adamant that things would work out eventually but Laurie would not change her mind. Frankie didn't know Rich well enough and Laurie could not take her advice on that basis. "You don't know him Frankie," she used to say. "You don't know what he is capable of."

And yes, over the years, as Frankie had spent time with Laurie and her family, she had admitted that Laurie had a point. Frankie disliked Rich intensely and saw how stubborn and contentious he could be. Frankie admitting this had made Laurie feel so much better as she felt her decision to stay had been validated.

"Well," said Frankie slowly. "You haven't been wasting your life, that's for sure. You brought your kids up as you wanted to. You have been there for them all the way. The choice you made back then has given them a solid, secure upbringing and you should congratulate yourself for that but..." Frankie shrugged her shoulders, "but, yes, *now*, I suppose I can see how you feel. The thing is, what are you going to do about it?"

Laurie had to laugh. This was Frankie at her absolute best. No messing, you have a problem, sort it! And Laurie loved her for it. "What *can* I do?" her look of bewilderment causing Frankie to sigh deeply.

"God, Laurie," Frankie said in exasperation. "You can do anything you want! Don't you see that?"

Shrugging her shoulders again and holding her hands up in surrender, Laurie could see how irritated Frankie was. "Yes, yes you're right, I know. But that's the problem. I don't actually know what I want and I just can't seem to get up any enthusiasm for anything these days, I just can't be bothered, to tell you the truth."

"I can see that Laurie," said Frankie sadly, taking both of Laurie's hands in her own again. "But, Laurie, you have a life to live still and you're only forty nine. You're *not* over the hill, however you may feel now, you have *years* left to

137

live and you don't need to waste them. Life *can* be enjoyed you know!"

"Not mine Frankie. It's too late for that now...far too late."

"No Laurie, No. It *isn't* too late. I have girlfriends in their fifties who tell me they are happier now than they have *ever* been! And you could be too!" Frankie urged.

They both went quiet, both lost in their thoughts. Laurie tucked into her quiche. It was really tasty and she could feel her appetite coming flooding back. "Very nice," she said as she finished. "God, I feel better for that," she added, smiling up at Frankie.

Shaking her head vigorously from side to side, Frankie looked over at Laurie. "I'm worried about you Laurie, you seem to have lost all your energy...all your spark."

Wiping her mouth with her napkin, Laurie smiled sadly. "I know," she agreed. "These sertraline certainly do the trick," she added. "I don't know what I want but frankly, I don't even care! I just get through the days in a little bit of a fuzzy haze. It's quite nice really!"

"I've got an idea!" said Frankie excitedly, jumping up out of her chair. "Why don't you come away with me? I've got two weeks off in September and I'm thinking of Thailand. It's beautiful there, you will *love* it!"

Laurie laughed, immediately dismissing the idea in her head. "I can't just take off, Frankie!"

Frankie looked at her incredulously "Why on earth not, what's stopping you? You've just said yourself you're not needed, your days are empty."

"You know *exactly* what's stopping me...Rich. He would go *crazy!*"

"Yes," agreed Frankie. "Of that, I have no doubt but what exactly could he do about it? How could he stop you?"

Laurie sat back in her chair. How *could* he stop her? He couldn't really, not unless he was to lock her in the house, she thought. He *would* go mad, that was for sure but he couldn't *actually* stop her from going! And the girls could all look after themselves. Smokey would be fine too as Marie loved him so he would get the odd walk at least. The house could look after itself for two weeks...okay...it would be a mess when she came back but so what? God, what would they eat? Who would make sure Rich had his tea ready, his shirts ironed?! Ha, he would have to do his own! This thought made Laurie chuckle and, feeling better than she had done for weeks, her food and wine helping her mood too, she looked over at Frankie. Her eyes twinkling, she nodded slowly. "You know what Frankie? I might just take you up on that offer!"

Laughing delightedly they clinked glasses together.

"Really!" exclaimed Frankie "Are you sure?" she asked, looking at Laurie in surprise mixed with disbelief.

"You know...I think I am," answered Laurie, a small bubble of excitement beginning to rise within her. "When are you thinking of going?"

"4th of September," answered Frankie.

"O....kaaay," said Laurie slowly, slightly taken aback by the date. The 4th of September was very special to Laurie and it was going to mark her twentieth anniversary...her best day ever...spent with Mike in Stratford. This was the date Laurie actually allowed herself to think of Mike...really think of him and *feel* her loss. Other than that day, Laurie had done everything in her power to move on and immerse herself in the life she had, trying not to think of Mike at all.

And she had managed this quite well, considering. It had helped tremendously with having a busy family life. Laurie had thrown herself into her children in such a way she barely had time to think, let alone reminisce. Her days had been filled to capacity and above. She used to get up in a morning, write as long a 'to do' list as she could think of and promptly get on with all her chores. She had been determined to be the best mum she could be and she knew

139

many of her friends admired her. All they could see was a super organised mum, three delightfully dressed and happy children, a nice house and a posh car. Yes, she could see their envy and Laurie had played her part to perfection. She told nobody of her troubles, the only link to her past being Frankie. "That's a Sunday isn't it?" she asked.

"Yes," replied Frankie in surprise and then, a dawning of realisation came over her. "Ah," she said, "Of course," she added. "I wasn't thinking. How long has it been?"

"Twenty years," Laurie whispered. "God...how I miss him still. In a way it feels like a lifetime but in another way it feels like it was only yesterday."

Frankie didn't know how Laurie spent that day and Laurie was not going to elaborate however there was no way she could go away that day. "I need time to think," she said. "I'm *really* tempted to come away with you but **not** on that day," she said emphatically.

Always ready with an answer to any of Laurie's protests, Frankie shrugged her shoulders. "Fair enough...That's perfectly okay, we can go on the Monday if you would prefer, Laurie. Quite frankly I don't care when we go, or where, really. I am happy doing whatever, so I'll fit in with you. I can always book a couple of extra days from work if necessary. I'm just absolutely delighted that you are even contemplating it!" she said, her voice rising in excitement. "We're going to have a great time and it will do us both the world of good."

Laurie felt bad then. Not for the first time, she had spent all lunchtime talking about herself and Frankie had her own problems too. "How is your dad?" she asked.

"Oh, he's doing okay, considering, but I'm struggling to look after him as well as working."

"I bet you are," acknowledged Laurie. "Can I do anything to help?"

"Not really, but thanks for asking. I've been looking into hospice care, certainly for when I go away but maybe even before. There's a wonderful hospice close to where he lives which he has stayed in temporarily already when I needed a break. They are *so* good and it perks him up tremendously. I was quite surprised, truth be told, I'd always thought of a hospice as a place people go to die, and whilst that's part of it of course, their ethos is fabulous. As far as they're concerned, whilst you may be dying, you're not dead yet and they have all sorts of activities taking place each day, always so positive too. Its actually a very happy environment to be in. I never fail to be uplifted there. Dad likes it too which is a tremendous relief for me. I don't feel bad therefore when he goes in and I have a break. So I've provisionally booked that for two weeks from the 3rd. I am a bit worried though. It's still a month away which is why I haven't booked Thailand yet. I was going to wait until nearer the time just in case he takes a turn for the worse," said Frankie, her lower lip trembling a little.

"Yes, of course," said Laurie softly, some of Frankie's words hitting Laurie hard. 'Whilst you may be dying you're not dead yet,' she mused. What a lovely way to look at death. In fact, they had turned it on its head. They are actually living *more* as a result of knowing death is close. Chiding herself for *her* continued negative attitude and lethargy, Laurie looked at Frankie, deciding in that moment that *she* was going to choose to live too, not merely exist. "It must be awful just watching your dad decline knowing you can't do anything to make it better Frankie and I can see you need a break. You've also made me think. So...yes...I will come with you. Not maybe, *definitely,"* she said, laughing. "That's a promise, I won't let you down," she added.

"That's brilliant! I must admit, I never mind going away by myself normally but I could certainly do with some company this year. Oh, wow... I'll start looking seriously then. What's your budget?"

Oh God, that's a point, thought Laurie. Rich would go mad if she took it from their savings, not that they hadn't got it mind, it would just be another thing for Rich to moan about.

But then she remembered something she had done years back, just after Rich's ultimatum. She had squirrelled money away, taking it from the housekeeping that Rich had supplied.

Ten pounds here and there had made a difference over the years and Laurie had managed to put away just over five thousand pounds into a savings account that Rich didn't know existed. She'd stopped eventually once she had fully come to terms with the fact that she was going nowhere, but it had certainly helped her feel better in those early years, allowing her to feel she had an escape plan should she need.

"I've got five thousand pounds that Rich doesn't even know about," Laurie answered. "So I suppose I could use that," she said, laughing delightedly. "Oh Frankie... I'm actually starting to feel excited! Wow, it will be a real adventure won't it?"

Laughing with her, Frankie nodded. "Absolutely it will!...And don't worry Laurie, five thousand will be more than enough, trust me. I'm not planning on it costing more than two! I'm single, remember, so as long as you don't mind budget accommodation, we're laughing!"

"I don't mind at all, as long as it's clean. That's all I ask, the rest of the detail I'll leave with you."

Picking up their bill and walking over to the till, Laurie felt better than she had in a long time. Frankie also looked happy and they gave each other such a hug before they parted ways, Frankie promising to call her as soon as she had further info so they could finalise all of their plans.

Chapter 26

Laurie awoke with a start. 7.15 am and she was fifty!!

She crept out of bed, not wanting to disturb Rich who was flat on his back, snoring noisily. She loved getting up earlier than everyone else. She loved the quiet stillness of early morning and would often take a cup of coffee into the conservatory where she would sit, undisturbed, Smokey by her side. It was so peaceful looking out over their garden, watching the birds, whilst listening to their morning chorus.

And today looked as if it was going to be a glorious day. Not a cloud in the sky! Wonderful, she thought as her coffee started making it's way through her body, awakening all her senses. She didn't like hitting fifty. She didn't suppose many people did, of course. Since meeting with Frankie, though, a fortnight ago, Laurie's life had taken an upwards turn. She had found herself feeling less down, less of a victim and was even reducing her anti-depressants, now down to one every other day. She was going to take them every third day from today and she was determined she would not be taking them with her to Thailand. No, definitely not. Laurie was choosing to live, she thought to herself, smiling delightedly and giving herself a big hug.

Their holiday was booked!!

Laurie still couldn't actually believe she was doing this and she felt an enormous amount of excitement, but also a little fear. Neither Rich nor her girls were aware yet. It had been booked for over a week now and Laurie *had* planned to tell them all straight away but she had ducked it, she thought, getting quite cross with herself.

She knew what she was doing and it annoyed her immensely. She was so weak! She did everything simply to fit in, never wanting to upset the apple cart. The girls brought plenty of drama into their home every evening and then...well...add Rich to the scenario too, who she knew full well would go ballistic and Laurie had simply not felt the strength she knew she would need.

So, she had said nothing! She *could* just go, she thought. Leave a note! Could she do that? Well, yes, of course she *could*, that was certainly a possibility but it wasn't right, she told herself firmly. But where had doing the right thing got her so far in life? she asked herself. Frowning slightly, she looked over at Smokey who had snuggled himself by her side, as close as he could possibly get, his eyes looking up at her adoringly. "What do you think Smokey?" she asked quietly. His tail wagged slightly, happy to be having attention as he began to lick at her hands. "Do I tell them and give myself a miserable couple of weeks before I go or do I just leave them a note?"

It *was* possible, she could pack whilst everyone was out. Their suitcases were in the loft, she could easily manage to retrieve one and pack it in the daytime, leaving it in the boot of her car. No-one would be any the wiser. It would certainly be easier, she thought, much easier than telling Rich! She wouldn't feel guilty just leaving a note for him. She didn't care for him any more and had little interest in how he, personally, would feel as a result. However, her girls...that was a different matter. They would find it all a little odd to say the least and then they would have to listen to their dad moaning about her afterwards

She could just imagine it, he would fill their heads with all sorts of rubbish...how their mum was ungrateful, how he worked all hours so that mum could just swan around at home, how crazy she was acting...yes...she could see it now.

And, of course, from the outside, looking in, it would certainly seem that way. Laurie would be the one in the wrong. Rich would present himself as the victim and the girls would fall for it, of course they would.

Could she inform the girls, but not Rich? To do that, she would have to explain to them how she felt and why she needed a break. That was a possibility, she mused, she didn't have to tell them *everything*. Maybe they would understand? Mmm, maybe not. She hadn't much evidence so far of any of them showing much empathy. They were all so wrapped up in their own lives, she reflected. In fact, Rich and Laurie had done such a good job of presenting a so-called perfect life, their children had lived the dream. Two parents at home, their mum always at their beck and call, no money worries, everything they wanted, they had! So, of course, Laurie had no idea how they might react. There had been little adversity in the girls' lives, she had not witnessed any particular mental strength from any of her girls as they hadn't had anything bad happen! So, in honesty, she didn't know how they might behave. She would like to think that they would listen to their mum and have some understanding of why their mum needed a break, even encourage her to do it! Yes, she would *like* to think that but she didn't feel overly hopeful, especially considering how spoilt they seemed to have become and how overly concerned with image they all were.

Now...Adam?...maybe he would understand. She felt very connected to Adam and pondered whether she could at least talk to him before she went. At least that way there would be a chance of the girls getting a different viewpoint from their fathers. Remembering Frankie's words though, she also told herself they were all grown up. Her job was actually done. No-one needed her anymore. But if she was going to worry to this extent, then she would totally spoil her holiday. There was absolutely no point in going if she was going to worry about what Rich was telling the girls every day!

Pulling herself up from her chair, she sighed heavily. If she was going to decide to choose to *live,* not merely exist, then there was going to be some trouble along the way. Of course the girls wouldn't like it! They were perfectly content with how things were! But Laurie had to start thinking of her needs too. So...she still hadn't answered her question. Does she tell them or not? She would stay quiet for now. It was her birthday after all and she didn't want to rock the boat today. Yes, that's what she would do...put it off for another day!

Cara walked into the kitchen as Laurie was unloading the dishwasher.

"Morning Sweetheart," said Laurie softly, smiling over at her youngest. Cara grunted something unintelligible and turned the kettle on, grabbing a large mug from the cupboard and popping a tea bag into it. "Kettle's only just boiled love," said Laurie, automatically wanting to step in and take control. "Sit down, I'll do it." Cara silently obliged, yawning loudly. She was not a morning person and Laurie was surprised to see her up, it was only 8.30 and a weekend too! "Didn't you sleep well?"

"Okay," shrugged Cara, picking up her phone. "Oh, happy birthday by the way," Cara added, her concentration clearly on her handset, not even a glance in Laurie's direction.

"Thank you Cara," said Laurie simply, as she handed the mug of tea over the kitchen table. She stood for a few seconds but realised Cara was not about to engage in further conversation. "So...Any plans for today?"

"Dunno," replied Cara with another shrug of the shoulders.

At this point Laurie decided to give up. She turned back to the task at hand, placing all the clean crockery onto her marble worksurface. Unloading the dishwasher was one of her pet hates. It always seemed to take an age and Laurie would have happily gone back to the days of washing up.

She thought back to when she had been a child, her mum washing, her dad drying and Laurie putting away. Many an evening had started in this way, with them all contentedly sighing as they took a cup of tea into the living room, their jobs done for the day and an evening in front of the tele to look forward to. They had always watched 'Coronation street' together, her dad moaning every time the music came on, but funnily enough knowing all of the characters as much as Laurie and her mum did! And then there had been 'Dallas' on a Wednesday night, 8pm, she thought, chuckling to herself. That had been a brilliant series. Everyone seemed to love it. It would be the topic of conversation in every school, place of work, hairdressers, everywhere you could think of on the Thursday morning. Things had certainly moved on since those days, she thought, and not always for the better. She couldn't think of many evenings her daughters spent with her now. Yes, they may have been in the same room, but everyone was in their own little world, phones or tablets never leaving their sides. It was rare for them all to enjoy a programme together anymore.

'X factor' had been brilliant a few years ago when her children were younger. They would all enjoy a take-away and then huddle on the sofa together to watch it. That had been nice. But now...well...they watched all they wanted on 'catch up'. Very rarely did she now sit and watch TV with her girls and she missed it....very much.

Laurie had trouble with anything 'techy'. Not having been at school when computers were regularly used...well...that was laughable...the only computer room she could remember was the language room where you would put headphones on and listen to a foreign phrase and then be asked to repeat it. Obviously she had been more in the know at 'Kays' but twenty years of not working, of not *having* to use a computer had taken their toll and she felt very left behind. These days she often had trouble even using the remotes for their TV and she would get very frustrated trying to work out which remote to use and whether it should be on DVD, VCR, HDM11 or 12 or whatever else it said!

Whatever had happened to the days of simply switching the TV on using the on/off switch! God, she was sounding old!

She remembered picking up Cara's phone a couple of years ago when she had been dusting in the living room. It was unusual for Cara to leave her phone anywhere and as she picked it up to take it into Cara's bedroom, she looked at the screen. 'Lifetime companion,' it said. Laurie had laughed at the time but she could see, more and more, that this was actually true! Yes, life was moving on at a pace and Laurie was not keeping up. She was aware that this was largely her own fault. So devastated had she been all those years ago and so completely defeated, she had allowed herself to drift.

Rich had taken control and Laurie had simply gone along with everything. She understood why, oh yes! She simply hadn't cared anymore. All she had left were her girls, or that's how she had felt anyway. On that basis it didn't matter what she did, where they lived, it all felt futile.

Rich had indulged in many affairs along the way, none of which she had cared about. She secretly hoped he would fall for someone enough for him to want to leave but that had never happened. Well, not so far anyway! You never know, she thought, one day maybe?

But this thought process was exactly what she needed to change, she thought in exasperation. Again, automatically allowing Rich to take control. *Hoping* he would leave! What was that about for goodness sake?

About time she started to take some control, she told herself, smiling. Yes, some of Frankie's words were at last getting through. She would be telling her to grab what was left of her life and live it, not for others, but for herself, and that's exactly what Laurie intended to do!

Chapter 27

That evening.

"Can I have your attention everyone?" shouted Rich, standing importantly at the front of the marquee Rich had arranged to have erected in their back garden. The marquee had been beautifully decorated, arrangements of flowers everywhere, tables each decorated in a rose gold theme, Tattinger champagne and canapés being handed out in abundance.

All went quiet as everyone turned to listen to Rich.

Smiling as he looked around, he beckoned to Laurie to join him.

Here we go, thought Laurie, attempting to plaster a smile on her face that she didn't feel. Taking Laurie's hand in his, Rich turned to her and smiled. God, he was a good actor, she thought. Everyone would be taken in, he came across as so charming and genuine.

Laurie felt sick, actually physically sick as she listened to Rich continue with his act. "I won't keep everyone long, I just want to say a few words. First of all, thankyou to you all for coming. I want you all to have a thoroughly enjoyable evening whilst you are celebrating my wife's birthday with us...fifty," he said, smiling indulgently at Laurie. "And still as beautiful as ever." God...She couldn't stand it, the smile on her face becoming increasingly difficult to maintain. She looked around at the group in front of her. Her girls were standing together, both Sarah and Cara tapping away on their phones...the rest of the crowd though, Laurie barely knew...neighbours she had only passed the time of day with to be polite and then all of Rich's work colleagues together with their respective partners.

Twenty years of business associates basically with their pompous attitudes!

Not even Rich's mum was there, off on another of her cruises! She searched for Frankie's face in the crowd. There she was. Thank God...a friendly face... someone who understood how much of a farce this party was, someone else who knew Rich was talking utter bollocks! And it *was* bollocks...all of this.

The party, the marquee, the speech. What was it all for? Not for Laurie, that was for sure! She had been adamant she hadn't wanted a party. Absolutely adamant! She couldn't have been clearer, but of course, she thought cynically, you can't have the big house and a successful family life and NOT have the big fiftieth bash for the wife! All for show, Laurie thought sadly. Rich hadn't called her beautiful in years!

Searching the crowd again, Laurie saw three women who she knew had had affairs with Rich...and that was who she knew!... How many more had there been? Those three knew this was all a farce. How many others were thinking the same thing? she mused. People talked, Laurie knew, so whilst Rich was presenting the perfect family life to everyone, Laurie felt that possibly the whole crowd in front of them knew differently.

She took a large gulp of her champagne.

"Yes," Rich continued. "I would like to tell you all how blessed I feel." He placed an arm around Laurie. "So, please, raise your glasses to my dearest wife...Laurie. To Laurie," Rich shouted, raising his glass in the air as Laurie watched all the crowd do the same.

"Speech, speech," she heard from someone at the back.

"There will be no speech," Rich announced immediately in an imperious tone. "Laurie doesn't like the limelight. Do you pet?"

For a brief second Laurie saw a nasty sneer appear on his face, quickly wiped away. She looked over at Frankie who was looking rather sad, she thought. Catching Laurie's eyes, she raised her eyebrows quizzically.

The combination of Rich's sneer, Frankie's urging, coupled with plenty of champagne stirred something deep inside her and a strength she hadn't felt in years surfaced.

Taking the mike from Rich before she had chance to change her mind, she scanned the crowd again. They were all beginning to chatter amongst themselves again but it was still reasonably quiet as she began to speak. "Actually," she whispered into the mike. No-one heard her though and Rich went to take the mike from her quickly, a frantic look spreading over his face. "What's the matter Rich?" she asked quietly. "Frightened of what I might say?" she added, looking intently into his eyes as he wrestled with her to try to get the mike out of her hands. Laurie held on firmly. She had finally had enough. She was going to speak and Rich was not going to stop her!

Taking a deep breath she scanned the audience again. "Actually," she repeated, louder this time and more firmly. "There *is* something I would like to say."

Her stomach was performing somersaults and she deliberately avoided looking in Rich's direction but stared over at Frankie as she spoke. "Firstly, I would *also* like to thank you all for coming... but let's be honest," she said, a sad, wry smile on her face. "This isn't a party I wanted...oh no...absolutely not."

The crowd fell silent, a small gasp heard from one of the women, one of their neighbours, Laurie believed. "NO" she said again, firmly. "This is a party organized by my husband because he feels it is right...the right thing to do...as always. He wants to appear to be the good husband, the provider, presenting to you our perfect life." She went quiet for a moment. "But it isn't perfect, in fact, far from it to be honest. And it hasn't been perfect in a long time," she added. The crowd all held their breath. A pin could have been heard, had one been dropped.

Laurie took another deep breath in and raised her voice. "And tonight, this farce stops," she announced. "So, whilst I'd like to re-iterate my thanks to you all for coming, I, myself, am leaving now. By all means, please feel free to enjoy the rest of the evening. Please...drink the champagne, enjoy your meal."

Dropping the mike on the closest table, Laurie turned and walked calmly out of the marquee. She could hear a few gasps and low whispering as well as Cara's voice shouting "mum" in shock and surprise, but Laurie was past caring.

Walking across the garden, she slid off her shoes...they were way too uncomfortable...and opened the back door into the kitchen. She walked past Smokey, patting him on his head and climbed the stairs.

She felt absolutely elated...free...she couldn't quite believe what she had just done but, boy, did she feel good! Honesty... that's what it was. For the first time in twenty years, she had finally been honest. Honest with herself, first and foremost, and then had the strength to be honest with the world!

Chuckling to herself she walked into the bedroom she shared with Rich, sliding out of her dress and choosing her pyjamas...baggy ones, fleece too. Pyjamas Rich hated. Tough, she thought as she put her head through the top. Flopping onto the bed, she sighed and noticed a deep calm beginning to descend, an inner peace she hadn't felt in years surging through her body.

Closing her eyes, she fell into the deepest of sleeps.

Chapter 28

Laurie awoke early. It was only 5.30am and for a few seconds it was another normal day...until the memories from last night came flooding back.

Her stomach took an immediate dive. Shit, she thought, what *had* she done?

Looking over to where Rich usually lay, she could see he had not come to bed. Oh fuck. He would be so pissed off. She had never behaved like that before and she could only imagine how annoyed Rich would be. Showing him up in front of everyone! He would be livid!

Tough shit, she thought to herself. She had spent too many years being the perfect wife and mother, better than a bloody 'stepford wife'!...Well, no more.

Thinking back to his speech, her anger resurfaced.

The indulgent look on Rich's face, his words, all lies, followed by that nasty sneer that only Laurie had seen, had all contributed to her response. She supposed also that her decreased use of the anti-depressants would be making a difference as she was fully starting to feel things again...Anger, certainly, she thought with a wry smile.

She felt as though she was waking up from twenty years of sleeping and she *did* feel angry. At Rich, first and foremost, but also at herself. She had wasted her life and last night had really highlighted to Laurie the farce they were living.

Sighing heavily, Laurie walked into their en-suite, peeing quickly. It had been one of the first nights Laurie could remember in a long while when she hadn't woken up in the night for a trip to the loo. As a result she was desperate.

154

She turned her shower on full blast, as hot as she could possibly take it and stood, enjoying the water cascading over her body for a full five minutes. Ahhh. It was beautiful, she thought. There was nothing like a hot shower to wake you up and feel better. If only it were that simple though. Wouldn't life be great if all could be sorted simply by taking a shower?! Wrapping herself in a large white fluffy towel, she padded into her dressing area.

She *loved* her dressing area. There were full length mirrored wardrobes all around her, plenty of storage space and even a whole wall for their shoes! All stacked neatly in see-through boxes, there was none of the trouble of ploughing through as she used to, all of her shoes jumbled together in a mess at the bottom of the wardrobe! She pulled open the drawers where her underwear lived...again...all neatly sorted...with lots of beautiful silk panties that had cost an absolute packet! They felt so lovely on her skin, so soft. That was the only reason for buying them though, certainly not for Rich's pleasure! She picked out a bright purple pair and a bra to match but avoided looking at herself in the mirror as she put them on.

Mirrors should be banned once you'd passed fifty, she told herself. She hated looking at herself now. All she saw was dry, wrinkled skin, her wrinkles around her eyes were actually meeting up to have a chat with those around her mouth! And her stomach! Well...God...what a shambles! Three kids later with all the stretch marks collected along the way! Add to that the extra stone she had gradually accumulated and she looked a right mess.

Stop it, she told herself firmly, she was getting older, yes, but so what!

She thought of what Frankie had said about her dad at the hospice. Their belief! Today they were alive and so they were going to enjoy it.

She was alive too! And so she would do everything she could to enjoy her day.

Pulling on a pair of stretch jeans and a loose fitting summer top, she smiled as she looked at herself again. What a difference...nice clothes disguising all her lumps and bumps and a smile which made such a difference to her face!

The weather was absolutely beautiful still and she could tell it was going to be another glorious day. It was still only 6am and all was quiet as she walked downstairs.

She assumed Rich had used their spare bedroom. It was a large room with it's own en-suite and they usually kept it for guests but Rich had taken to using it more often these days. Not that Laurie cared. She much preferred it and hated it when he came back into their own bedroom. He only did so for appearances sake as he wouldn't want the girls to think there were any problems between them. Well...they would know differently now wouldn't they? she thought as she put the kettle on for a cuppa.

Laurie felt bad about that and some of her fight within her receded a little.

She loved her kids so much, she only ever wanted perfection for them. But she was also beginning to realise that this was not actually possible. Perfection didn't exist, maybe momentarily, but never for long. Real life was not like that and she had actually not helped the girls any which way by trying to protect them from reality. She was going to have to speak to them all today if that was possible, try to give them an understanding of where she was coming from and why.

How could she possibly explain twenty years of misery and pretence away? She had no idea...no idea where to even start...how much to say? Feeling tears sliding down her cheeks she realised the enormity of the situation as she grabbed Smokey's lead from the utility and called to him quietly. "Come on Smokey, let's go for a walk."

Smokey, who hadn't even raised himself from his bed yet, perked up at the word 'walk', pricked up his ears and stretching himself, padded over to her eagerly, his tail wagging.

Laurie hugged him tightly around his neck, breathing in his doggy scent, just like she used to when the girls were babies, she thought. Opening the front door, she walked outside, breathing in the fresh morning air...Beautiful, she said to herself as she walked up the drive and along the path into the village centre. A walk Smokey knew so well, he didn't really need his lead on.

Walking back into the house an hour later, Laurie felt wonderfully calm. A good job, she thought to herself as she walked into the kitchen where Rich was sitting at the table, a look of absolute fury on his face.

"How could you?" he shouted as soon as Laurie walked in. "How *fucking* could you?" he shouted again, louder this time.

Laurie didn't respond as she walked past him to give Smokey some water.

"*Don't* walk by me as though I'm not here," he shouted, rising from his seat. Grabbing her shoulders he stared at her. Quietly this time he repeated the question "How could you Laurie? All I do for you. All I have provided for you! In front of all our friends...how could you?"

He looked quite hurt and Laurie was astounded. He did seem to actually believe what he was saying! It amazed her. Their marriage was an absolute sham. He didn't respect her, didn't even seem to like her and yet he believed she had done him wrong. He looked down on her continually, put her down whenever he could, showed her up in front of the girls all the time...and yet...and yet...he still believed she was the one in the wrong and he was a complete innocent.

Amazing! She was culpable, she knew. After all, it *was* her who had had the affair. But twenty years for God's sake! For twenty years she had allowed him to play the victim and she had felt a tremendous guilt. He never mentioned Mike...not once...but Mike was always there...in the tone of voice Rich had used ever since. Rich had never forgotten, never forgiven and never would.

But Laurie also realised that she had also never forgotten or forgiven Rich for how he had behaved at the time. As far as she was concerned, his behaviour had been as bad and, using the girls in the way he had, she had found deplorable. An act she could never get over.

A certain clarity descended in that instant, a clarity Laurie wished had come an awful lot sooner. They were stuck, both of them, neither of them making any effort in all those years to come together again, communicate, attempt to appreciate the other's feelings. Had they done this, gone to counselling, whatever, then *maybe* they would have stood a chance. They had loved each other once, she reasoned. So there had been affection at one point! How sad, she thought, how so, so sad.

"I'm sorry Rich," she said softly.

"I should fucking think so," he shouted indignantly, puffing himself up to his full height in righteous indignation.

"No," Laurie said firmly. "No...You misunderstood me," she said sadly. "I *am* sorry, yes, but not sorry about last night. That was well overdue."

Rich's face went purple with rage.

"Listen to me Rich," Laurie said firmly. "I'm sorry we have ended up this way, it's so sad and we are both to blame for it. And yes, I'm actually going to speak of Mike," her voice trembling a little at his name, a name she had never dared mention in all these years.

Rich took a step back as though he had been hit.

"Sit down Rich," Laurie said quietly. "Sit down please," she urged. "If you have any feelings for me at all still, then please, hear me out."

Her heart was pounding and she was sweating profusely but she knew she needed to carry on.

Rich sat back down and Laurie took the opportunity to speak.

"This is from my perspective, Rich. And then, I'd very much like to hear it from yours if you can. Are you ready to listen?"

He looked absolutely astounded and Laurie was not sure what on earth he was thinking. Seconds rolled into a full minute as Laurie waited with bated breath.

"Go on," he said finally, sitting back in his chair, his arms folded, a tight expression on his face.

Laurie had to smile. It was as good an opportunity as she was going to get. Of course he would feel defensive, she reasoned. But at least he hadn't stormed off. "When I met you Rich, I loved you...so much...and I truly believed we would live happily ever after," she said softly, a small, sad, rueful smile on her face. "And we *were* happy in the early days. Well, I was anyway and I think you were too? But things got complicated Rich. We both seemed to want different things from life, have differing needs. You wanted me at home. I wanted to work."

Rich opened his mouth to speak.

Putting one of her hands up toward him, Laurie continued. "No, hear me out Rich. This is not about what's right and wrong. I'm simply trying to get you to see things from where I'm coming from, that's all."

Rich nodded as he looked over at Laurie. He looked quite surprised, she thought. Surprised that Laurie was taking the lead she supposed. Defeated as well.

"As I was saying," she continued. "Things were not good between us as a result, as well you know. Mike came along at that time...a time when I was vulnerable and I fell for him...hook, line and sinker. I **loved** him Rich. I loved him so much."

She went quiet for a while. Was she going too far? No. She was simply telling the truth and it actually felt good. Like a cool balm on her skin. Twenty years had not lessened her feelings for Mike in any way and she could feel tears filling her eyes. "What you did Rich," she said, looking directly at him, "your ultimatum...it killed me. Actually killed any feeling I had ever had for you. You gave me **no** choice that day, as well you know. You fought for me and you won! You knew I could never leave my kids after what you said. But what *exactly* did you win Rich? As far as I can see, that day, we both lost! Let's face it, neither of us has been happy since have we?" she asked softly, looking over at him.

Rich was giving nothing away so Laurie continued. "Yes, we have the big house, the posh car, lovely holidays too. But **no** love Rich, not on either side. I know you've had affairs, I'm not daft and, truthfully, I don't actually care! So, why are we continuing like this eh? Why? Just so everyone else thinks we have a perfect life?"

Again, Rich said not a word and Laurie still had no idea what he was thinking. Rich was always the vocal one, the one with a quick temper, an answer for everything so Laurie was feeling increasingly unnerved by his lack of response. She realised she was waiting for his explosion. Had she said too much? No. All she had done was spoken the truth and it felt good. "Well?" she whispered.

"You showed me up," he said flatly.

"What?!" she exclaimed incredulously.

"You showed me up last night," Rich repeated. His voice was stoney calm.

"Oh, for God's sake Rich," she shouted in utter exasperation. "Is that all you can say, all you care about? How sad is that? There were no *friends* there last night, they are all just acquaintances. Who cares about what they all think?" she shouted, feeling as though she herself was going mad.

She couldn't seem to reach Rich. Here she was, trying at last to talk about their *real* problems and all Rich seemed concerned about was last night!

"*I* care," he shouted. "I care. And I've got to show my face tomorrow at work knowing everyone will be talking about me, or, more to the point, about *you*...how mad you are...how ungrateful you are, how...."

Laurie had had enough, there was clearly going to be no meeting of minds here!

No shock really, she thought sadly as she quickly walked away, hands to her ears in an attempt to block out the rest of Rich's tirade.

Laurie felt a sadness so deep. For a moment there, she felt as though she might actually have a chance of getting through to him. She had been hopeful of a proper, honest talk. Rich, listening to Laurie and she, in return, listening to Rich. But it clearly wasn't to be...not even after this many years and she knew, deep in her heart that they could never move on, either of them.

Rich was stuck in the past, so bitter. And Laurie was stuck too...also bitter.

Well, she had tried. Rich was unwilling, or unable? to talk about the past. Too proud a man, she thought sadly as she began to tackle the pile of ironing sitting in the laundry basket.

Chapter 29

Same day.

"Well...what was all that about mum?" demanded Sarah, plopping herself down on the sofa. "God, how embarrassing!" she added, rolling her eyes dramatically.

Laurie had been ironing for an hour by this time and had immersed herself into the news in horror. A suicide bomber at a Turkish wedding. How awful, she thought. How on earth could anyone even *consider* doing something as awful as that? A day that should have been so special, taken over by evil. How does someone get to that point? She had absolutely no idea how anyone could go through with it, to *actually* put a suicide jacket on, knowing you were going to blow yourself up! It was unbelievable. Not to mention the hatred that person must feel to be willing to take so many innocents with them! What *was* the world coming to?

So immersed was she in the news and so upset by the thought of at least fifty lives having been taken so unnecessarily, she had not looked over at Sarah as she had walked in. Neither had she noticed her tone. "God, Sarah, have you heard about this?" she asked, spraying water onto one of Rich's shirts in an attempt to get some of the creases out. She should iron his shirts whilst they were still slightly damp. Made such a difference. But she hadn't and now she had seven shirts to iron, all so creased it was untrue! "This suicide bombing, it's awful! At a wedding too. Can you believe it?" she asked, talking to herself as much as to Sarah.

"Muuum," shouted Sarah. "Are you for real?" she asked, her eyes like saucers. "I can't *believe* what you did last night. It was awful mum. How do you think I felt standing there after you walked out? Everyone was looking at us! I could have *died!* I mean...really...what were you playing at mum?" Without waiting for her mum to reply, Sarah continued. "And as for dad! Well, I felt *so* sorry for him. He didn't know *what* to say, it was excruciatingly embarrassing for him too. God!" Sarah shouted "What's up with you for Christ sake?" she asked, her hands lifting into the air in a questioning manner.

Laurie sighed heavily. A suicide bomber in Turkey meant nothing to Sarah...absolutely nothing...and this shook her. Had she been the same at that age? Maybe...but she didn't think so. She had been married, having just had Sarah. She believed a suicide bomber would have had *some* impact at least.

"Sarah, I'm sorry," she said, putting the iron down on the ironing board and looking over at her eldest daughter. Sarah was beautiful, she thought. A willowy frame and lovely tanned, smooth skin. She had no idea of her beauty, thought Laurie.

Sarah said nothing, just looked at her mum reproachfully.

"I'm *really* sorry," Laurie repeated. "And I need to talk to you properly, I understand that...your two sisters too."

"Well," demanded Sarah, sitting back, her arms folded in a not dissimilar manner to her father, she noticed.

How much did she say? thought Laurie. God, this was so difficult! She never wanted to tell the girls anything which she knew would upset them. She only ever wanted them to be happy. But she realised that honesty was badly needed and long overdue.

"Sarah," Laurie said softly, sitting down beside her. "I'm sorry about last night. I really am. It wasn't planned and I certainly shouldn't have done it. But I hadn't wanted this fiftieth bash. I'd told your dad on many occasions I didn't want any fuss but he went ahead with it regardless. So, I was angry, I guess."

Sarah opened her mouth to speak but Laurie shushed her. "No, Sarah, let me speak. Let me at least try to explain...Please," she pleaded. Sarah's mouth closed. "Yes,

I was angry...sad too. I know you are finding this difficult Sarah, of course you will be. But please can you try and see this from my perspective too? I haven't been happy in a *long* time. I'm actually on anti-depressants, I have felt so low."

Sarah looked shocked but said nothing as Laurie continued. "I'm trying to come off them, so don't worry," she added hastily. "But last night everything got on top of me. So much! As I said, I hadn't wanted a party, I'm not that type of person am I really? But your dad...well...he just went ahead and I stupidly went along with it just to keep the peace! But what your dad said Sarah. It's just not true and I lost it, I suppose. The truth is, love, our marriage is *not* idyllic...far from it...and I am really struggling at the moment. But I don't want you to worry love. It's not for you to worry about."

"How can you say that Mum?" Sarah scoffed. "Of course I'm going to worry. God!" she shouted, standing up in exasperation. She paced the room.

"What are you actually saying mum?" she whispered, looking over at Laurie, fear evident in her eyes.

"I don't know Sarah, I really don't actually know what I'm trying to say. I'm just trying to be honest, that's all. Last night's behaviour was inexcusable and I feel quite ashamed now. Thinking of you and your two sisters having to deal with the aftermath. And I don't know what's going to happen going forward. As I say, I'm in a bit of a mess. Perimenopause, the doctor tells me, but that's no excuse."

"Are you and dad going to get a divorce?" asked Sarah, her voice raising several octaves.

Laurie shook her head, tears filling her eyes. Her automatic response was to shake her head vehemently, wanting to protect her daughter, wanting to deny this possibility. But she didn't. "I don't know Sarah," she said sadly. "I really don't know what's going to happen. I'm so tired, so desperately, desperately tired of it all."

Laurie put her head in her hands and started to sob, quietly at first and then as she felt her daughter's arms around her, she sobbed uncontrollably, her heart feeling as though it would break, her loneliness so acute.

Chapter 30

All was quiet. The front door had slammed firmly shut at 8.15am as Cara left for work. Rich had left as normal at 7.30am and Marie not long after him.

Cara only worked in Worcester, twenty minutes by car. She worked at M&S, having landed a job there when she left school at eighteen. Cara had never shown any interest in going to uni, Marie either and they both seemed perfectly content. Cara loved her job, she said. It was quite busy during the day but she felt no stress, liking the fact that once the day was done, she had nothing to worry over. She could come home and simply enjoy her evenings.

Rich had tried, unsuccessfully, to persuade each of the girls to come and work with him. He could find them a job, he would say. But her girls weren't daft, thought Laurie, a smile on her face. A place of work where your dad was the boss? How could they flirt with anyone? Have a laugh and a joke? No...they had all resisted and chosen their own paths.

Marie worked for a charity, working in their offices, spending the majority of her time on the phones, dealing with all manner of fund raising activities and she seemed perfectly content too. So Laurie had no particular concerns over either of her youngest girls, despite them having chosen not to go to uni. She marvelled at how they had both settled into a work environment and it was a constant source of satisfaction to her. So...all was quiet...thank God, thought Laurie as she sat down in the conservatory with her second cup of coffee of the day.

Well, what a mess the weekend had been, she thought. Rich had studiously ignored her the rest of yesterday. After having given instructions to the team dismantling the marquee, he had gone out, golf clubs in the boot of his car.

Sarah had taken Laurie by surprise though. Yesterday had been a first...Sarah comforting Laurie...this had never happened before. The arms Sarah had put around her mum had shocked Laurie, but comforted her too...enormously.

Not much more had actually been said, but when Sarah left later that day to go back to Birmingham, she had hugged her mum tightly and asked that she phone her every day. Laurie had said she would and had to smile at this turn around. Crikey, it hadn't been many moons ago that Sarah had told Laurie off for doing that. "God mum, you don't have to phone me every day, I'm perfectly ok" she had said. And so, the phone calls had dropped off over the last year or so, but still, whenever Laurie *had* called, it had always been about Sarah...Was she eating enough, sleeping ok, where was she going out, how was work? Very little two-way conversation. So...the thought of Sarah actually asking her mum to phone showed how concerned Sarah was. And getting more mature too, thought Laurie proudly.

Laurie hadn't managed to speak to Cara or Marie though.

Marie had not been at home, presumably having chosen to stay out of the way. She assumed she had stayed at Adam's overnight, having come back late last night and run straight into her bedroom before Laurie had a chance to catch her. This was quite typical of Marie. She was quite capable but she liked to sort things out in her own mind first and Laurie decided Marie would come to her in her own time as and when she felt able to do so.

Cara worried her though. She hadn't spoken to her mum yesterday, ignoring her completely on the two occasions they had bumped into each other.

Taking another sip of coffee, Laurie sighed heavily. She felt particularly low this morning. She had woken up feeling this large black cloud hanging overhead and it had followed her from the bedroom into the kitchen and now into the conservatory. Her stomach was playing her up too. It always did when she was upset and she hadn't been able to face breakfast.

She felt so, so alone, she thought, looking out of the conservatory window. She didn't know what to do with herself, she thought desperately. No-one understood her, no-one cared enough to try and for the first time in many years she allowed herself to think about Mike. Mike had been the only person throughout her life, her parents excepting, who had really truly made her feel loved...properly loved...someone who would have cared for her no matter what...and she really needed that now. Hugging herself tightly she tried to stem the tears filling her eyes but she couldn't stop them and they streamed down her cheeks, falling onto her dressing gown. She felt extremely vulnerable, so sad too and she fell from her chair onto the cold conservatory floor, her crying getting louder, not even noticing Smokey's pitiful whining and pawing on her back.

It was now 11am. Laurie had cried until a beautiful, cathartic numbness overcame her, temporarily blocking her pain. She felt strangely calm now, she thought, as she walked back through to the kitchen. She knew she had decisions to make...big ones too regarding her marriage, but she could also see that nothing needed to be decided today. She had lived through twenty years, she could put up with it for a little longer... but the girls? She was worried as to how the weekend would have affected them. They were obviously now aware that all was not well, to put it mildly, but to be fair, the weekend had not fundamentally changed anything. Her chat with Rich had simply made things between them even frostier but nothing she wasn't used to.

But the holiday...well...that was another thing entirely. That *did* need addressing...and soon! She was supposed to be going in less than two weeks! She couldn't tell them now though, not after the weekend. She simply wasn't up to it and couldn't face the idea of nearly two weeks listening to their moans and groans. They wouldn't be happy, she knew that. They would be concerned about their dad. Rich, too, would be angry and she hadn't the energy to deal with anything more right now. Maybe she should drop it on them at the last minute? Tell them it was an impulse decision after speaking to Frankie. She could even use Frankie's dad as an excuse...tell them Frankie badly needed a break and hadn't wanted to go by herself? Anyway, she would worry about all that another day, she thought wryly. Her immediate concern was how she was going to get through today.

Picking up a pen and paper, she wrote a long 'to do' list.

11.05 Washing in

11.10 Dust and Hoover living room

11.30 Hoover hall, dining room, kitchen

11.40 Dust dining room (she hated dusting so had to spread it out)

11.50 Clean kitchen

12.20 Lunch

1.00 Hang out washing

1.10 Clean windows in kitchen/ living room / dining room

2.10 Tea break (read paper)

3.00 Peel potatoes / veg

3.20 Ironing

4.00 Put meat in with roast potatoes

There...that would keep her busy. And such a tight time scale there would be no time for feeling morose, she thought as she turned on the radio.

Chapter 31

Sunday 4th September 2016.

It was early. 7am and Laurie was up, butterflies in her stomach. She showered and dressed quickly, finding herself in her car by 8 am.

This was *her* day...the day Laurie allocated to Mike...and she always spent it the same way, taking herself down memory lane.

She returned to Stratford.

It was the only time she ever went there. In all the years since, even though Stratford was virtually on their doorstep, Laurie would never visit, despite her girls having asked to go on a number of occasions. Cara had once been on a school trip when she had been about twelve and had returned, raving about the place asking repeatedly to go back there, but Laurie had always resisted, coming up with all sorts of alternative suggestions...Warwick castle, Hereford...anything else... but not Stratford. No...that was for her and Mike.

Having arrived and parked by 9am, she strolled around the town. She would spend at least thirty minutes simply standing outside 'Ann Hathaway's cottage', trying to bring back all her feelings on that day twenty years ago. God, she even tried to work out *exactly* where they would both have stood, wanting to stand in the right spot! In the early years she had entertained the notion that maybe Mike might actually turn up! How crazy was that? she thought sadly to herself.

Mike had left 'Kays', Frankie had told her, just a few months later so Laurie had no idea where he lived or worked anymore. Him turning up here therefore had been

Laurie's only hope...a hope she soon realised was not going to materialise.

So.. she took what she could from the day. She always took a boat ride on the river, come rain or shine, and would sit in quiet contemplation, replaying their conversation and allow herself to simply *feel*. She would then take herself to their hotel, booking exactly the same room they had been in all those years ago.

The hotel had changed over the years of course and each year, Laurie felt increasingly removed. The first few years the hotel had remained the same...the smell, as she remembered...the decor not having been changed, and Laurie would gain an immense comfort simply from being there. She would slip into the bed, close her eyes and imagining Mike's arms around her, feel such love.

But things had moved on. The decor had been changed four times now, each time, Laurie feeling a little more removed and disappointed. She still derived some comfort however. Mike had been in that room, his DNA still in there somewhere, she told herself. It was the closest she could ever get to him and the routine she had established brought a sense of familiarity and comfort to her despite the continued changes.

Room five, it was. On the ground floor.

Using her key card, she entered, holding her breath. Fabulous, she thought, breathing a sigh of relief. No changes to contend with this year, she thought as she walked over to the window. The view was over the car park. Not really a view at all but so familiar for Laurie and she could still recall looking out over it that first time, anxious about the time as she remembered not wanting the sun to set...wanting time to stand still. How magical would that have been, she thought sadly. Shivering slightly, she closed the curtains even though it was still bright daylight. This was her routine. She wanted to shut the world out and take herself back in her mind. Taking off her top, bra and Jeans, she slid between the sheets in just her panties.

Lying on her back, she replayed her day with Mike, replaying her feelings, allowing all her emotions to come to the fore and when she replayed their lovemaking, she could recall it as though it had only happened yesterday. Mike had been so loving, so tender, and yet made love to her with a passion she hadn't known existed. And it had been beautiful, she thought longingly, sighing deeply.

The last two weeks had been horrendous for her. She had stopped taking her anti-depressants and had done it without consulting her doctor. She knew her doctor was busy and she hadn't wanted to be a bother. But she felt anxious all the time, agitated over even the slightest thing and felt herself being taken down. If she could describe it to anyone, she felt she had fallen into a deep pit with no-one able (or bothered) to hear her cries for help and Laurie had no idea how to begin the process of climbing out by herself.

She was past crying, she felt absolutely nothing at the moment, totally void of any feeling. Leaning over, she took out two packets of sertraline from her handbag, tablets left over from her prescription, together with forty eight paracetamol she had bought over the last few days. She then reached for her hip flask, a present Frankie had bought her as a laugh. The hip flask was filled with 'cherry brandy,' a liquor Laurie loved.

She picked up her phone. What about her girls? What would they think? Should she message them or not? She hadn't an answer to this. Feeling as low as she did, she felt they would be far better off without her anyway but still...how could she not leave them some sort of message? What would she say though? That she loved them? She often messaged them but normally after a phone call, not just a random text message like this! Oh God, what to do?

Impulsively she messaged the three of them. "I love you all...so much. Live your lives, always follow your heart. Mum xxxx."

Then she turned the phone off, placing it back into her handbag.

She looked over at the tablets lying on the bedside table, ready for her to take, and gulped. This was a big deal, she thought. How would it feel? Would she be in pain? Or just simply fall asleep? She didn't like pain, even discomfort in fact so she was hoping the tablets would send her off into a really deep sleep from which she would just never wake up.

But what if they didn't, she thought, feeling suddenly anxious. She knew nothing about medicine and their effects did she? But *surely* all these tablets would do the job? Especially with the alcohol too.

Her first gulp of cherry brandy slid down marvellously, feeling lovely and warming as the effects spread through her body. God, that was better, she thought, especially on an empty stomach! Oh yes! She took another gulp, together with two tablets. God, was she doing the right thing? She was sweating profusely...another bloody hot flush, she thought irritably. Grabbing another two tablets and swallowing them down with another gulp of alcohol, Laurie's thoughts turned to Mike. She would be with him at last, she told herself. In her dreams at least. This thought made her smile. No-one could take her thoughts away from her. In her head, she could be wherever she wanted to be and that was with Mike.

Placing another two tablets into her mouth and swallowing them down, she had to smile. God, this was going to take forever at this rate. She hated taking tablets at the best of times and she hadn't thought it through properly. The paracetamol she had bought were large and tasted vile on her tongue. She should have bought the capsules. That would have been much easier. She could only take two at a time as it was and it was going to take forever! Typical, can't even get this right, she thought, chuckling a little to herself. The alcohol was certainly having an effect though, a certain calm contentedness sweeping her body.

She then jumped out of her skin...the sound...a piercing shrill sound she was finding hard to ignore ringing in her ears. God, it was so loud! She held her hands over her ears in an attempt to block it out. It would stop in a minute, she told herself. Just a standard test they had to do, maybe? Mind you, she couldn't recall them saying anything about one when she checked in. It was not stopping either. Shit, she thought. Shit. It's not a false alarm, it's still ringing! The noise was piercing... a noise she could not ignore, however much she was trying to do so. Surely it was going to stop? She sat stock still, listening to the noises in the corridor. It was clear people were vacating their rooms now. God, could it actually be a real fire? She had a fear of fire, had always held an irrational fear of being trapped in a burning building. She found herself laughing at the irony. Here she was, planning to take her own life. Did it matter how it was taken? Oh yes, she thought. Absolutely!

Leaping out of bed, she hastily threw her clothes back on and ran from the room.

"Are you okay?" asked the lady, standing patting her on the back.

"Yes thanks," mumbled Laurie, wiping her mouth with the back of her hand after being violently sick.

"You must have picked up a bug or something," the woman continued.

"Yes. I think I must have. I feel a bit better now though."

"Come and sit down pet. We can't get back in yet and there's a lovely bench in the sunshine free."

Laurie followed the lady over to the bench and sat down gratefully. She had lied. She felt awful still. Her stomach was rumbling, complaining bitterly no doubt, thought

Laurie. Taking a few deep breaths, she felt a little less sick and, looking over at the woman who had helped her, smiled shyly. "Thankyou," she said again. "Thank you for caring."

Laurie felt a large lump in her throat.

This stranger had cared sufficiently to come over and help Laurie out, putting arms around her which had comforted Laurie enormously. There were nice people in the world, she thought. Some people *did* care and Laurie was taken by surprise by how much a small act of kindness could feel so huge.

It was a lightbulb moment for her.

Instead of continually looking inward, maybe she could look outwards, look to others for help and support.This was not something Laurie had given any thought to in all her fifty years. She had never needed others...not at school or since...or so she had believed.

But where had that thought process got her? Here, she thought sadly, that's where. On her own, in a hotel room, looking at taking her own life! Oh my God, how on earth had she reached this point? She could blame no-one but herself and it had only taken one kind act from a stranger to show Laurie that it didn't have to be this way.

Her tears began to fall.

"Hey, it's okay," the woman placated, putting her arms around her again. "You'll soon feel better. It's not nice is it? Being sick. But better out than in though. That's what my mother used to say anyway," she continued, chuckling to herself.

Laurie smiled as she wiped her eyes. Her tears had been brought on by relief mainly...relief that she hadn't actually gone through with the deed, mixed with tears resulting from the woman's kindness. She was being so nice, just like her mum would have been and Laurie felt an immense comforting presence around her as they both sat in the sunshine waiting to be allowed back into their respective rooms.

Chapter 32

Tuesday 6th September 2016.

WOW, thought Laurie, as she dragged her case behind her, following Frankie through arrivals in Bangkok airport. It was *chaos*!

Laurie had never seen so many people in one place at one time before and the noise was horrendous! The heat too, she thought as she loosened the scarf from around her neck whilst struggling to keep up with Frankie. She certainly didn't want to lose sight of her! Talk about being out of her depth! Without Frankie, she wouldn't have a clue *what* to do. She didn't have any Thai baht with her and neither did she know where they were staying. No...keep her in sight, she told herself, quickening her pace despite the stifling heat.

Frankie had been to Thailand many times before and, as a result, knew exactly what she was doing, so, within minutes, they were both safely ensconced in the back of a taxi, Frankie having bartered with the taxi driver to such an extent they were laughing with each other. It's as though she knew him! "God, how do you *do* that Frankie?"

Frankie smiled widely. "Welcome to Asia, Laurie! They expect it, it's how they operate. They initially ask a ridiculous price, knowing some people will just pay it, but as soon as they realise that you know the score then they will barter and it becomes a game. They love to barter and you know what they say...when in Rome..."

"God...This is all so different, it's unnerving."

"There's no need to feel unnerved. They're lovely, gentle people on the whole, you'll see."

"Right," answered Laurie unconvincingly.

She felt exhausted but could not stop looking out of their car window in fascination as the taxi sped away from the airport. It all felt quite surreal at the moment. She was here! She was actually *here*. She couldn't believe it and the sights...the traffic! Oh my God, how on earth did they not have an accident? There were cars literally all around them, horns honking relentlessly. It was absolute mayhem! She felt a small bubble of excitement in the pit of her stomach and she smiled over at her friend. "We're here," she whispered, taking Frankie's hand in hers. "We are actually here," she said again, laughing out loud as she hugged Frankie tightly.

"Yes we are and we're going to enjoy ourselves too. I know you need it, that's plain for all to see but I need it too. I can't wait...a break from my routine...and my dad," she added, her smile wavering slightly.

"He'll be fine Frankie," soothed Laurie, patting her on the arm as she pulled away from their embrace. Seeing the look of concern still on her face, Laurie continued. "He'll be *fine*," she repeated firmly. "He's being well looked after and had given you his blessing too, didn't you say? So, make the most of this break and when you get back you'll be able to cope with him so much better as a result."

"Yes, I know, you're right," mumbled Frankie, sitting back in her seat and closing her eyes.

The last forty eight hours had been an absolute whirlwind for Laurie. She hadn't given herself time to process the events on Sunday and she felt particularly bad too, that she had been so low, she hadn't given poor Frankie a thought!

She had nearly taken her own life, she thought to herself, horrified that she had come so close to it. The two previous weeks had been terrible for Laurie and she had sunk deeper and deeper into a dark place. No-one seemed to care. Rich didn't, that was evident. Sarah cared but her phone calls she had promised daily soon diminished. Let's face it, she had her own life and it wasn't as though Laurie was actually *talking* to her so the calls became laughable. "Are you okay?" Sarah would ask. "Yes...fine, thank you," Laurie would reply. This was an absolute lie but Laurie was so used to playing everything down in front of her girls, she simply couldn't allow herself to burden one of her daughters. **FINE**...mmm.

And where did Sarah go from here? She normally talked about events going on in her own life for a few minutes and then made an excuse to finish their chat.

So...whilst Sarah *meant* well, it was excruciatingly awkward for both of them and Laurie had been pleased when Sarah's calls dropped off a little.

Her two other daughters had pointedly ignored her. They were always polite but it was obvious they didn't really know how to deal with their mum. They were probably still in shock. Let's face it, until their mum's birthday bash, all had been perfect in their lives. Laurie's outburst had come completely out of the blue for them and they were dealing with it the only way they knew how. To be fair to them, they had no doubt been speaking to their dad who would definitely have sugar coated the whole event. He would have blamed Laurie...the menopause, "You know what women of a certain age can be like," he would have said jokingly. Yes... He would have trivialised it and her girls would have been only too happy to believe him. Normal order resumed, she thought bitterly.

Sunday had actually been a huge blessing...Oh, the irony! In a perverse way, she felt Mike had sent her a message on that day and she felt enormously comforted by this thought. She still couldn't believe what had happened. Was there a bigger picture to life? Were there such a thing as guardian angel's? She had always scoffed when people talked about that kind of thing....hippies, she would think derisedly. But, hey, look at Sunday...a chain of events having to happen simultaneously. The fire alarm, followed by such a kindly woman. Add to that the time spent sat on a bench in the sunshine, calming her nerves had allowed Laurie to see some kind of beauty to life again.

That woman had been Laurie's guardian angel that day, she felt, talking to her calmly and gently whilst Laurie got better, the warmth of the sunshine wrapping itself around her as much as the arms of a stranger.

So she had raced home, feeling exhilarated as well as immensely relieved. Finding the house empty, she had taken the stairs two at a time and flung open her wardrobe doors, grabbing handfuls of summer clothes and throwing them onto her bed. She had then successfully manhandled one of the smaller suitcases from the loft and thrown her stuff into it. She hadn't had time to pack carefully. As long as she had her passport and money with her, then that would do. Anything else she had forgotten, she could always buy and she was well aware she had very little time on her side. Dragging her case down the stairs and out of the front door, she heaved it into the boot of her car, breathing a huge sigh of relief when her car boot slammed shut. Passport and credit card safely ensconced in her handbag, she then hurried to prepare some tea.

Rich had arrived home at 8pm, not ten minutes after Laurie had finished and her heart was beating furiously by this time. But she had done it and Rich was none the wiser!

Frankie had instructed her to meet at Shrub hill station at 11.55 am on the Monday morning, their train due to depart at 12.10 pm. Laurie had gone away many times over the years with Rich and the girls and not once had she started a holiday from a train station! They had always taken their car and paid for parking.

"Not a chance," Frankie had remarked when Laurie had suggested it. "I've already booked the train tickets anyway...they only cost £12.50 each...you get deals if you state the train you want to be on, especially when you're not travelling at peak hours. It's an awful lot cheaper this way Laurie and not half as much hassle either. But we can't miss the train, that's the thing, otherwise we will have to pay to get onto the next train and that would cost us a fortune, so 11.55 am Laurie! Don't be late!"

So...the train it had been, and actually their journey had been surprisingly hassle free. No motorway hold ups to contend with either!

They had arrived at Heathrow airport just after 3pm and enjoyed a wonderful late lunch together with a bottle of red wine whilst waiting to be called through to departures.

The direct flight had been good too, Laurie thoroughly enjoying immersing herself in the in-flight entertainment, catching up on some of the recent movies that she had seen advertised but not gone to see. "They will soon turn up on TV," Rich used to comment whenever she suggested they went to their local cinema. "I'll be buggered if I'm paying a tenner just to watch a film a few months earlier," he would grumble. "Bloody ridiculous price," he would then add.

And so...here she was, she thought to herself, in wonder again. It was getting increasingly built up now and Laurie didn't actually know where to look, there was so much to take in! What hit her the most was that there was so much life...in all it's chaotic vibrancy and Laurie's excitement built.

The taxi pulled up on a main road and Laurie looked around her anxiously. Oh my God, she thought, the hotel can't be here, it was a dump!

The buildings were all in various degrees of decay and the traffic was horrendous, exhaust fumes fighting for space as Laurie stepped out of the taxi. God, it was so hot here too, so humid! How did people manage?

Fanning herself desperately, she felt sweat tricking between her breasts. Her shoulder length hair was sticking to the back of her neck and she felt decidedly uncomfortable. She would just have to put up with it for now, she thought, as she glanced over enviously at Frankie. Her hair had been cut into a short pixie style only the other day and she was looking altogether more comfortable in her surroundings.

Seeing Laurie's face, Frankie smiled at her reassuringly. "I know what you're thinking! It doesn't look much does it but you wait and see, the hotel's just down this alley," Frankie said gesturing over by a canal.

Laurie picked up her case and followed Frankie down some steps. The water was to her left and was giving off a very strong unpleasant odour but the further they began to walk away from the traffic, the quieter it became. They walked past one or two shacks which were clearly peoples' homes and Laurie felt cheered by their welcoming smiles.

An old lady of an indeterminate age was crouching down, a bowl of some sort of indescribable vegetable in front of her and she was peeling the skin off, throwing it to her side. How could she crouch like that? thought Laurie in amazement. She hadn't been able to crouch in that manner since she had been a toddler! The old woman grinned, displaying many gaps and a few black teeth. Laurie smiled at her and gave her a hesitant wave. She was rewarded with a full sentence, the lady gesticulating loudly, her arms thrown out wide.

Laurie laughed in delight. She hadn't a clue what the old lady was saying but she could tell it was simply friendly banter and it warmed Laurie to realise how friendly the old lady was being.

They walked past many bare footed children also, all grinning from ear to ear and waving in delight at these two foreigners. Laurie began to feel a lot less anxious. It was a delightful place, she thought. Everyone seemed so happy, laughing, playing or just simply getting on with their day.

The old lady clearly had very little if the hut she was sitting by was anything to go by. Her clothes had seen far better days too, but she certainly seemed content. Laurie

181

couldn't help but compare her to many of the old women she came across at home and couldn't recall a time when she had ever encountered an older lady with such a grin on her face. Oh no...they were always moaning, she thought. Yet, compared to this old lady they had everything they could ever have wished for.

Five minutes after walking along the canal side they reached their hotel. It was beautiful! They were greeted with a most welcome cool drink as two men relieved them of their heavy cases and, whilst Frankie checked in, Laurie looked around her.

It was a small hotel, nothing elaborate, but calming...an oasis, she thought, in comparison to the chaos outside. To her right there was a small restaurant area, beautifully set out, soft music playing in the background. To her left was a small pool, a covered wooden roof, but open to the elements also, beautiful ornate shrubbery surrounding two sides and welcoming loungers scattered around. Laurie could feel a welcoming slight breeze as she stood waiting for Frankie.

Fans overhead also helped, she thought as she grabbed a banana from a bowl of fruit she had spotted on a low table close to the reception desk. Oh my God...the banana was delicious, a very small one but *my,* she had never tasted a banana as tasty.

"Wow" she said, throwing the banana skin into the bin. "That's the best banana I've ever tasted Frankie. Have you tried these?"

"Yes," replied Frankie, laughing as she took one herself. "Gorgeous aren't they? Makes our bananas at home seem really crap," she added, laughing again. "You wait until you try some of their food Laurie, it's out of this world. Let's drop our bags off in our room and get a bite to eat in the restaurant, what do you say?"

"Sounds good to me. Then maybe some time by the pool?"

"Sure," answered Frankie easily. "Will do us some good to get some rest, get over the jet lag a bit too. And then we can plan...I've loads of ideas, I can't wait to tell you about them," said Frankie enthusiastically, wrapping her arm around Laurie's waist as they walked over to the lift.

Chapter 33

It was late afternoon and Laurie and Frankie had been enjoying an hour by the pool. Having cooled off in the pool, they were now lying on sunloungers in the shade.

They had eaten a wonderful meal in the hotel restaurant. Laurie had ordered 'pad thai' with chicken and she had loved it. The veg was so fresh and therefore extremely tasty. Laurie was not a 'foodie' and she had never really enjoyed cooking either, seeing it as more of a chore than anything else. She enjoyed a roast, she supposed, but that was about as far as it went but this thai food was something else! And healthy too! She had often scoffed at home whenever she had listened to food advice. Five veg a day! Were they having a laugh? And now people were suggesting you needed more than that! It was impossible...bloody boring too, she used to think. But she'd had five veg in her 'pad thai' alone! And enjoyed it!

"Right," announced Frankie "Are you ready to listen?"

Laurie groaned loudly. God...what was Frankie going to come up with? She dreaded to think! Laurie was perfectly content exactly where she was...here...it was a lovely hotel, had a pool, a nice restaurant, she had also noticed some English novels sitting on a shelf by reception that had obviously been left by previous holiday makers. What more could she want? This was a perfect tranquil spot in which she could wind down and enjoy some well earned rest.

But no, she told herself. It wasn't to be, she thought despondently as Frankie began to speak. And Frankie came up with a whole host of ideas, none of which included staying put!

"We're not staying here," said Frankie emphatically, seeing the look on Laurie's face. "This hotel was a treat...to get you acclimatised, get over the jet lag, that's all. We're only booked in overnight. Besides, I can't afford this for two weeks."

It was fifty pounds a night and Laurie had not given a thought to it. She felt instantly guilty. Frankie was not well off and Laurie had to remember that. She had probably only splashed out on this hotel for Laurie's sake. So, sitting up, she apologised and listened again to Frankie's ideas, this time listening with serious intent.

"Right," Laurie said slowly, feeling more than a little stunned. "Right," she repeated. "Wow," she then added.

Frankie's list had not been too long but oh my God, it was nothing like Laurie's idea of a holiday.

Volunteering at a children's orphanage.

Three days trekking in Chiang Mai (the north of Thailand apparently)

Volunteering at an elephant sanctuary for a week!

Volunteering in Bangkok working with street children.

Volunteering to work with street dogs.

Where was the beach in all of this? thought Laurie despondently.

"Well?" asked Frankie. "What do you think? What do you fancy?"

"God, Frankie, I've no idea, to be honest. What do *you* fancy?" she asked, passing the buck.

Laurie was not used to thinking for herself, she realised and she didn't actually fancy any of her suggestions if she was being honest. But, equally, she didn't feel as though she was in any position to complain. It would be really ungrateful of her and Frankie had been really good to her. It was only two weeks, she told herself miserably. She would just have to get through it as best she could. It would soon pass.

Chapter 34

Friday 9th September 2016.

It was *hot*...so bloody hot, thought Laurie but, despite the heat, she was absolutely loving it. Smiling delightedly, she couldn't believe where she was and what she was doing.

It was 10am and she was trekking in the hills of Chiang Mai.

They were in a group with ten other tourists and two guides. The scenery was absolutely breathtaking, overlooking rolling hills and small villages as far as the eye could see.

Villages? Well, not as Laurie thought of as a village, there were more livestock than people, Laurie noticed, and all of the houses were built from wood. Many on stilts with their livestock living beneath them. Laurie had to laugh because even though their houses were as primitive as she had ever seen, they all had satellite dishes! Hilarious, she thought to herself.

They had started their trip yesterday morning and had begun with an elephant ride. And what an experience that had been! She couldn't believe how high she was when sat on an elephant with Frankie and had laughed continuously as their elephant had negotiated the hilly landscape, screaming on more than one occasion as they had walked down into streams, Laurie feeling as though she was going to be thrown forward over the elephant's head on more than one occasion.

Their elephant was gorgeous, so gentle, she thought, for such a huge animal. Following lunch that day, they had set out on their trek. It had been in the heat of the day and began with an uphill climb. Laurie was not the fittest of people and had found herself breathless within the first 15 minutes.

They were climbing, literally, at times, and Laurie was struggling, using her hands often to help haul herself up. The younger guide brought her a walking stick he had made when he saw how she was struggling and that had helped enormously. At first she had wondered what he could be doing as he began to hack at a tree branch with a machete. A machete! She had only ever seen one on the TV, never in real life. Within seconds, the branch had come away and he had used a knife to blunt any jagged edges before passing it over to her, a huge smile on his face.

And so, the afternoon had continued, Laurie still out of breath as they had climbed, but managing much better now she had her crutch. She hadn't taken in her surroundings, so busy was she putting one foot in front of the other and she had never been so relieved when they had arrived at their overnight camp.

The last two hours of their trekking yesterday had been in the hills, much of it flat, certainly not the steep climb they had endured most of the afternoon. And once Laurie had found her breath, she had at last been able to look around her and admire the beautiful views. She had never done anything like this in her life and had been immensely concerned at first but Frankie was having none of it when Laurie had tried to protest. "You'll love it Laurie," she had simply said. "Trust me," she had added for good measure.

And once they had reached their camp, Laurie had been horrified! She had been so relieved to eventually rest, her calves in agony, but their camp! Well....Oh my God...talk about basic! It was a shed! With a bamboo floor to boot. No walls, they were open to the elements, just a roof over their heads to keep out the rain. And then their bedding! There were a row of simple mats, a blanket folded on each one. No privacy at all!

Frankie couldn't help smiling as she had looked over at Laurie's expression. "It's not what you're used to, I know," she got in before Laurie could speak. "But I'm so tired I'll sleep anywhere...and I think you will too!" she had added.

Laurie had not been so convinced and, when she was then shown their facilities, she very nearly went into meltdown. Their facilities were fifty metres away from their shed, down the hill and Laurie's heart leapt into her mouth as she took in the small wooden structure, inside consisting of little more than a hole in the ground for their loo and a hosepipe hanging on a nail for their water. Cold water obviously. At least there was some electric, a bare bulb hanging down, she thought, trying desperately to console herself. Oh my God, she had thought, how much worse could this possibly get?

Close to tears as she had retraced her steps back to their shed, she hadn't trusted herself to say anything positive so had chosen to say nothing at all as the ten of them sat around a camp fire waiting for their food to be cooked.

Everyone else had seemed to be taking it all in their stride, she had thought, looking around her. Mind you, they all looked the type...all dressed in correct trekking gear, lightweight dark trousers or shorts, long sleeved lightweight shirts, all wearing strong looking walking boots. All younger too, she noticed, the closest to her must have been at least ten years younger.

She had been handed a mug of wine which she took gratefully and peered into the distance. She had to admit, the scenery was stunning and it was all very peaceful as everything around her seemed to quieten down, the sort of stillness that seemed to occur anywhere in the world as the sun set. Taking a few deep breaths, she had begun to calm down a little and, feeling the alcohol seeping into her body, she smiled as she took in her own clothes.

Not having given any thought to what they would have been doing on holiday and not in her wildest dreams seen herself in this situation, Laurie had not brought the 'proper gear' with her and had had to settle for 'good enough'...something she had never felt comfortable with. She was wearing her trainers, bright pink, some light grey linen trousers and a short sleeved pink flowery cotton top.

"You'll be fine," Frankie had assured her. "It's not a fashion show anyway and it will do," she had added.

To be fair, the guides were not exactly in the 'appropriate' gear either. One had trainers on like her, the younger one only had flipflops! Then just shorts and old battered 'T' shirts.

And she *had* been fine in what she was wearing, the trainers having been perfectly adequate and her clothing sufficient.

Frankie had brought with her some super strength mosquito repellent which Laurie had used liberally all over any bare skin and so far she had not noticed any bites, thank God.

Once their meal had been consumed, Laurie had found herself feeling so much more mellow. It had been a gorgeous meal, simple, but, oh, so tasty. Chicken with an abundance of fresh vegetables and then mango to follow. She had never tasted such sweet, juicy mango in her life.

The talk around the camp fire had become more interesting as the food hit the spot and the drink continued to flow.

Strangers in the morning, they now felt connected, the sort of connection that only comes after an arduous time together. A younger woman of about forty years of age had particularly shocked Laurie. Initially, meeting only this morning, Laurie had her neatly in a box, an immaculately presented woman, in control, displaying such a confidence that Laurie had taken an instant dislike. Displaying an arrogance not unlike Rich had not helped her case either and Laurie had pointedly ignored her all day. Of course, she had been one of those who had always been striding out at the front of their group, seemingly not at all affected by the strenuous trek, or, indeed the extreme heat. Finding herself sat next to her by the campfire however, Laurie had been forced to be polite and Laurie had heard enough to make her feel thoroughly ashamed of herself.

Anne, it was, and she was forty five. (Older than Laurie had thought.)

And yes...she had a job that did not take Laurie by surprise at all...banking in London. No surprises where the arrogance came from then, Laurie had thought bitterly as Anne had begun speaking. She then went on to discover she was on this trip alone, having taken a year out from working. This was her third month away and she had already visited Vietnam, Laos and Cambodia.

Laurie couldn't help raising her eyebrows at this. Wow! Travelling alone...to all those countries? Why? Anne had then gone on to tell her that her only son and husband had both been killed in a car accident last year. Her son had been twenty and he had been driving. He had taken a bend in the road too fast and crashed head on into a tree.

The impact killed her husband immediately, her son living for another twelve days before he died from multiple injuries.

Fuck! Laurie had thought. What on earth could she say?

Anne had been openly crying at this point.

Reaching over to her, Laurie put her arms around her and hugged her tightly. It was the only thing Laurie could think to do. There were no words were there when faced with such a tragedy? How did anyone carry on after something as catastrophic as that?

Thinking of how she would feel should this have been one of her own children, Laurie was hit by a tremendous feeling of guilt. Her own problems were insignificant compared to Anne's. *And* they were all of her own making. Nothing awful had happened to Laurie until her parents had been killed and yes...whilst that had been a tragedy, it hadn't actually affected her day to day life.

For Anne, however, it had. Her whole life had changed...just like that...one day, she had everything, the next...well...it had all been taken away from her. Yet she was here. She was choosing to live, or at least trying to, Laurie thought...trying to find a different path.

If someone like Anne could do that after such a tragedy then there was no reason why Laurie couldn't get her life back on track either!

And so here she found herself the following morning, with a huge smile plastered on her face as she walked, taking in her surroundings.

Laurie had slept really well last night, Frankie had been right about that. Ok, the bamboo must be the most uncomfortable material to lie on...hard wearing apparently, no fucking wonder, she had thought! It didn't give at all, so hard on her body.. and sleeping in a row like that had taken Laurie back to her teenage years when she had had sleepovers.

But there was such a simplicity in this way of life and Laurie felt a certain amount of freedom and lightness as a result. Just covering the basics...food, drink, shelter...it really made life so simple and Laurie was loving it.

It had been pitch black last night, so quiet and peaceful that she had slept like a log. Not even her very quick cold shower this morning had dampened her sprit.

Laurie couldn't remember the last time she had felt so good, she thought delightedly, just putting one foot in front of the other, not a care in the world, even if just for today.

Reaching a waterfall around lunchtime, Laurie had shrieked in delight. Realising they were staying here for their lunch and seeing two young boys already in the water, she wasted no time herself. She scrambled down the rocks as quickly as it was possible to go and sat down heavily on her backside as she undid the laces on her trainers. Peeling her damp socks off and throwing them into her trainers, she jumped into the water.

It was gorgeous, so cold but so welcome after the heat throughout the morning. Beginning to swim, she dived under the cool waters and swam like a fish. Surfacing, she heard the group laughing at her, exclaiming she still had her clothes on. Who cared she thought, they will soon dry anyway in this heat. Swimming further away from the group she lay back and simply watched the boys playing.

Following another simple, but delicious meal of chicken and rice, wrapped up in a banana leaf, they were off again, Laurie's stick helping her tremendously as they negotiated some tough, steep, narrow walking trails.

And Laurie had been right. Her clothes had dried, albeit slowly, which had kept her cool enough in the heat of the day to really take in all the hills Chiang Mai had to offer. She was living in the moment, so to speak, a phrase she often heard nowadays but something she had never really mastered the art of doing. This is what she needed more of, she told herself. This was *living* as Laurie had not dreamed possible and she wanted more of it!

The second night was not dissimilar to the first but Laurie was more prepared and fully engaged in the evenings activities, even taking a beer when offered one and thoroughly enjoying its coolness as it slid down her throat, laughing alongside Frankie and Anne as they all had a sing-a-long.

Going to sleep that night, Frankie snoring gently on one side, Anne murmuring a little in her sleep on the other, Laurie felt content. She felt connected to Frankie, Anne, even their guides who were being so kind to her, always asking how she was doing as they walked along. Yes...she felt connected to the world again, in a way she hadn't in a long time.

Turning over, desperately trying to ignore the hard floor and the rough grey scratchy blanket she had been given, she found herself smiling as her eyes closed and for once slept the sleep of the dead.

Chapter 35

Monday 12th September 2016.

"So...how many day you want stay?" asked the lady looking directly at Frankie.

"A few days," answered Frankie. "Maybe all week if that is possible?"

The lady smiled up at her and bowed her head slightly as she replied. "Yes, of course, you let me know soon. Now, let me take you to children...come," she commanded, walking away, beckoning both Frankie and Laurie to follow behind her.

They followed the lady out of her office.

They were in an orphanage. It looked like a school, lots of grass and many ugly concrete buildings built around it. Some appeared to be classrooms, others sleeping quarters, Laurie thought, noticing rooms with row after row of bunk beds.

Turning a corner, the lady walked them over to a slightly quieter spot where Laurie could see what she thought to be a pre-school area, the garden having baby swings and a small slide in it, together with a couple of tricycles and small toys strewn all over.

No children were outside though, no surprises really, it being so hot.

The lady walked them over to a door and as soon as it was opened, Laurie smiled. Oh yes, there were definitely kids in there, the noise was deafening! Seeing the expression on their faces, the lady smiled. "Yes" she said, nodding her head vigorously. "They noisy," she added, wagging her finger. She sounded cross but it was said with a smile as she encouraged both of them to follow her inside.

As soon as they entered they were ambushed from all sides. One little girl of about three was tugging at Laurie's skirt, another trying to jump up into her arms, having wrapped her arms as high as she could around Laurie's stomach and, wrapping her legs high around Laurie's legs she was slowly inching her way up. Wrapping her right arm around the child's backside, Laurie hitched her the rest of the way up until the child was sitting comfortably on her waist and gave her a great big smile.

Looking around her, she took in the rest of the room. The children were all of a similar age, between two and three years, she guessed. They all had the same haircut, all the boys had shaved heads and all the girls a very short bob. It looked as though they had literally had a bowl placed over them and a cut around the bowl! They looked hilarious, but so cute too.

Frankie had got down on her knees and had at least five of them clambering all over her, touching her face, her hair, her clothes. It was chaos! But a wonderful chaos....all the children so excited to see some new faces, they could barely contain themselves. Frankie was being buried amongst a sea of little arms and legs, snotty noses too, no doubt!

Laurie remained standing, the little girl in her arms seemingly content just to stay where she was. Amongst the chaos, she spotted one little girl, lying listlessly on the hard concrete floor. Her legs and arms were pitifully thin and she was covered in spots, red, angry spots, all over her face as well. Her eyes were open but she didn't seem to be aware of her surroundings. Her eyes were blotchy, dried tears evidenced on her cheeks.

Laurie moved over to her, still carrying the other little girl in her arms. Sitting herself down by the poorly girl's side, she stroked her face softly with her fingers, speaking to her quietly and gently even though she knew she would not be understood. "Hello sweetie," she whispered tenderly, caressing her cheeks some more. There was no response at all, her eyes looking completely dead, even though they were wide open.

In contrast the girl clinging on to Laurie for dear life was full of beans, her bright eyes darting all over Laurie, grabbing her dress, her bra strap, fiddling with the chunky necklace around her neck, her smile so bright, Laurie could not help but smile back.

But Laurie was taken by the poor sickly girl beside her. Never had she seen such a blank dead look before and certainly never on a child of such a tender age and Laurie wondered what on earth could have happened to her as she continued to sit, stroking her face and speaking softly to her. Catching the attention of one of the Thai ladies, Laurie pointed down towards the child. "This child," she asked "What's her name?"

"Dang," whispered the lady "she sick, have medicine soon," she added.

"Ahh, I see," answered Laurie. Thank God for that at least. They were clearly aware and seemed to be looking after her as far as the medicine was concerned anyway.

What perturbed her though was the fact that she was just being left, lying on a hard, dirty floor. Placing the more boisterous girl down gently and sitting her by her side, she quickly undid her necklace which she gave to her to appease her. It seemed to do the trick, she grabbed at it greedily, holding it to her chest, a huge grin over her face.

Relieved, Laurie then picked up Dang. Spotting a tiny seat in the corner, she walked over with her and sat down, wrapping Dang in her arms and rocking her gently from side to side. Dang's eyes flickered a little, as though in recognition of her change in circumstances, the faintest trace of a smile evidenced on her lips. Laurie continued rocking Dang, fighting the tears that wanted to fall. Poor little thing, she thought. No parents to look out for her and so sickly. She needs love and care as well as bloody medicine, she thought sadly, a feeling of immense helplessness overcoming her, a single stray tear sliding down her cheek.

Laurie sat like that for the rest of the day, helping give her the medicine when the same lady came over to her. Dang hardly moved as Laurie sang to her and rocked her incessantly, until, finally, Dang's eyes began to shut and she fell into a fitful sleep.

Thank God, she thought, sleep being the best thing for her, Laurie believed. Her nappy hadn't needed changing, Laurie noticed. It was still bone dry. She must try to get some water down her when she woke up, she resolved.

Meanwhile, not wanting to disturb Dang, Laurie sat backwards against the hard cool wall and spent her time simply watching the other kids.

She loved kids, she loved their enthusiasm for life and felt she could just sit here and watch them for ever, so happy they were, in their own little worlds, playing either on their own or in groups. Looking over at Frankie she smiled. Frankie returned her smile whilst continuing to play with the crowd of children she had attracted. Frankie was boisterous with them, tickling them, playing tig, dancing.

Funny, thought Laurie, how we all naturally revert to type.

It would never have dawned on Laurie to play rough and tumble with these kids, she automatically went to the children needing love and care. She knew why...sitting here, Dang in her arms, Laurie felt an immense sense of calm, reminding her of how she used to feel when her own were little, sitting in that rocking chair in their bedroom. She felt the same loving, calming feeling here with Dang also. Breathing in deeply she found herself smiling again.

She had been in Thailand for a week now and she couldn't quite believe all they had done in that time. Laurie had loved the trekking she had done and it had provided her with some valuable time to simply feel and reflect.

197

Yes...feel...instead of trying to sort out her problems by thinking and analysing, she was simply allowing herself to feel again and she felt so good.

Laurie would not, in a million years have suspected she would enjoy this type of holiday. She had only ever previously been to five star resorts and never really contemplated any other holiday she could take. And, whilst it was all a little too basic for Laurie's tastes, she had to admit that she was really enjoying herself. She felt *alive* as well as calm, a feeling Laurie had not experienced in a long time. She couldn't actually remember feeling like this since she had been a child herself and she liked it tremendously.

It had all been such a whirlwind since they had arrived and Laurie had not given much thought to home. It seemed so far away and she realised she was not missing it at all.

Home had in fact started to feel more like a prison the last few years, something she had not realised until now. She was aware she needed to contact everyone but as usual, was putting it off. Stupid, she thought, and irresponsible too, she told herself. What sort of a role model was she being to her girls? Not much of one, that was for sure. Time to contact them!

Frankie had brought her phone with her as well as her tablet and was on the internet every evening skyping people back home.

Laurie hadn't given a thought to communicating when she had been packing...understandably so, in the circumstances...so had only got her phone with her which had been turned straight onto flight mode to avoid any phone calls from Rich. She *could* take flight mode off, she supposed and call her girls, that *was* a possibility but maybe email would be better...give her a chance to explain things properly and the girls time to take it in. Remembering a conversation with Sarah, only a few weeks ago, Laurie smiled ruefully. Sarah had been encouraging her to get 'WhatsApp' on her phone, saying how much Laurie would like it but Laurie had stubbornly refused. Surely phoning, texting and emailing were enough weren't they? How many modes of communication did youngsters actually require these days? Hmm, maybe she should have listened. Still, she hadn't, so email would just have to do!

She hadn't actually checked her email since she had arrived and she felt bad about that. What if her girls had been trying to get in touch?

She had only left a brief note on the kitchen table when she left. It said little really, just that she was badly in need of a break and had taken up Frankie's offer of a two week holiday in Thailand. The rest of the note was all about the frozen meals she had left in the freezer and instructions as to how to cook them. So...that wouldn't have gone down too well, Laurie thought wryly. It wasn't as though she had just popped out to get some milk, for goodness sake! Looking down at Dang, she gently stroked her cheek, watching her eyelids flutter as though she was dreaming. "You sleep little one," she whispered into her ear. "You sleep," she repeated, holding her tightly to her chest.

Yes, she would contact them tonight. Explain as well as she could and give them her news. They would be amazed, she thought, laughing to herself. She had some wonderful pictures she had taken too. Maybe Frankie could show her how to send them. God...she was pathetic! She knew so little about stuff like that. Not being interested over the years, letting Rich take charge had had a very negative effect on her and she realised how left behind she had become.

And there was no need for it really. She was perfectly capable, she thought, thinking back to when she had worked at 'Kays'. She had been more capable than most there and there had been no one who had balanced work and home life in the way she had! HA! she thought...well...for a while anyway!

199

But there was nothing to be gained from looking back, she told herself firmly. What she needed to do was look forward. Have a plan, whatever that was going to be! She felt mentally stronger now, she realised. Things had gotten really bad at home and Laurie felt horrified to think that she had actually contemplated taking her own life. No-one knew. Not even Frankie, and it was going to stay that way as far as she was concerned.

But *she* knew. She *had* to start looking forward, things could not continue as they had and this thought frightened her to death. No way was she going to return to Rich. Her and Rich were over. Had she held any doubts on that score then the last conversation she had had with Rich had been the final nail in the coffin.

She finally had clarity, they would *never* be on the same page and Laurie couldn't bear the thought of spending the rest of her life with him.

She wasn't even going to email him, he didn't deserve it, she thought bitterly.

But the girls...well, yes, she needed to contact them as soon as possible.

She was worried as to how they all were and it was time to face up to them, no matter how they felt towards her.

Chapter 36

Same day.

'WTF !!!!!!!'

Laurie had to laugh. Rich's email! That's all it said. Nothing else! Typical really, she thought, angrily pressing the 'delete' button.

'Are you ignoring me????'

Really? she said to herself sarcastically, "whatever gives you that idea Rich?" she hissed, again pressing the 'delete' button.
And so it continued...there must have been at least fifty emails from him, all growing in anger as his frustration had taken hold. Laurie had taken great delight in deleting each and every one of them. She cared so little, she realised, not even bothering to read the majority.
But she *did* care about the ones from the girls.

'Are you okay mum? I've been trying to call you. Dad says you've gone off to Thailand with Frankie. You didn't say anything! And that last text message you sent worried me too. Let me know how you are as soon as you can, I'm really worried mum. Sarah xxxxx'

'Mum, please call me as soon as you get this...getting *really* worried now. I can't get any sense out of dad whenever I phone him. He sounds so angry every time I mention you. Its horrible to listen to him. Call me mum!!!! Sarah xx'

'Hey mum, what's going on? Dad's being really vile. He's so angry all the time and he keeps ranting about you, it's horrible here! Really horrible! I'm staying with Tom. At least it's pleasant there. His mum is looking after me. Whatever she thinks though, I have no idea. God, it's *so* embarrassing!! Cara'

'PLEASE let me know how you are mum. God, I hope you are okay? Just email me if you don't want to call...you don't have to tell me anything, I just want to hear from you. I'm really worried mum. I love you. Sarah xx'

And later yesterday...'Please mum!!!!!! Sarah xx'

Oh **shit!** thought Laurie, feeling really bad that she had not looked at her emails any sooner. She understood why, she had been in such a state after leaving and then, add to that the jet lag, as well as being in such a strange country and being so busy...but even so...she felt guilty.
She hadn't given any thought to how her kids would be feeling and she had completely forgotten the text message she had sent to them all...shit, she thought again.

'Hi Sarah, it's your mum! I'm sorry, so sorry not to have emailed you sooner. I would have done so obviously had I even looked at my inbox. HATE the thought that you have been so worried. Please don't be, I am fine, absolutely fine. I needed a break and Frankie's offer to accompany her just came at the right time, that's all. I will be back before you know it. Love you so much. Mum xxxxxxxx'

Laurie had wanted to tell Sarah everything she had been up to, but it felt awkward to be doing so when Sarah would be worrying about her dad too...insensitive, Laurie thought, and she didn't want to upset Sarah any more than she already had so had kept her reply very simple. There would be plenty of time for her to tell her all about it later anyway.

'Cara, it's your mum. Sorry I haven't replied earlier. This is the first time I've looked at my emails otherwise I would have done so. I know this is all very weird for you and can only imagine how upset you are and I'm really sorry Cara. I've come away with Frankie because she offered and I badly needed some time away. I know you don't want to hear this but it's time there was a little honesty Cara. Me and your dad are going through a difficult time and I have been struggling massively the last month or so. Probably my age as well! I won't go into detail but please try not to worry about everything. I'm glad you are staying at Tom's...maybe for the best right now. I'm sorry you feel embarrassed though Cara. To be honest, I don't really care too much what Tom's mum thinks! And I don't think you should either Cara. It's really none of her business! I am fine and enjoying some time away. I love you Cara, hate that you are upset by everything. I would dearly love to be able to put everything right for you like I did when you were little but I can't. Speak soon. All my love. Mum xxx'

Laurie sighed, re-reading her email to Cara before pressing the 'send' button. Was she sounding a little too harsh? Maybe. And she didn't want to upset Cara, but at the same time she felt a bit pissed off at Cara's attitude. It smacked so much of Rich. Embarrassed! Really! For God's sake, talk about her father's daughter! Not for a second had Laurie expected Cara to ask after her but she did feel a certain disappointment. She was only twenty one, she told herself and a young twenty one at that, she reasoned.

But time, nevertheless, for Laurie to question Cara's attitude, she told herself fiercely. Spoilt, she was! Laurie felt her anger rise towards Rich. He had spoilt them. Of that, she had no doubt. But was she also culpable? Of course she was. She had brought them up too! If they were incapable of showing any empathy then maybe she was also to blame, she thought sadly. Her decision to take a back seat...to let Rich spoil them...her lack of energy certainly made her complicit. Twenty fucking years! What an idiot she had been.

Pressing 'send,' she put her head in her hands. God...what a fucking mess, she thought miserably.

And Marie?...well...she had heard nothing from her. Now she had replied to both Sarah and Cara, she knew she would have to write to Marie too. Her girls would talk to each other and Laurie didn't want Marie to think her mum didn't care.

Her head was pounding. It had been quite a day. Seeing the kids at the orphanage. They were all so vulnerable, so sweet and so many of them! Where were they all from?

It was exasperating for both Frankie and Laurie as they could speak no Thai between them and none of the staff seemed to speak much English. Even the lady they had first met!

On their way out at about five o'clock, Laurie had tried to ask about the orphanage and she had got nowhere. She had also tried to ask about Dang, where she had come from etc. but she simply got a similar reply to earlier. "Dang? Yes, she sick."

"Yes I know, but what is the matter with her?" Laurie had asked again.

"She sick...have medicine."

"How long has she been sick?" asked Laurie, trying a different tack.

"No understand," said the lady. "She sick...yes," she repeated.

"You're wasting your time Laurie," placated Frankie. "Come on, let's go. We can come again tomorrow if you'd like."

Sighing, Laurie had smiled a goodbye to the lady. "Okay, we see you tomorrow, yes?"

"Yes, yes, good, good," the lady replied, a broad beam spreading across her face.

"God, it's infuriating when you can't converse properly!" Laurie had moaned as they'd walked up the path, out of the orphanage.

"It is, yes," agreed Frankie. "I'm not sure she *can't* communicate though. It may be that she simply doesn't think it's any of our business."

"What do you mean?" she had asked incredulously. This was not something she would have considered.

"Well...this isn't our country is it? Who are we to be asking questions?"

"Yes, I know that, but did you *see* Dang today?" enquired Laurie, completely perplexed by Frankie's comments.

"Of *course* I did but they do things differently here. We may not ever get to understand why things are happening as they are here. This is a different society to ours. They have different ways to ours and I think we have to respect that, that's all," answered Frankie, shrugging her shoulders.

"*What!*" Laurie had exclaimed indignantly. "And leave poor kids like Dang just lying on a concrete floor!"

"Yes, absolutely. It sounds harsh I know but like I say, they have their own ways. She's getting medicine, she's being fed and watered, she has a bed to sleep in at night I assume, or at least a roof over her head anyway," she had acknowledged. "There's not much we can do Laurie, apart from what we have done today. Crikey, you sat with her all day. She had love and comfort from you which she wouldn't have had, had you not been there. We're going tomorrow, you can do the same again," she had added, glancing over at Laurie. "But, you know," she continued gently, "We will only be here for a short time and Dang has to get on with her life without you...and she will...she'll be fine I'm sure."

Laurie had been very thoughtful all the way back in the 'tuk tuk'.

It had been overflowing and they had all been packed in like sardines. Seeing an old lady climbing in too, Laurie had looked around her perplexed, wondering where on earth the old woman had been expecting to sit. On seeing this, the girl next to Laurie had promptly picked up a child of about ten years and sat him on her knee, gesturing to the old lady to sit down where the young child had vacated. The lad had not batted an eyelid at having a stranger grab him and sit him on her knee. Could she have imagined that happening in England?! God, no way, they would have been done for child abuse! And she knew they didn't know each other, Laurie having seen the child get on at the last stop on his own. Mmm, she had reflected, she could see Frankie's point.

It *was* a different world, that was for sure. Laurie had swung from seeing something she had deemed to be cruel to something so kind and caring...all within the space of a couple of hours.

And they *were* caring, she had noticed. Far more likely to smile at you and help you, Not at all like us. In fact, maybe they actually saw us as cold and hard, just out for ourselves. Everyone for himself is our motto, Laurie thought sadly.

Sighing again, she looked around her. Their room was basic but clean. Two single beds, a small, dark brown wardrobe, two bedside tables and a lamp on each. Not that Laurie's lamp worked mind! En-suite too, as well as a small kettle and two cups.

They had taken to buying sachets of '3 in 1' coffee. It was a lovely comforting drink, sufficient sugar in it and lovely and creamy. Filling the kettle, she emptied a sachet into a cup and went in search of some ibuprofen. She would take two, have a coffee and hopefully her headache would ease. It was pounding so much she could hardly think straight.

Frankie had gone out. She wasn't sure exactly where and she had been gone about an hour now. This suited Laurie, she was used to her time alone and had been a little concerned as to how she would get on being in Frankie's company 24/7. But that had not proved to be a problem at all. Frankie, clearly also liking her own company, took herself off most days.

So they had settled into a very harmonious way of living. Frankie didn't pry either. It was obvious Laurie was distressed but Frankie just let her be, she certainly wasn't a typical female in that respect, and, for that, Laurie was exceedingly grateful. Laurie knew Frankie would be all ears as and when, but she was also perfectly content with Laurie's silence.

Sipping her coffee, Laurie felt herself relax a little. She was fully over the jet lag now and feeling slightly more comfortable in her foreign surroundings. She didn't like the heat. God, she had difficulty with hot flushes as it was! As soon as she left her air-conditioned room, she would find herself sweating profusely, her hair sticking to her face and neck, her clothes wet to the touch within minutes. There was little point in putting any makeup on, bar some face cream. Eyeshadow, mascara...they both looked ridiculous on a sweaty face! She didn't try to dry her hair much either as she had found it wouldn't style as it did at home. Must be something to do with all the humidity, she thought, simply resorting to tying it back in a ponytail.

So...her normal routine at home was no longer!! And the freedom! Wow. It was really quite liberating to be ready to go out of the door so quickly. Showered, teeth brushed, clothes on, hair tied back and job done!

This must be what it felt like to be a bloke, she thought wryly.

She had lost weight too, her muffin top receding before her eyes. It was just so much easier to eat healthily here...all fresh produce and very little stodge.

"Hi," smiled Frankie, dumping her bright shoulder bag onto her bed. "God, it's crazy out there, so many *people*! I've walked miles too, my feet are killing me," she groaned, throwing herself on her bed beside her bag.

"Where have you been?"

"All over, couldn't tell you now. I love just wandering, getting lost. Could do it for hours...well...I could if my sandals were comfier anyway! What have you been doing?"

"Oh, just emails. Thought it was about time I checked in. Feel a bit bad...there were loads from Rich, not that I give a shit about them," she added bitterly, "but also from Sarah and Cara."

"Oh yes?" enquired Frankie slowly. "And..."

"As you would expect I suppose. Sarah's are fine, she is simply worried, but at least I had spoken to her before I left. Just the day after my fiftieth actually," she added, looking over at Frankie, a sheepish smile on her face.

"Right...I can imagine that was a difficult conversation then," laughed Frankie. "God, I will remember that night until my dying day," she added. "Go, Laurie, I thought it was brilliant...long bloody overdue too in my opinion."

"Yes, I know," agreed Laurie, chuckling as she remembered. "But for the girls it wasn't so clever was it? They were devastated. Anyway, as I say, I spoke with Sarah and didn't tell her everything obviously but enough for her to know how I'm feeling. She was good too, really understanding. I feel quite proud of her, truth be told. She's growing up I suppose."

Frankie pulled a face. "Of course she is, you muppet, she's twenty five! What were you doing at that age?"

"Yes, I know...still took me by surprise though," acknowledged Laurie, with a slight shrug of her shoulders.

"So, as I say, Sarah's fine. Cara's not though...far too concerned by how embarrassed she is!"

Frankie scoffed but before she could say anything Laurie continued. "She's only twenty one but still, it's hurtful."

"Of course it is," acknowledged Frankie. "But she'll get over it. Shit happens Laurie, as well you know and your girls will deal with it, don't worry so. And Marie?"

"Nothing at all from her...not surprisingly. Both her and Cara avoided me after the party. I should have made the effort to seek them out but I got so down myself, I wasn't thinking clearly. And now? Well, it's really difficult to communicate via an email and I don't want to call her. It's selfish of me, I know, but I don't want to take the chance of Rich getting hold of me. It's typical of Marie though. She's a deep thinker, she's probably still processing everything. Anyway," said Laurie more stridently, "I've emailed Sarah and Cara already so there's only Marie to do now."

"Excellent. Well, when you've done that, how about we go out for some fodder? I really fancy some fried chicken with cashew nuts followed by a banana pancake."

"Oooh, sounds lovely. Ok, give me fifteen minutes and I'll be with you," she answered enthusiastically as she began typing. She felt better after talking to Frankie.

Her headache had cleared and the thought of some delicious food brought a smile to her face.

Chapter 37

Tuesday 13th September 2016.

It was 9am and they were knocking on the orphanage door, Laurie desperate to see how Dang was doing.

Opening the door, a young Thai girl they hadn't seen yesterday smiled as she let them in.

They received the same response as yesterday, a whole hoard of kids rushing at them, eager to get to them as fast as possible. Laughing, Frankie knelt down immediately to say 'hello' to them all but Laurie only had eyes for Dang.

Surveying the room, she saw her in almost the same spot as yesterday, lying listlessly on the floor again. "Hello sweetie," she whispered, picking her up gently and looking into her eyes. Dang appeared to recognise her as a very slight smile flashed over her face and her eyes brightened a touch. "How are you today eh? Any better?" she cooed, walking over to the comfiest seat she could find and sitting down to inspect Dang properly.

Her legs and arms looked so sore, so heavily covered in spots, Laurie could hardly see any skin. She was so frail too, bless her and Laurie's heart burst for this little scrap of life.

She resolved to spend the rest of the day with her again, ensure she got food and medicine as well as a massive dose of love and care.

She also decided she was going nowhere the rest of the week. She had been pestering Frankie for a few days by the beach but that would have to go by the wayside. She wasn't leaving this little mite.

Dang slept a lot, which Laurie was pleased with. She also ate a little food which she hadn't done the previous day, her little smile appearing on more than one occasion which delighted Laurie and as they walked into their room that evening Laurie asked Frankie if she would mind if they stayed the rest of the week. "I mean, you can go if you wish, I'll understand."

"No, of course I don't mind," answered Frankie briskly. "I love it here myself so I'm happy to stay. Did you write to Marie yesterday by the way?"

"Yes I did," answered Laurie, taken by surprise by Frankie's abrupt change of conversation. "Similar to what I told Cara but I haven't heard anything back yet. Not from Cara or Marie. Sarah's come back to me...not saying much, just asking me to keep in touch."

"Have you thought about what Rich might be saying to them?"

"What do you mean?" asked Laurie, perplexed.

"Well...you indicated how angry he was. He might be giving them his version of events, you know, before you get yours in."

"What? you mean telling them about Mike?" asked Laurie, a trickle of fear seeping into her bones.

"Er...yes!" Frankie replied, talking to her as though she was a simpleton.

"Shit, I hadn't given that a thought. Do you think he would? No, don't answer that, of course he could and I wouldn't put it past him." Laurie stayed silent for a moment. "Are you saying I should tell them everything, Frankie?"

The thought alone panicked her immensely and she struggled to calm her breathing as she waited for Frankie to reply.

"It's not for me to say Laurie but it's worth considering. You know what they say, honesty is the best policy."

"Well yes, I know *that,*" Laurie bit back huffily. "But, for God's sake, how much honesty when you're talking to your kids? About your sex life?! I don't think so!"

"It's up to you," replied Frankie calmly, getting up from her bed to nip to the loo, "but they are not kids anymore," she sang as she shut the bathroom door.

Laurie found herself smiling at Frankie, despite feeling so panicked. How would she ever cope without her friend? She loved how calm she always was and even in a situation like this, she could still make Laurie smile.

She lay back on her own bed. God, she was tired, she could fall asleep right now. Looking at her watch though, she chuckled. It was only 7pm.

Two full days working had taken it out of her. However would she cope if she had to work full time? Mind you, maybe she needed to start to think about that as a possibility.

This frightened her. She had been out of the workplace for such a long time now. What on earth could she do? Still...what this holiday had shown Laurie was that it was perfectly possible to live a simple life. Not only that, she had actually enjoyed getting back to basics. She would be fine, she told herself emphatically. She only needed a shop job, that was all. She could get by on very little if need be. At least she would be free of Rich and that would be worth eating beans on toast for the rest of her life if necessary!

She also gave some thought to Frankie's comment. Would Rich tell the girls? She didn't know. She hadn't exactly spoken to him about anything to do with leaving had she? Would he be expecting her back? He was so into appearances, would he tell the girls on that basis? Or is he waiting to see Laurie's next move? She had no idea and she was worried.

He obviously hadn't said anything to Sarah but she wasn't at home like Cara and Marie. But they would have been straight onto Sarah if he had, she reasoned, so she didn't think he could have...yet. It was immaterial really, she told herself. She wasn't going to stay with Rich and as soon as he knew that for certain then he would play dirty all the way! And she was just going to have to accept the consequences. However much she herself would do anything to protect the girls, Rich would do anything to hurt Laurie and she knew that if the girls got hurt along the way, Rich would see it as collateral damage. Not only that, he would simply blame Laurie. She could see it now. "If you hadn't fucked around, the girls wouldn't be upset." Yes, she thought. Rich had a very odd way of seeing the world and seemed quite incapable of seeing anything from anyone else's point of view. She used to think he was just unwilling to do so but, being fair to him, she now believed he was actually just utterly incapable of it.

Anyway, tough shit, she told herself. His problems were for him to sort, she had enough of her own!

"Have you thought about trying to find Mike?" asked Frankie, coming out of the bathroom, drying her hands on her dress.

"*What*!!" shrieked Laurie incredulously, looking over at Frankie in complete and utter disbelief. "Where's *that* come from?" she asked eventually, when she had finally found her voice again, pulling such a face, Frankie laughed.

"Well, I really don't know why you're sounding quite so surprised. What's up with my suggestion?"

"EVERYTHING Frankie, for *GOD'S* sake. You're a complete *nutter*. Of *course* I haven't thought about contacting him...I mean...it's been twenty years!!!"

"So," answered Frankie belligerently. "Look Laurie, plenty of people contact their ex's nowadays. It's a lot easier now with the internet. And why not? Whoever knows, he could be footloose and fancy free still," she added, a delicious grin all over her face.

Laurie laughed loudly. This was ridiculous! "Ok, even if he *is* still single, what on earth makes you think he'd be interested in me now...after what I did to him. God Frankie, I don't even like to think of it now, even after all these years.

His face that evening, how distraught he had sounded, it's haunted me ever since. He probably hates me," she added, her face etched in misery.

"Okay," said Frankie carefully. "But you have no idea really do you, let's be honest. He never had the chance to tell you how he felt so you are just guessing. Anyway," she added briskly, "just a thought. I'm off for a wander, see you in about an hour, okay?" And, leaving Laurie with that thought, she grabbed her bag and a bottle of water. Shutting the door gently behind her, she left Laurie in complete shock.

Laurie had never given a thought to contacting Mike and felt a little annoyed at what she felt to be Frankie's simple attitude to life. She always made everything sound so black and white and life wasn't like that. In fact life was so many shades of grey, it would be impossible to count them all.

Sighing, Laurie lay back on her bed in an attempt to shut her eyes for a while before she had to face the world again.

Chapter 38

Wednesday 14th September 2016.

Dang was still so poorly, it was breaking Laurie's heart. She showed no enthusiasm for any food offered to her and seemed even more listless than usual. "God, look at her Frankie!"

"She does look poorly, that's for sure. Is she keeping down her medicine?"

"Yes, she is, thank God but she's not eating anything. She ate yesterday, only a little but still...I had thought she might have been on the mend," answered Laurie, tears brimming in her eyes.

"Is she drinking?"

"Just some water...I keep giving her sips. She mainly wants to sleep though. I just feel so helpless."

Gesturing to one of the ladies, Laurie pointed to Dang. "Can I take her outside? Get some fresh air?" The lady smiled but didn't answer, clearly not understanding what Laurie was trying to say. Frustrated, Laurie tried again. Pointing outside Laurie gestured to Dang and asked again. "Outside?"

"No, she sick" answered the lady once she had understood.

At this response Laurie felt an immense anger. "Yes," she stated firmly. "Dang *needs* fresh air. I go outside," she repeated, gathering Dang up, together with her bag and striding toward the door. Her heart was pounding, she was taking Dang outside whether they liked it or not, a stubborn streak coming to the fore.

A streak she couldn't recall acting on since childhood!

Opening the door she stepped outside and looked around her. There was a small park area, with some children's swings, but nowhere shady to sit down so she walked to the left of the classroom, noticing a metal seat, completely in the shade underneath a huge tree.

Sitting down, she sighed. Ahh...beautiful, the breeze was delicious as well as the absolute peace. The chair rocked slightly too, an added bonus.

The lady she had had an altercation with had followed her out but on seeing where Laurie had gone, had simply shrugged and left her to it.

And so, there she sat, the rest of the day, simply breathing in Dang's scent, singing to her whenever she appeared restless and allowing her to sleep as much as she wanted.

They had only four days left, thought Laurie. God, she couldn't imagine leaving this little mite just yet...not whilst she was so ill. Just the thought of Dang lying alone on the floor inside tore at Laurie's heartstrings. She couldn't possibly see how Dang would be well enough for Laurie to leave her in just a few days time. "Oh Sweetie," she whispered into Dang's ear. "You poor, poor thing," she said quietly, sighing deeply. "You must get better," she repeated over and over again.

Walking out later, Laurie was in floods of tears. She had hated leaving her...hated handing her over, suspecting that as soon as they had gone, Dang would be back on the floor again.

Pragmatic as ever, Frankie was doing her best to reassure her. "They'll be having tea and putting them to bed shortly," she placated. "And they *do* have beds, I asked today," she added, smiling at Laurie. "I found someone who spoke a tiny bit of English and she showed me where they all slept. You should have seen it Laurie, loads of little beds all in a row," she added, chuckling. "You'll be back tomorrow too," she added. "Try not to worry."

But Laurie *was* worried. They had been there three days already. Their flight was booked on Sunday from Bangkok. That only left Thursday and Friday really, maybe some of Saturday at a push, but they had to get to Bangkok from Chiang Mai. They had travelled up on an overnight train and it had taken thirteen hours!

"I haven't sorted anything out yet," replied Frankie when Laurie questioned her. "But it's always best to get to Bangkok the day before our flight just in case, so I was looking at leaving on the Saturday at the latest. We could always get a flight I suppose but that would be quite expensive I imagine," frowned Frankie.

"Yes, I expect it would," acknowledged Laurie. She was aware of Frankie's tight budget and didn't want to make her feel guilty by insisting on a flight. They could even have booked a flight on the Sunday, that way they would have all day Saturday here. "I don't know how I'm going to leave her, I'm not sure I can!" she sighed.

"Well, don't," answered Frankie. "Why don't you extend your stay? I mean, what exactly have you got to go back for? You've already said you need to leave Rich, so you're just going back to some shit anyway. So...what difference does it make if you stay a few more days?"

"*You* can't stay though can you? And anyway, what about my flight home?"

"No, I can't, but what's stopping you staying here by yourself? It will be easy to amend your flight and I'm sure you'll be able to extend your stay in our room here. That's as long as you can afford it of course?"

Laurie hadn't given any thought to extending her stay but why not? She still had plenty of her savings left, thanks to Frankie's frugal ways.

But *could* she stay on her own? Without Frankie?

The thought frightened the life out of her, but equally she didn't believe she could abandon Dang either and she was far more important.

And, *of course* she would be okay, she knew the area well enough now, she would be fine. She actually felt a frisson of excitement about the thought. "It's actually not a bad idea you know, I just might sleep on it," she said, smiling widely over at her friend.

"Excellent. Well, be quick about it as we will need to change your flight and the quicker we do that, the cheaper it will be," answered Frankie, as forthright as ever. "Now, where are we eating? I really fancy 'chicken pad thai' especially from that place over the road from us. God, it was gorgeous the other day. How about you? What do you fancy?"

Smiling, Laurie said the 'chicken pad thai' was fine by her. She was happy to go wherever Frankie preferred, food not being quite so important to Laurie as it seemed to be for Frankie. Laurie had lost count of the number of conversations Frankie seemed to have about food. She teased her about it regularly, noting how the first thing Frankie would discuss every day was what they would be eating, not what they would be doing! Frankie had agreed with her wholeheartedly, and without any shame, a fact Laurie admired immensely.

Having had a shower, they were now both tucking into their 'pad thai' along with a large glass of somewhat suspect wine. "I think I *will* stay Frankie. I think I have to. Dang is really poorly still, and whilst I know they will give her medicine, I think she needs more than that. Just sitting with her today outside, you know, she had love, fresh air, peace and quiet too. I was also able to get her drinking a little too. She needs that, most definitely, she needs 'one to one' and I can do that."

"I think you're absolutely right. It's definitely the right decision. Fabulous! I'm dead pleased. I must admit, I'd stay with you too if it wasn't for my dad...well, work too," she acknowledged. "But that's brilliant Laurie," she said, clapping her hands delightedly. "Right," she added, standing up to leave. "Let's get back, extend your room and cancel your flight. I looked into it for you whilst you were in the shower. We can't get a refund unfortunately. I wondered whether that might be the case...I always book the cheapest flights but that often means no amendments are allowed. So we'll just have to cancel it and then you will have to book another flight as and when. It will cost you though Laurie. I'm sorry, I feel really bad about that."

Laurie shrugged. "That's okay, bit of a bummer but there you go...I'm still not leaving."

Writing to her girls later that same evening, Laurie *did* have a wobble.

Was she doing the right thing? She hadn't heard anything from Marie or Cara since her email so she had little idea of what may be going on at home and her natural maternal instincts were kicking in as she thought of them.

But then her mind turned to Dang...a very sickly little girl who seemed to have no one else on her side.

Her need was greater, even if she wasn't blood.

And...as she kept being reminded by all and sundry, her girls weren't little any more!

So she wrote, to all three of them, stating that she hoped they were all okay and that she was extending her stay...only for a week at most, she had added. She gave them as much information as she could about Dang and how she would find it impossible to leave her at this stage. She added that she hoped they would understand and that she loved them all dearly.

Pressing 'send' she sat back on her bed, letting out a deep sigh. Well, she thought, that's done it, no going back now, she told herself. She knew she was doing the right thing though and couldn't wait to get back to the orphanage tomorrow.

She would sit with Dang all day and all night if necessary. Dang was going to get better if it was the last thing Laurie ever did! Smiling to herself, she rested her head on her pillow and fell into a deep, peaceful sleep.

Chapter 39

Thursday 15th September 2016.

Laurie was up early, 5am!

She had slept soundly, but once woken to go to the loo, had given up trying to get back to sleep. A mixture of excitement at her decision to stay, mixed with apprehension as to how the girls had taken her email, made further sleep impossible.

Reaching for the phone, she couldn't resist seeing if she had received any replies.

YES! One from Sarah *and* Marie. Oh God, she thought, opening Marie's with a certain trepidation.

'Hi mum, Sorry I've not emailed earlier. It's all been such a shock for me...what, firstly with your 50th party and then, well, you just going off! Especially after that weird text you sent! Dad is really mad. At first I felt really sorry for him but he's still so angry and I don't like how he only ever has horrible things to say about you. It makes living here at home very miserable. I hate to see him so upset, but equally I hate that you have felt the need to take off on your own. Adam has been really good, he says it's no surprise at all for him and that you and dad never seemed very happy together. I feel quite bad about that as I'd never noticed. It all seemed normal to me but I believe he may have a point. Anyway, what you said about that poor little girl! I feel so sorry for her and of course you must stay, as long as she needs you to. I love you mum. Please stay safe though, I couldn't bear to think of life without you. Marie xxxxxxxxxxxx'

Oh, the relief! It was immense! Re-reading it, she felt so proud of her daughter. She was growing up, that was obvious. And Adam, what an astute man he was! How she hoped Marie would make it with him.

'Hi mum. Just a quick one, I'm dead busy at work. Wow, sounds great what you are doing for that little girl. Keep me posted. Sarah xx'

Smiling to herself, Laurie put the phone down. Well...two out of three! That wasn't too bad was it? Maybe between them they would be able to talk some sense into Cara as well?

Now, what to do about Rich? she pondered. Lying back in bed, thinking back to the day Rich had given her that impossible ultimatum, Laurie's heart hardened. Nothing, she thought. She wasn't going to do anything. She just wouldn't turn up on Sunday. Frowning, she then thought how Rich would react and realised she couldn't do that to her girls. She didn't know whether Cara was still at Tom's or not, but Marie hadn't indicated that she was staying at Adam's and so she would be at home and would therefore bear the brunt of Rich's anger. She couldn't do that to her, she would *have* to email him, she thought miserably. If only to prepare him. At least, that way, the girls may not see him lose his temper. She'd do it tonight, she decided, have him receive it whilst at work, not at home.

Having made her decision she slid out of bed and went to watch the sun rise on their balcony, a '3 in 1' coffee comforting her immensely.

Dang was a little better again today, similar to how she had been on Tuesday.

Laurie took her outside as soon as they arrived, sitting on the same rocking chair, enjoying the beautiful breeze as well as the shade. It was so peaceful, Dang in and out of sleep, looking up at her with the largest brown eyes Laurie had ever seen whenever she woke, a small smile appearing once or twice. Her eyes were gorgeous, thought Laurie, in contrast to the rest of her, both her arm and legs still painfully covered in angry spots.

She was so glad she had made the decision to stay...it felt right and Laurie felt good about herself for a change.

"Hello," said a lady, coming and sitting next to her on the chair.

"Hi," answered Laurie with a smile.

"Who have we here then?"

The lady was in her fifties, Laurie believed, English like herself. "This is Dang, she's really sick as you can see. That's why I'm out here with her, trying to give her some fresh air as well as peace and quiet!"

"I know, it's manic in there isn't it?" agreed the lady, nodding over to the classroom. Smiling broadly she continued. "Well, she couldn't be in better hands, I wouldn't have thought. I noticed you out here yesterday. I'm Deborah by the way...And you are..?"

"Laurie," she answered. "Sorry, how rude of me...I didn't notice *you* yesterday."

"Oh, that's okay, you were clearly engrossed, so much so I didn't want to disturb you! I couldn't resist this morning though, too nosey for my own good," she added, smiling. "I come here three days a week, Wednesday to Friday...trying to teach the little buggers some English. It's no easy task though," she chuckled. "But, even if only some sinks in, I figure it'll be worth it when they get older, don't you?"

"Yes, I expect so. Gosh, what a lovely thing to do. How long have you been here?"

"This time?...one month so far, staying another month though. Managed three months last year," she frowned. "Just depends on how much time I can get off from work."

223

"Oh wow! How lovely!" exclaimed Laurie. "Where are you from?"

"London. I work in the city, in insurance. Worked there for years, hate every minute of it," she added wryly. "But it pays well, allows me to do this every year, so it's not all bad."

Laurie was intrigued. Her experience of the orphanage so far had been a little negative.

Not being able to communicate, finding it very frustrating, she couldn't help wondering how this Deborah had managed to get an agreement for her to teach.

As if reading her thoughts, Deborah continued. "I've been doing this for eight years now and they are *slowly* beginning to trust me," she laughed. "I'm even allowed to take some of the kids out for the day sometimes. Not all of them at once," she added, seeing Laurie's shocked expression. "Just three or four at a time. It does them good I believe, to see the outside world, gets them away from same old, same old."

"They're not very trusting are they," commented Laurie dryly.

"Oh, they are when they *know* you," Deborah responded. "Remember people come and go all the time, most staying for just a day or two, some simply to be able to say they've 'volunteered.' Some are nice of course, but not all, and these kids are already damaged. They're only watching out for them."

"Yes, I suppose," acknowledged Laurie reluctantly. "Ignore me, I'm just frustrated, that's all." Looking sideways at Deborah, she noticed how well put together she was, even in this heat. She had an air of calm about her and Laurie could see how she had been able to integrate here. "So, how do *you* find it here?"

"In what way?" Deborah asked, looking perplexed.

"Well....Regards how many children are here?....how they are looked after? I mean, only yesterday I saw them chuck a bucket of water over a child, after taking his nappy off!" Laurie's voice was rising with indignation.

Deborah smiled and shrugged her shoulders. "I find this place okay actually. Not all the kids are orphans, some come because their parents can't feed them, they are so poor. Here, they are safe, fed and watered. So yes...on the whole...it's not perfect but God, it could be a lot worse for them all!"

Laurie looked down at Dang and sighed heavily. "I expect so," she acknowledged reluctantly. "It's my western ways, I suppose. Never seen a child had a nappy change in such a way before," she added, smiling.

"And the harm? Its not exactly cold here is it? bet its quite refreshing for them and at least they get properly cleaned. There's a lot of them, if you noticed," she added wryly. "Not your three to one ratio our kids have back in the UK is it?" she challenged.

"No, you're right there!" Laurie conceded.

"That's where the likes of us can come in, you, giving Dang one to one is *exactly* the right medicine, so try to keep positive," she added, standing up and looking to her right. "Right, I'd best be going, get organised. I've got fifty of them today," she added, laughing." Maybe see you tomorrow?"

Nodding, Laurie said that would be lovely, her attention turning to Dang who had just woken up. She was lying still, her eyes not particularly focusing on anything. "Come on, little one, let me take you for a walk," she said softly as she struggled to get up from the chair.

Ambling around the gardens of the orphanage, Laurie did her best to draw Dang's attention to all the different flowers there were as well as pointing out all the birds she could hear tweeting above their heads. But Dang was still clearly ill, she showed no interest, seemingly content simply in Laurie's arms, safely protected and soothingly rocked.

At lunchtime she managed a small mouthful of sponge cake, which she sucked at for the longest time before finally swallowing it down. "Bloody sponge cake," moaned Laurie to Frankie. "There's nothing else I could find for her. Have you noticed how much sweet crap these kids are being given?"

Nodding in agreement, Frankie sighed. "Yes, I have. It would be nice to see them having a bit more fruit and veg wouldn't it? Still, better than nothing," she added, as positive as ever.

She stood up, rounding up as many kids as she could manage. "Come on kids, let's go and play on the swings. Not for long, mind, it's way too warm!"

And off she went, trotting with at least eight kids in tow.

"Right Dang, what are we going to do eh? Back to our lovely quiet seat, I think, and maybe some more sleep after your medicine? What do you think?" She knew Dang couldn't understand her but she was convinced her gentle voice would comfort Dang as much as her medicine would.

God, she had been hopeful of an improvement by now but at least she wasn't getting any worse!

'Rich. Will not be back on Sunday. Just wanted to let you know. Will be back within a week, I would have thought. Will let you know exactly when in due course. Laurie. P.S There should be plenty of frozen meals still in the freezer.'

Pressing 'send', she found herself smiling. She couldn't help do the 'looking after' bit. I mean, he wasn't a *complete imbecile*! He would know there were meals in the freezer, obviously. And, anyway, even if there weren't, he would survive. She could always send him a map of the kitchen! Point to where all the saucepans were kept! Anyway enough about him. Job done!

"Where do you fancy tonight then?" asked Frankie, clearly sensing Laurie had finished.

Laurie shrugged, as was her way. "I don't mind, you choose."

Never one to be told twice, Frankie made a suggestion which Laurie readily agreed to and off they set.

"Mmm..delicious," remarked Laurie, wiping her mouth with her paper napkin. Taking a large slug of wine, she looked over at Frankie "What time is your flight on Saturday?"

"Early, 7ish, made it cheaper," she answered brightly.

"Right...so we only have tomorrow then," said Laurie, a feeling of dread filling her body. "God, I hope I'll be okay by myself," she muttered, almost to herself.

"Course you will. It'll feel odd at first but whenever you find yourself having a wobble, just think of Dang. You're doing *wonders* for her, you know. God...what you're doing, I couldn't do it!"

Laurie looked puzzled. "Of course you could. I'm not doing anything anyway," she added.

"I think you are. And when I say I couldn't do it, I mean it. I couldn't just sit for hours like you are doing, I'd die of boredom, even if I knew it was necessary. You're a born natural with kids, you know, I feel quite jealous of how easily you bond with them. And you love it too, I can tell. Watching you yesterday, you looked so serene, so calm with Dang. You're so, so good at that sort of caring, that's your calling in life."

"I *do* like 'looking after,' you're right," agreed Laurie. "And it's something I miss now the girls have grown up. There's only the dog left!" she added, laughing.

"Well, maybe that's something to think about when you get back home. There's plenty of opportunities for 'caring' roles...Nursery nurse?...no...'childcare practitioner,' that's what they call themselves these days!"

"I'm not qualified at anything though," replied Laurie despondently.

"Oh, for God's sake Laurie!" Frankie said, impatiently. "No, you're not but that doesn't mean you can't care for someone! You're doing it now, here, aren't you?"

"Yes, but it's different at home, you know how prissy everything is."

"You just need to get your foot in some doors, that's all. Make some phone calls, make things happen," insisted Frankie.

"Crikey, if necessary, offer to volunteer somewhere first. Doors will open for you then, given time. You'd be surprised. *And* you could get some qualifications under your belt."

Listening to Frankie, Laurie had to agree. She *would* be good as a 'carer', whether to the old or the young. Yes...maybe something to explore, she decided, another small sliver of excitement flowing through her at the thought of all the possibilities life might have to offer.

If only Laurie was willing to take the first steps...and she would, definitely, she told herself.

She would have to, anyway, she would need to earn some money at some point if she was going to stand on her own two feet.

"There's something else too I've been meaning to say but I haven't dared."

"What?" asked Laurie slowly with trepidation. God, what could it be? A problem with one of her girls? Was one of them sick? Or Rich? Surely he hadn't contacted Frankie?

"Well, promise you won't shout at me?"

"Just *tell* me Frankie, you're making me bloody nervous!" Laurie answered, feeling irritated as well as worried, getting up from her chair in nervous anticipation.

"I've contacted Mike."

"What!" stated Laurie incredulously, "What the Fuck!" she added, sitting back down again, her legs too shaky to hold her upright.

Putting her hands in the air in mock apology, Frankie grinned. "I know, I know, I should have run it by you first, but I didn't. I didn't think you'd let me," she added sheepishly. "Anyway, don't you want to hear about him?" she added playfully.

"This is *so* not funny Frankie...not funny at all!" Laurie felt exasperated as well as very angry. This wasn't a *game*! How could Frankie do this?

"Oh come on Laurie, lighten up," urged Frankie. "Okay, okay, I'm sorry. Maybe I shouldn't have done it and I apologise," a trace of a very small smile on her lips. "I won't mention it again. Come on, let's get the bill, we both need our beauty sleep," she added, standing up, placing her bag on her shoulder and picking up her scarf.

They did not speak at all, as they walked back to their hotel. Neither did they as they both showered and climbed into their beds.

Laurie was still fuming, there was no way she would be able to sleep now. Mike! Just the thought of him still made her stomach do somersaults. And Frankie had actually *contacted* him! OMG! She wondered how he was doing now, what he might look like, whether he still had that slow smile she had loved so much...his passion for life, his naivety, as she saw it. But naivety that had a definite honesty with it. He had been adamant they could have made a go of it and nothing put him off. Not Rich...not the girls. She had thought him too simplistic at the time but had he been? Had he been right all those years ago, could they have made it work?

No, she still believed not. Laurie hadn't ever had any doubts she and Mike would have worked but Rich?! Well, Mike hadn't known him, hadn't realised how stubborn and unpleasant Rich would have been. Only she knew what Rich was capable of and she still believed that, had she chosen to leave that night, she would have been walking away from her girls too and THAT, she could never have done.

She allowed herself to think of Mike as she lay there, trying to bring his face to life. She couldn't anymore, he was just a blur...but it wasn't just the physical aspects, it was how he made her *feel*...and that, she could never lose, she thought, wrapping her arms around herself.

God, what she would give to feel loved like that again, she thought miserably.

"Are you awake?" whispered Frankie.

"Yes."

"Thought so. Do you want to talk?"

"Okay," answered Laurie reluctantly.

"Do you want to know what happened when I got in touch with him?"

"Go on," she whispered, a feeling of incredible fear and excitement hitting her stomach.

"Well, first of all, let me tell you he was more than happy to hear from me. I found him on 'Linked in'. Not that it matters how I found him but it's an app for professionals more than anything else, you know, to increase their profile, give them more opportunity for jobs. Anyway, that aside, he responded immediately. Cut to the chase, he would love to be able to contact you so I said I would ask you if I could give him your email address." She sighed. "I'm sorry though, maybe I should have kept out of it all. It's none of my business." Sitting up in bed suddenly she sighed again. "I get *so* frustrated though. I mean, it's clear you were meant for each other and it's not as though you are happy is it? And, anyway, what's to stop you now? Rich can't use the girls anymore can he? So why not? What have you got to lose? Nothing, from what I can see. God! You frustrate the hell out of me Laurie! He actually wants to get in touch, that's amazing *and* he's single, if that's what's worrying you!"

"Okay, okay, I get the picture," Laurie answered softly. "We're just different, that's all and you took me by complete surprise and...I don't know...can you really resurrect the past so easily? God, so much water under the bridge for both of us. I mean, he might not even fancy me anymore, I'm not exactly the girl he met am I?"

"And neither is he. And love is more than that isn't it? Real love? More than just the physical?" Pausing, Frankie then continued in her normal direct manner. "Anyway if you don't pursue it, you'll never know will you. It's time you started taking some chances in life, don't you think? Stop playing safe."

Frankie had a point, Laurie thought. Playing safe had not exactly worked too well so far, had it? Could she get back in touch? Oh, she would absolutely love to, she couldn't think of anything else she would like better, she thought, hugging herself tightly, as excitement surged through her body.

Chapter 40

Friday 16th September 2016.

"Okay," said Laurie, as they were sitting, squashed up in a 'tuk tuk' on their way to the orphanage.

"Okay what?" asked Frankie, puzzled. Frankie was busy on her phone, sorting out her travel plans for the following day.

"Okay for you to give him my email address," Laurie answered, in a tone that suggested it was obvious.

"Thank fucking Christ for that!" Frankie replied quietly, putting her phone down on her lap.

"About bloody time...you've finally seen sense!"

Laurie had to laugh at Frankie. She loved her, loved how she always knew exactly where she stood with her. Frankie didn't have agendas, she didn't play games. It made her very easy to be with. Laurie knew Frankie only ever had her best interests at heart. And so, whilst Laurie felt Frankie had overstepped the mark, she couldn't feel angry with her.

"God, it scares me to death though," she added, ringing her hands together. "Did he say anything else? You know, like what he's doing now, where he lives, how he is?"

"Nope, he was just asking about you that's all. I only know he's single from his profile.

"What was he asking?"

"He was asking how *you* were. I didn't say much, don't worry. I just told him that we'd come away together and a little bit about what we've been doing here, told him about the volunteering we're doing at the orphanage, a little bit about Dang too. Might have mentioned you weren't happy though!" she added mischievously. "Just take it one step at a time, see where it goes. You have nothing to lose, but possibly everything to gain. And I saw you together, remember. You were made to be with each other then, that was obvious to anyone who had half a brain. You fit together so nicely, like you were *meant* to be."

Laurie smiled. Frankie was right. That's exactly how they had been. But what about now?

"I know, but can it still be the same after all this time?" Laurie asked, a worried frown on her face.

"Do you still feel the same about him now as you did then?"

"God, yes of course! Maybe more even!"

"Well then! It's not, therefore, beyond the realms of possibility that he still feels the same way too is it? I mean, he answered me very promptly when I contacted him. Stop fretting so, just see where it goes. That's what I would do anyway... 'go with the flow' as they say in my yoga class."

Yes, Laurie decided. Frankie was right. What *did* she have to lose? She hadn't got Mike now anyway so if it didn't amount to anything then nothing would have been lost would it? Mmm, not so sure about that though, she thought to herself. Hope... that's what she could lose....at the moment a wonderful bubble of hope sat inside her heart, growing more and more as she thought of him. Could she bear life again if that bubble of hope was distinguished forever?

Sighing heavily, she bent her head into her hands. She didn't think she could. She didn't believe she would have an ounce of strength left to cope should that hope die.

"Hello Sweetie," she said, greeting Dang in her usual manner. "Any better today?" she asked, scrutinising her whole body in a matter of seconds. Was it her imagination or did those spots not look quite so angry today? A flicker of a smile again too! Yes, she recognises me, thought Laurie delightedly, picking her up in her arms and taking her outside again for her daily dose of fresh air, peace and tranquillity.

"Hi Deborah," whispered Laurie, noticing Deborah walking over to her.

"Hello again, and hello Dang. Ahh, she has her eyes open," she exclaimed. "Wow, what beautiful eyes she has," she whispered as she sat down beside them. "How is she today?"

"Oh, not too bad actually. I think she may be a little better. I mean, she has stayed awake a while this morning, she's looking around too. It's the first time I've noticed her taking in her surroundings so that's got to be a good sign hasn't it?" she asked a little anxiously.

"I would have thought so," Deborah agreed. "Her spots don't look quite as bad either," she added.

Laurie beamed. "Oh, that's what I thought earlier. Only I was starting to wonder whether I was just kidding myself," she chuckled.

"So, how long are you here for then Laurie?"

"Well...I was supposed to be leaving tomorrow, but I've cancelled my flight. Because of this little one," she added, looking fondly down at Dang.

"Really?! Oh, that's good of you. Mind you, I'm not surprised, seeing how you are with her. I couldn't imagine you being able to leave her just yet."

"God, no. I couldn't possibly. I just hope she gets better soon...for her sake, obviously. But, for mine too. I have to go home soon and there's no way I can go until she's a lot better."

Laurie was feeling quite worried about this. She had indicated she would be staying for no more than a week. But she had been here for five days so far and seen little improvement in Dang. Would another week be enough? Well, she would cross that bridge when she came to it. Meanwhile she *was* here and giving Dang all the love and care she could.

As Frankie would have said, there was little more she could do.

"She'll get better. As I say, her spots look better already. And kids can improve overnight can't they? Crikey, I remember my son when he was little. At death's door, I sometimes thought, and then, overnight he was bright as a button! Never failed to amaze me. Wish it was so at my age," Deborah added wryly. "Any slight cold I get these days stays with me for weeks!"

Laurie laughed. "Yes, that's true, does with me as well."

"Oh, the joys of being older eh?" chuckled Deborah "Still...there are advantages too."

"Are there?" asked Laurie, a sceptical look on her face.

"Oh absolutely! Don't you think so?"

"Not really no! What are the advantages? God, I'm fatter, way more stressy about everything and get so tired. Never used to. And that's before I get started on the hot sweats!"

Laughing, Deborah had to agree. "Well, yes, okay, there are those downsides but the ups need not be forgotten. You're wiser, that's for sure, you know what you *don't* want even if you don't know what you *do* want. And you're invisible."

Laurie spluttered. "Oh...charming! Invisible? How is *that* an advantage?"

Deborah laughed. "It is!" she insisted. "You can use that. No one notices you...that makes you free. Free to do whatever you want in life. Go where you want, live how you want."

"Really?!" asked Laurie incredulously.

"Oh absolutely. You have no men chasing you, controlling you, ordering you about. They are too busy chasing the younger models," she added ruefully. "And, as I say, there's a certain freedom in that. We are such a nonentity as far as society is concerned therefore there are few expectations of us. And that can be a positive if we think of it that way. I certainly feel so much freer these days. Maybe that comes with not caring so much about what others think either. And *that* has definitely come with age! Gosh, is that the time?" She asked, looking at her watch, her voice rising an octave or two in surprise. "Crikey...I must go, they'll be waiting for me," she added, rising hastily from her seat. "See you next week," she added as she rushed off at a pace of knots.

Smiling to herself, Laurie acknowledged Deborah's comments. She wasn't actually right as far as Laurie was concerned but neither was she wrong. They were her opinions and the positive attitude Deborah decided to take on life only enhanced it for her. Yes, she was aware of all the negatives but she didn't dwell on them, that was for sure. She looked at a glass half full as opposed to one half empty...or empty, thought Laurie wryly.

Sitting here, listening to Dang's gentle breathing, Laurie acknowledged for the first time in her life that her attitude to life was not as good as it could be...well...okay, it was shit!

She was starting to realise that she was indeed allowing others (Rich, her girls) to control her and that she was culpable. She had *allowed* others to treat her that way. She had *allowed* herself to be a victim. She found this thought most disconcerting and didn't like to admit it, even if just to herself. And how easy had it been as a result? Always someone else to blame. Never having to take any responsibility herself. But it hadn't brought happiness had it? She was living a 'half life' and it had to stop.

She was afraid, she realised...afraid in case everything went wrong...and her fear had led her to being controlled all her life. That way she could always point the finger if necessary. Never *her* fault. But what a cop out! As she'd just said. It *had* to stop!

Her thoughts turned to Mike. This was another example. Here she was, afraid of having contact...just in case it didn't work out! She exasperated herself! "Time to grow some balls Laurie," she said quietly. "Time to *live!*" she added. If little Dang can still smile when her world is so crappy, then about time she learned to do the same, she thought.

She would write a list! She was good at those. But this list would be about stuff that *mattered,* not just everyday chores! And she would visit it every day, making sure she was going in the right direction.

Grabbing her bag, she found a pen and a crumpled piece of paper. Nothing like starting as you mean to go on, she told herself, manoeuvring Dang over slightly so she could write. Right...What do you want from your next thirty years Laurie? And think BIG! Feeling a beautiful breeze on the back of her neck she began to compose her list.

Be proud of myself.
Have my girls look at me with pride.
Get fitter.
Feel healthy.
Feel alive.
Love again!!!

Mmm....okay...all well and good but How? Breaking it down she began to write again.

Proud of myself. How?... Sort Dang out, get her healthy again. Maybe come over here regularly like Deborah did and look after others who were sick?

My girls looking at me with pride?... As above.

Get fitter?...Join a gym.

Feel healthy?... Five fruit and veg every day.

Feel alive??? Well, all the above will help!!

Love again? Don't be afraid of Mike's contact. If it doesn't work out then what the hell! Find other love!!!

Wow! Her list had been written in minutes. Was it that easy? Why not? It's a start anyway. And yes, she was going to laminate it and look at it every day. No twenty four hours would pass without Laurie feeling as though something was being achieved towards these goals. Baby steps every day. In fact, she walked past a yoga studio every morning to catch the 'tuk tuk'. So tonight on her way home she would go in, see when classes took place. No time like the present! And Frankie going home tomorrow? Instead of dreading it, she was going to look at the positives. Frankie was fabulous but Laurie just followed in her footsteps. With Frankie gone, Laurie would have to start making her own decisions for a change. And about time too!

"You and I against the world Dang," she whispered. "And what a team we are going to make," she added.

Again, she noticed a flicker of a smile as Dang's eyes opened and stared up at her. "Come on Sweetie, let's go and fetch you some food. And I'll be damned if it's just bloody cake!" she added, striding purposefully towards the classroom.

Chapter 41

Saturday 17th September 2016.

Well, she'd gone!

And Laurie felt lost.

Sitting on her bed, she looked around her. The whole feeling in the room had changed completely. Complete silence. Oh my God, how was she going to manage on her own? She took a few deep, calming breaths. She mustn't analyse, she told herself, she must keep busy! Picking up the list she had written yesterday, she read through it again. She just needed to keep taking baby steps, that's all.

Right, okay, what could she pick on? She had two hours before she needed to leave for the orphanage and she was damned if she was just going to sit here getting increasingly morose. Well, she thought, poring through her list, I'm doing what I can with Dang, so it's either fitness, healthy eating or love!

Love, she could do nothing about, so a yoga class followed by a healthy breakfast would have to do. Not giving herself any time for further reflection, she jumped off the bed, grabbed her purse and proceeded out of her room.

Arriving at the orphanage later that morning Laurie felt great. Her yoga class had been superb. She was so pleased with herself. She had simply turned up, grabbed a mat, placing it at the back of the room and done what she could. Some of the poses had been way too difficult and Laurie hadn't even attempted them, choosing to go into 'child's pose' on more than one occasion. And the instructor had been really encouraging. "That's good," she said. "Do what you can but don't listen to your ego, come out of the pose at any time. It's your body, you know best." How lovely, Laurie had thought. What an attitude! The times Laurie had been tempted to go to a yoga class over the years, only to tell herself she wouldn't be good enough, or flexible enough.

And who cared? Nobody there, that was for sure. Nobody even looked over at her, they were all too busy doing their own workout.

Then she had indulged in a tasty breakfast, fresh fruit and yoghurt, and as a result felt quite wonderful.

Two things on her list!! Babysteps, yes, but babysteps she was determined to continue making.

Walking into the classroom, Laurie immediately looked around for Dang and was delighted to see she was actually sitting up...okay...propped up with cushions, but sitting up nonetheless, her eyes wide open, taking in her surroundings. "Hello Sweetie, wow, look at you!" she exclaimed, being rewarded with a huge smile. "Hey, you look a little better today, oh I'm so pleased," she gushed, picking Dang up and cradling her in her arms. "And guess what I have for you today?" she whispered. "I have fresh mango and a tomato. Oh yes, and an egg. I'm going to get you better, I promise. And no crappy cake!" she added, laughing.

Thinking back to yesterday brought a smile to Laurie's face. One of the ladies had brought Dang a slice of cake over for lunch and Laurie had refused to take it. "No" she had said, shaking her head firmly. "Dang needs good food, not cake."

The lady had looked at her in surprise, but simply shrugged and turned away.

"Fruit!" Laurie had shouted to the lady's back, "You have fruit? Or egg?" she added, trying to think of anything light but good for her too. Getting no response, Laurie had tried another of the ladies, an older lady who she felt may understand more. Pointing to Dang, she repeated her request. "Fruit? Egg? Not cake, no good for her," she had added. Seeing the lady's perplexed look, Laurie tried again. "Mango? Papaya? Pineapple?"

"Mango," the lady stated.

"Yes, yes," Laurie had shouted eagerly. "You have mango?" And Dang had loved it, sucking on the succulent fruit with an eagerness Laurie had not seen previously.

Yes, thought Laurie to herself. She had been stubborn yesterday, persistent too, and it had worked. Whoever knew whether Dang's improvement was down to that or not but all these little things added up and were bound to be helping overall and Laurie felt an immense pride.

"Come on," she said. "Let's go outside to our normal spot, away from this mayhem," she added, chuckling.

Her day had continued in the same vein as all her other days with Dang, sitting outside, watching Dang sleep mostly, but also noticing that, when Dang *was* awake, she was a little more alert to her surroundings.

She ate some of the fresh food Laurie had brought in, drank a little more water than previous days and smiled on a number of occasions.

By the time Laurie left her that day she felt immensely comforted. For the first time since seeing her all those days ago, Laurie allowed herself to think that Dang would get better and that was a fantastic feeling, she thought, walking quickly to catch the 'tuk tuk' she knew was due.

Well... her first day by herself and so far, so good! She would grab some food on her way home – she was feeling quite exhausted and the thought of having to get ready and go out again held no appeal. Wanting some familiarity, she returned to the restaurant they had eaten in only last night, even ordering the same meal, chicken with cashews. It was just as nice and two glasses of wine later, Laurie was feeling quite mellow.

Planning to get home, jump in the shower and dive into bed, Laurie paid the bill and walked briskly back. It was only a two minute walk but she felt wary. It was dark now and she was alone. Head down all the way, she breathed a sigh of relief when she entered her sanctuary. Closing the door firmly behind her, she laughed loudly. "Stupid girl," she said to the room. God, look at all those women she had met over the last fortnight. They were alone and they survived! It was just different, that was all, she told herself. And she was tired too, that never helps, she thought as she pulled her sweaty clothes off quickly and jumped into the shower.

Sat in bed, she looked at her watch. It was only 8pm. That meant lunchtime at home. Dared she look at her emails? She had hardly allowed herself to think of the possibility that Mike might had been in touch. She had deliberately not looked this morning, not feeling able to cope with having her hopes dashed, telling herself it would be way too soon (God, she'd only given Frankie permission to pass on her email address yesterday!)

There was Cara too...she hadn't heard a peep from her and everytime she looked, she felt hugely disappointed, worried too, wondering how Cara was feeling.

Taking a deep breath, she opened her in-box.

Nothing!

She sighed deeply. He wasn't going to get in touch, she told herself, feeling a deep pit of despair wrap around her. Of course he wasn't. Bloody Frankie! Getting her hopes up! How bloody stupid she'd been, thinking he would be interested in her after all these years. Why would he be? All the younger models he could have his pick of!

Nothing from Cara either....not even one from Rich...well, that was a blessing at least, she thought, throwing her phone down on her bedside table.

God, she felt so alone!

Listening, Laurie heard not a peep. This was the trouble, this complete and utter silence. She had never experienced this before.

There was always stuff happening around you when you were part of a family and with Frankie...well...she made enough noise for two! But this...she didn't like it...not one bit.

She had never been alone, not really, going straight from her parents to married life with Rich. It wasn't just the lack of physical presence around her which she found unnerving but the thought that no one would know what she was up to. She could sleep, cry, sing, listen to music, go out and no-one would be any the wiser. No-one but her would know! And that was weird. She had forever had someone around, someone to care, even if it was only the dog sometimes, so she was finding this 'being alone' malarkey scary.

Add to that, the huge disappointment and upset she felt over Mike and she felt completely overwhelmed. So, so lonely. She wiped away the tears that were beginning to fall. God, she was crying *again*. How many tears could she possibly have left?

A small voice inside her told her to review her list, pick something to do, change her environment, do something, *anything,* to make her feel a little less lost.

But then thoughts of Mike forced themselves into her mind and she fell back into a deep despair. Frankie had lit a small flame of hope in Laurie's heart and she couldn't bear the thought of it being extinguished. "Please Mike, please contact me," she begged, sobbing loudly now into her pillow.

There she lay, her pillow getting soaked until finally, exhaustion overcame her and she fell asleep.

Chapter 42

Sunday 18th September 2016.

Laurie was numb, a numbness one could only feel after sobbing so much.

She showered quickly and threw on her yoga clothes without giving herself time to think. She simply forced herself to put one foot in front of the other until she found herself lying on a yoga mat, in the same spot as yesterday morning.

And the yoga had done its job, much to her amazement. A different practitioner today, this lady had concentrated far more on the mind, less on the body. *And* she was positive, thought Laurie. So calm and gentle. Content and serene, that's how Laurie would describe her. The class had started with her repeating the date and time, pointing out what a beautiful day it was and were we aware it would never be this day and time again! "So listen to the day," she had said. "Take it all in, don't let it simply pass you by in a haze. What a shame that would be!"

Smiling, Laurie felt so much better, lighter even, as she left the studio. There was definitely something in this yoga, she decided. It had certainly made her feel so much better this morning...more accepting.

And Mike? Well, what could she possibly do? Nothing, that's what!

So, she would force herself to look forward, concentrate on things she *could* control...like Dang! She loved that child now. How strange, she had only known her for six days. But love was like that...a connection of souls, that's all. It could happen in a heartbeat. There was no explanation, it was that random.

So, Laurie was determined to do her best by Dang. She would get her better first and then investigate what else she could do, what other help she may be able to give, going forward. After all, if Deborah could do it, then why couldn't she?

She was delighted. Dang was sitting up, no cushions supporting her and she gave Laurie a huge smile when she saw her, making Laurie's heart sing. Not only was she smiling but her arms were out, gesturing to be picked up!

On doing so, Laurie danced her around the room, causing a couple of the Thai ladies to laugh and smile at them both. "She's getting better," she sang. "Look at her!" she added.

"She good," smiled the lady who had fetched her the mango the other day. "She good," she repeated.

The red spots were still covering her arms and legs, but were not now so livid. Thank God for that! "Come on Dang, let's get you outside again. Let me show you all those birds I've been trying to get you interested in," she said, taking her away again from all the noise and smells typical in a room full of toddlers.

They sat on their bench, Laurie talking softly to Dang, telling her what a pretty girl she was and Dang seemed to be drinking it all in. She couldn't understand, obviously, but she certainly seemed to be enjoying the love and attention she was getting, even mumbling a few intelligible words herself and whenever Laurie laughed, Dang chuckled a little too.

And, so they sat...until Dang's eyes went heavy and she fell asleep.

"Hello again," shouted Deborah, approaching Laurie at speed.

"Hi," smiled Laurie, taken by surprise. "I didn't think you came in today?"

"No, I don't, you're right. Well...not to teach anyway. I'm taking a couple of the kids out with me. Thought I might take them to the zoo."

"Oh, lovely!" exclaimed Laurie, wondering how on earth Deborah had managed to sort that out with the powers that be. "You don't speak Thai do you?"

"God...I wish. But I've learned a little over the years, enough for me to get by anyway. How's this little one today? She asked, changing the subject. "She's fast asleep I can see!"

"Yes she is now, but you should have seen her earlier, she was really quite bright, chuckling even! She's so much better, I can't tell you how relieved I am."

"I can imagine," acknowledged Deborah. "So, how much longer are you planning to stay then?"

"God, I have no idea," answered Laurie. She couldn't imagine leaving yet. She certainly wasn't prepared to consider it until Dang was better. But then, what would Dang think? All of a sudden Laurie would just stop turning up! She couldn't explain to her, she would feel abandoned! Mmm, at some point, Laurie was going to *have* to leave.

Up until now Laurie had been so concerned with getting Dang better, she hadn't given a thought to what would happen afterwards. In all honesty, until a few days ago, she had wondered if Dang would *ever* improve!

She looked over at Deborah who had plonked herself, unceremoniously, by her side and smiled ruefully. "I can't imagine leaving her now. God, this is all so difficult isn't it? I mean, I'm going to have to leave her some time. And whatever will she think?" her voice rising a little with her distress.

"I know," acknowledged Deborah. "It's difficult isn't it? For Dang's sake I would suggest you wean yourself off her slowly."

"How on earth can I do that?" asked Laurie, outraged. "She's still not right, I couldn't possibly! That would be so cruel!" she added, annoyed at Deborah's suggestion.

Raising her hands in surrender, Deborah backed off a little. "I don't mean right this minute," she said, smiling. "Just over the next few days. As you see her improving, that's all. Maybe less time here, one to one. Maybe some time spent with the other kids too. You'd still be there to keep an eye on her."

"Mmm, it makes sense I suppose," she said grudgingly. "But not today though," she added, grinning. "Today, I'm going to enjoy her all to myself. But yes, from tomorrow, as long as she's still improving, then that's what I'll do."

"Good. I think that's the right call. Don't forget, I'm here for the next couple of months too. I'll keep an eye out for her, so don't worry so," she added. "Well, I'd best be going. See you later. I'll be back around 4ish, I would have thought. Will you still be here?"

"Of course," replied Laurie. "They have to literally throw me out!" she added with a laugh. "The later I can get away with staying, the better."

"Yes, I can imagine," Deborah said, laughing with her. "How do you fancy some food with me later then? I'll be starved by the time I get back from the zoo and there's a lovely cafe just down the road."

"That's a wonderful idea. Yes thank you, I'd love to. See you later then. Enjoy!"

Watching Deborah march off with purpose, Laurie went over what she had said and knew she was right. The only way Laurie could imagine walking away from Dang was if she felt, firstly, that she was well enough and secondly, if she knew she could hold her own in this environment. And that meant playing with the other kids and re-integrating in the classroom.

In order for that to happen, Laurie needed to put Dang's needs before her own.

Which got Laurie thinking about herself. She was starting to realise what a buzz she got out of caring for others, how much more alive she felt when doing so. In fact she would forget her own worries for a while, so immersed was she in the caring. She always felt so good afterwards, a warm, fuzzy feeling.

She would have to leave Dang but that didn't mean she couldn't come back.

And she would, she promised herself.

Tucking into their sweet and sour chicken that evening, Laurie found she was thoroughly enjoying Deborah's company. She was not dissimilar to Frankie in many ways, more polished, definitely, but with the same 'no nonsense' forthright manner that Laurie admired so much.

She was obviously drawn to a certain type, maybe seeking out characteristics she would like a good dose of herself!

"Anyway, now I've filled you in on my day, how about you? How's your day been?"

"Oh lovely," answered Laurie enthusiastically. "Dang is so much better. I kept her with me today but I'm going to do what you suggested from tomorrow. It makes sense and I can't stay here forever. But I will be coming back, most definitely!" she added, as much to convince herself as Deborah.

"Oh, that's excellent. Well, we must keep in touch, it would be nice to come out at the same time, don't you think?"

"Yes, that would be lovely," replied Laurie, sounding a little unsure, thinking of all the chaos she was going back to.

Picking up on Laurie's sudden change of mood, Deborah cocked her head to one side. "Are you okay?" she asked, smiling over at Laurie.

"Oh yes, ignore me. It's just things are not so good at home at the moment. Well...that's an understatement if ever there was one!" she added. "And I don't know how things are going to pan out, so I'm not sure I could come back even if I wanted to...you know, financially...and workwise too."

"What do you do?"

"I don't do anything at the moment!" laughed Laurie bitterly. "But I will be needing to find work soon, that's for sure."

"Ahh, you're going through a divorce then?"

"Divorce! Well, yes I expect I will be. Jeez, I've not thought that far ahead!" Looking quizzically over at Deborah, "That's very astute of you?"

Deborah smiled. "Well, you have a wedding ring on but you never mention your other half. So, I've kind of put two and two together." Holding her hands up, she added, "But you don't have to tell me, I'm sorry, it's your business."

"No, no, it's fine Deborah. Anyway it's good to talk sometimes. And yes, you're right. I left to come on holiday with one of my friends and didn't tell him...Rich, that is, my husband. So when I get home it's all going to be a bit of a mess. He's a bit of a control freak and he's furious with me. But, that aside, I'm definitely leaving him and will need to find work. God knows what though! I've been looking after the girls for the last twenty years. Not earned a bean! Not had to. And just the thought of the mess I'm going back to, well, its all a bit overwhelming to say the least!"

"Oh dear Laurie. I'm sorry. It's always a sad time splitting up, but exciting too, don't you think?...just a little?"

Laurie smiled sadly. "Well, a little I suppose."

"And your husband...Rich? He's done well I take it?"

"Oh yes, he's done very well, I can't complain there! We have a beautiful home, three lovely girls, but..."

"Yes?" prompted Deborah.

"But there's no love, hasn't been for years. I don't even like him!"

"And how does he feel? Do you know?"

"Oh yes, I know!" Laurie scoffed. "He has no time for me whatsoever. He's had many affairs, speaks to me like I'm a piece of dirt and I've finally had enough!"

Deborah looked puzzled. "Well, what's the problem then? If neither of you are happy?"

"You don't know Rich," Laurie answered despondently, pulling a face.

"He's very much into appearances. And control. I mean, if he decided to leave *me*, then that would be okay, but for me to instigate it! Oh no! He will *never* allow that to happen, certainly not without a fight."

"Mmm, one of them is he? You say he's done well in his career?"

"Yes, he's a partner in a law firm."

"Arrogant too then, I'm guessing?"

"Absolutely!" agreed Laurie. "He won't make it easy for me, not at all! He won't just let me walk away."

Deborah was quiet for a moment. "Do you mind me asking how long you've been married Laurie?"

"Twenty six very long years!" Laurie replied.

"And your girls? How old are they now?"

"Well, the youngest, Cara, has just turned twenty one," Laurie answered proudly. "And then my two older girls are Sarah, who's twenty five and Marie, twenty three. Why?"

"Just asking. So there's no 'children' involved...well, at least not as far as the law's concerned anyway. Any mum knows they're still kids way into their twenties!" she laughed. "But, regardless, I wouldn't have thought you would have any problems from everything you've told me. You're entitled to half the equity in the house, which I assume will be a decent amount. You could still try for maintenance, at least for a little while, until you've had the chance to find decent work. You've invested twenty five of your years caring for his children, that's not to be sneezed at, it comes at a price, don't forget that! All you need is a good solicitor. If I were you, I'd sort that as soon as you get home. It will certainly make you feel better when you know where you stand. Knowledge is power, so the saying goes," she added, smiling.

"Crikey, you make it sound so simple!"

"It is. The difficulty is making the decision to split. You've already done that...the rest...well...that's just detail," she added. "Trust me, I've been there!"

"Really?"

"Oh yes!" Deborah answered vehemently. "To a right testosterone filled, arrogant control freak too!" she added, laughing. "Been single eight years now and I've never been happier. I love my freedom. I'd never have done half the things I do now, had I stayed married. I have no regrets at all...and...if you're wondering about other men? Well...they seem to come out of the woodwork with amazing regularity!" she chortled. "The difference now though? I'm in the driving seat!"

Laurie smiled. She had to admit, Deborah did seem to be perfectly content. "Eight years you say? Is that when you first came out here then?"

"Yes. Not a dissimilar story to yours. I needed to get away and I sort of stumbled on this place at the right time. Thailand always brings me back to the basics, what's *actually* important. Working in London, its crazy all the time. Always working to impossible deadlines, always being asked for more than you can give. Its toxic. Here is the complete opposite, allows me to recharge my batteries. It feeds my soul!"

"Wow! I see what you mean though. I feel the same too. Obviously I don't have the pressure you have, work wise, but I love the simplicity here, it's so nice. Far more about a roof over your head and food in your mouth and that takes away an awful lot of stress. Plus everyone is so friendly, I can't believe I've only been here for a couple of weeks, it feels like home already to me."

"You'll come back, I can tell you right now," stated Deborah. "You've fallen for the place, just like I did. And, financially, you don't need much here, you know. I rent a lovely place for just over three hundred pounds a month. Has two bedrooms, a kitchen. Perfectly adequate. So, all I need on top of that is enough for my food (flight too, of course.) I spend very little when I'm here though, far less than at home."

"Just three hundred? Really?" asked Laurie.

The room Laurie was in cost much more than that which is why she was so surprised.

"Oh yes. Just ask for the monthly rate and you'll be surprised. It normally comes in at a third of any nightly rate quoted...makes a big difference. Anyway, let's keep in touch and then, as long as you can come out the same time, you could always stay with me. It would make a lovely change having company. And you *are* needed at that orphanage, those kids need as much love as we can give them!" She yawned loudly. "Oh dear, those kids have worn me out today. They dragged me all around the zoo at breakneck speed and then wanted to go round again!" she said, getting up from the table "Let's get the bill shall we?"

"Yes, absolutely." agreed Laurie, gathering her stuff together. "And thank you Deborah, I've had a lovely evening. See you Wednesday?"

"Yes, definitely. And thank *you* too. I enjoy a good natter," she added as they walked along the road looking out for a 'tuk tuk.'

Laurie felt so much better when she walked into her room that evening. Being alone opened opportunities too, she realised. Had Frankie still been around, Laurie doubted very much that she would have ended up eating with Deborah, and even if they had, the conversation would likely have been a lot shallower. Far less likely to open up in a group of three, certainly for Laurie who was naturally very private.

And opening up more was what she needed to do!

Deborah had given her plenty of food for thought and had left her feeling positive for the future. *And* she was right! Instead of feeling fearful, maybe it was time Laurie allowed herself to feel more positive...God...even excited!

This was the second time in her life that she had been advised to get a solicitor and she wasn't going to ignore it this time! Had she listened twenty years ago, who knows what might have transpired?

So, overall, today had proved to be a good one. Her yoga was helping her feel calmer, Dang was vastly improved and tonight had allowed Laurie to see a glimmer of hope regarding her future. The thought of returning here on a regular basis excited her.

She would be okay financially eventually too. She hadn't given a thought to that side of things until Deborah had enlightened her. The house must be worth at least £600k by now and she knew they only had a small mortgage remaining, no more than £150k, she reckoned. So yes, over time, she would be fine.

Just the thought of selling up made her feel guilty though. What would the girls think? They certainly wouldn't like it. But she had to begin to look after *her* needs too. She certainly couldn't stay with Rich for the rest of her life just so the girls could keep their childhood bedrooms! Rich might buy her out anyway, she supposed, if it mattered that much to him to keep it. Yes, she decided. As soon as she got back, she'd get onto a good solicitor. In the meantime however, the best bet was not to alert Rich to her thoughts. She didn't want to get home only to find herself locked out.

Had she followed Frankie's advice and locked Rich out all those years ago, maybe everything would have turned out differently then? Really? No, probably not, she perused. Rich would have just broken in, so angry he would have been. A locked door would not have deterred him!

But Laurie wouldn't be breaking in would she? So where would she go if that happened? Mmm, she needed to start thinking a little more slyly.

She decided, therefore, to email him, try to keep him oblivious to her longer term plans. At least, that way, she could return home and plan accordingly.

There were many things in her home that were precious to Laurie. Not necessarily always expensive but precious nonetheless. All of the family photos of her girls for instance...some jewellery too, especially some rings from her mum. Yes. She wanted time to go through things and take what she wanted before Rich caught on.

Rich had always scoffed at Laurie's sentimentality and the first thing he would do is take the photos, not because he valued them himself but more because he would relish preventing Laurie getting her hands on them.

Her last email to Rich had been on Thursday. At least it had been polite, she thought. But she hadn't had a reply and had no idea of his feelings at the moment. She imagined he would be spitting feathers though, so she decided to attempt to calm the waters a little.

'Hi Rich. Sorry I've had to delay my return. Hope you're okay? And the girls too? The reason I put my flight back is because I've been volunteering at an orphanage. You should see the kids! They are delightful. But so many of them, all without parents, it's really quite heartbreaking. Anyway, to get to the point, I've been heavily involved with the looking after of a very poorly little girl, she's called Dang. She can't be more than 3 years old, I would guess, but it's so difficult to tell and its nigh on impossible to get any information from anyone in authority. But the point is, she has been so sick and I have been giving her all my time, you know, love, food etc. She's a bit better today, I'm delighted to say, but I obviously can't leave her yet. I need to make sure she's definitely on the mend first. Anyway, I felt I needed to fill you in. Will keep in touch. Let you know how things are going. Laurie'

Was that okay? She didn't know. She had ignored so many of his emails, treated him with such little respect that she thought he might indeed smell a rat. Reading through it again, she decided it was okay. It was Laurie, that was all. She *was* naturally chatty, so he wouldn't be taken aback by that and he knew how soft she could be around kids. She pressed 'send' quickly before she could change her mind.

Whilst on her emails, she allowed herself a quick glance at her in-box.

Holding her breath, she hardly dared to look. What she would give to hear from him!

She felt sick to the stomach. Just to hear from him after so long, that's all! To know he was alive and well even...nothing more! Well...okay, she'd love more obviously but her love for him ran so deep, her first concern was simply Mike's wellbeing. She was dying to know how he was faring. She could move on in her life on her own if need be, she was just so desperate to hear from him, just once more! It wasn't asking for much was it?

What was confusing her was that Frankie had been adamant that Mike had wanted to get in touch! Why ask for her email and then not get in touch. It was too cruel!

But there was nothing from him and her disappointment was immense.

Turning off the phone, she lay on her bed. She was gutted! "Fucking hell Frankie!" she shouted to the room. She felt so angry with her and wished with all her heart she had not interfered. That was the trouble with confiding in others, they then think they have a God given right to take over!

Her anger was misdirected though and on some level she knew that. She couldn't blame Frankie for the position

Laurie found herself in. She could blame Rich, yes. But the real blame lay with herself! Her natural thought process allowed her to become the victim, it was always someone else's fault as far as she was concerned! But it wasn't, she realised. She needed to challenge that thought process every step of the way. No more being a victim! She needed to continue taking charge of her own life.

Sitting up, she retrieved her list she'd put together only the other day. Reading through it, she couldn't help smiling. Actually she was doing okay! Dang *was* getting better, Deborah *had* made it seem possible she could continue making visits here, helping out on a longer term basis too and she *did* feel proud of herself. *And* she was doing all she could on the health and fitness front! So, all in all, not too bad really. Picking up her pen, she added one other 'to do'.

GET TOUGH...PLAN YOUR LEAVING STRATEGY. GET A SOLICITOR!

'Laurie. I don't give a flying shit about a Thai kid. Get back here as soon as. You've made your point, for fuck's sake. Let me know when you've booked your flight'

HA...Well, her email got a response at least! Wow! He was vile. However had she been attracted to him? she asked herself incredulously. A Thai kid?! He couldn't even be bothered enough to use her name! She shook her head in disbelief. It wasn't even worth a response. God, she felt so frustrated, irritated with him too. Who the fuck did he think he was? His tone was plain ugly.

Looking at the last line on her 'to do' list, she sat back down and took a breath. She needed to play him, remember! So, let's be calm, she wanted to move things forward in a way that would achieve the best possible outcome.

'Rich. I'll be back in a few days, I promise. Laurie'

Well, that should appease him a little, even though it didn't actually say anything. God, he was horrible. She had a battle on her hands and this was just the start. Laurie needed to toughen up and be quick about it if she was going to be able to cope. Thinking back to Dang's wonderful smile earlier on, she bristled. A Thai kid!! She would have the last laugh, she thought bitterly.

'Just book a fucking flight!!'

This email, she ignored, turning off the phone and hoping she would be able to get some sleep but fearing sleep would elude her tonight.

Chapter 43

They were sat on their bench again, Dang sitting up, looking quite cheery.

She had just enjoyed a banana Laurie had brought in with her and she was playing with Laurie's wedding and engagement rings, turning them around and around on Laurie's finger.

Laurie had decided they would have an hour together this morning and then another hour this afternoon but she was going to ensure that Dang mixed with the other kids the rest of the time. It would be hard on Laurie but she needed to make the break for Dang's sake. Dang's needs were far more important than hers, and so she was going to have to be tough with herself!

And she had been!

And actually had found herself enjoying engaging with some of the others.

Whilst none were ill, there were two or three who simply wanted cuddles and she was more than happy to oblige! Dang came over to her often, sitting on her knee, even pushing one of the others off at one point. But Laurie firmly told her "no" and simply made room for them both on her knee. It was lovely to see Dang engaging a little, even playing with a younger toddler for a few minutes. But she soon tired and when Laurie saw her fit to drop, she took her back outside, where Dang promptly fell fast asleep, clearly relishing a cuddle, together with some peace and quiet.

Laurie was delighted. She had achieved something again today...okay...still only babysteps, but still, it felt good. She could see that Dang was improving and had also evidenced how Dang simply got on with things. She hadn't cried when Laurie had put her down to play and seeing how she interacted with the other kids had been really satisfying.

Watching Dang play, Laurie had marvelled. A book Dang was holding in her hands was attracting the attention of one of the little boys and he snatched it from her. Laurie's initial reaction was to tell the boy off but she had resisted, wanting to see how things developed. Dang had not reacted initially and Laurie had felt quite upset for her but, after a couple of minutes, Laurie saw Dang grab the book back fiercely with both her hands and toddle off with it at a pace. Well...Go Dang, she thought to herself like any proud mum. Dang had just been waiting, biding her time for the right opportunity to present itself. As soon as the boy's attention had been elsewhere Dang had swooped in.

She was definitely on the mend!

'Hi Frankie, Hope you got home safely, bet you are shattered eh? Are you at work today? How's your dad? Sorry, don't mean to bombard you. Good news!! Dang is so much better. You should have seen her today! She's quite a character, stood up for herself against another boy, fighting over a book. I was dead impressed! Still tired though, still needs some love too, but I am making a determined effort to let her get on with things a little. I can't stay forever and I can't take her with me so I need to make sure she'll be okay here without me. Anyway, I just wanted to check in with you. Hope you had a good flight home. See you soon. Laurie xxx'

'P.S Oh yes...and Rich is being a complete DICK still! No surprises there. Telling me literally to "book a fucking flight home"...Charming.'

'P.P.S Oh yes...also..."he couldn't give a flying shit about a little Thai kid!" Isn't he lovely?...NOT!'

Laurie took herself off to an evening yoga session as well as the one she attended every morning. Following that, she enjoyed a Thai yellow curry, not a dish she had tried before and it had been so tasty. Finishing with a bowl of watermelon, Laurie looked around the restaurant. It was a different one to any she and Frankie had eaten in, deliberately so. She was trying to be more adventurous and eating on her own, somewhere new, *was* adventurous for her!

Ridiculous really, but she found she was enjoying herself, sitting, quietly observing those around her and taking in the scenery. A song came into her head from years ago and she started singing it softly. "I'm a big big girl in a big big world, it's not a big big thing if you leave me." Yes, she thought, that's *exactly* what she was. She *would* survive, she told herself, feeling a very gentle strength and conviction she had never previously experienced. She thought of what Deborah had said about men. "Coming out of the woodwork with amazing regularity" had been her words! Well, Laurie didn't know about that, but what she realised however, is that she was open to a different life. One where she could grow and get to know herself better. Maybe even to love again? Well...maybe...but no-one would take Mike's place. No-one ever could, she thought sadly.

And she had still heard nothing from him.

She was going to *have* to stop checking. He had had plenty of time now. She needed to accept that, for whatever reason, he had chosen not to contact her. At least she knew he was alive. That was something, she supposed.

Arriving back in her room, she opened her emails again. 'Well, when are you back?'

Oh, here we go. God, he was like a dog with a bone. He never let up, thought Laurie, sitting on her bed. But she had a plan now and she knew she needed to keep him sweet.

'Hi Rich, I promise I will book a flight soon. I just need a few more days to make sure Dang is going to be okay, that's all. Anyway, how are things at home? The girls? Laurie'

At least her emails were polite, not like his!

She found it difficult to even sound civil, she certainly couldn't bring herself to ask how *he* was. She didn't care. But she needed to keep him onside.

She wanted to be able to get back into her house and make a proper plan to leave, without him suspecting anything. She was starting to realise that, not only did she want to sort out photos etc, but also that she would need time to get some money out. She still had a couple of thousand left but if she was going to rent somewhere she would need money up front, not to mention living costs until she found paid employment!

She therefore wanted chance to get hold of some of their joint savings and she was well aware that once he got hold of her plans to leave, the money would be the first thing he would stop her having access to. So she needed to play a very delicate game.

But she was feeling positive, stronger, more in control already. Just a few days on her own had done her the world of good. For the first time in her life, she was taking control and it felt so good.

Another email appeared from Rich.

'Laurie. If you cared how things were at home you would be here! Fuck's sake! You fuck off without telling me and you won't tell me when you're coming back! What the fuck's wrong with you??? I'm getting really pissed off Laurie. Book a flight. Tell me when. No more stalling. I'm not going to stand for it. As for the girls, how do you think they are??? Wondering what the fuck's up with their mother, that's what!!!'

'Rich. Okay, I'll sort something out tomorrow. It's evening here and I'm just off to sleep. Laurie'

Sighing, Laurie put her phone down. Well, she had stalled until tomorrow at least. Then she would book one for a few days from now. He wouldn't be happy but if he had a definite date then at least he wouldn't keep pestering. The good news was, he was clearly just expecting her to come home. He hadn't given a thought to the fact she may have other plans! But he wouldn't would he? He was so dismissive of Laurie, he didn't believe she had it in her to do anything else.

And she needed to ensure she kept it that way!

Chapter 44

Tuesday 20th September 2016.

"Hi Deborah, you're here again? You can't keep away," chuckled Laurie.

She was having her allotted hour outside with Dang and they had been playing 'pat a cake.' Well...Laurie was! Dang was simply trying to follow, chuckling away, her stick thin hands never quite in the right place at the right time. It was so nice to see her like this, she was making an amazing recovery.

"Hello," answered Deborah, sitting beside her "No, I can't, can I?" she added, smiling. "I'm only popping in today though. To be honest I've come to see you more than the kids. How are you doing?"

"Ahhh...that's nice of you! I'm really good thanks. I'm finally starting to take control. I'm going home in the next few days, not because I want to, but because I need to and I now feel strong enough to cope with it all. I was actually going to ask you if you would recommend your solicitor. I know you've gone through a divorce. Was he good?"

Deborah beamed. "She, not he," she corrected. "And yes, she was fabulous. A 'no nonsense, take no prisoners' sort. A bit intimidating but that's exactly the sort of person you want. I'll email her today, see if she's still working. Haven't spoken to her for a few years."

"That would be wonderful, thank you. And I suppose if she's not practising, then perhaps she could recommend someone else?"

"Of course she would. I'm so pleased Laurie, you seem like a different person today?" she added, her head cocked to one side, inquisitively.

Laurie laughed delightedly."Yes, I know. I feel different. I think I've been living aimlessly for long enough. It feels good to have a plan for once. It also feels good to finally make some decisions and get on with following them through. I feel really quite excited. I'm actually losing my fear. I've always been a 'what if' sort of person. But, you know, who cares 'what if?' Whatever happens, I feel as though I would be able to cope now."

"Course you could, you're not daft. And not only cope but thrive!"

Laurie laughed. "Well, we'll see about that! And thank you, you've helped me look at things differently. I admire what you're doing here and envy your freedom. And I want some of that for myself."

"Good, I'm glad to have been of some help! Right...well...I'm going to leave you to it. I've got loads of stuff to do today, not least getting my laundry done! I'm down to my last pair of knickers!" she announced, a big smile on her face.

Laurie watched her stride off. Deborah always seemed to walk with purpose. Never just an amble! Always gave you the impression she was a busy person, even if it was just to wash her knickers!

"Come on then Dang, time's up," Laurie said regretfully. "Let's get you back inside."

Walking back into the classroom, Laurie had two kids make a beeline for her. They were the two from yesterday and had clearly cottoned on to where they could get an endless supply of cuddles. The Thai ladies were also getting friendlier. They had obviously seen her with Dang and were showing her a little more respect now, which was nice.

Deborah was right in what she had said. They *did* care for the kids, that was obvious when Laurie took the time to see them interracting with them. However, they did not have much time, they were always busy, either changing nappies, preparing food or cleaning.

And this was where Laurie could add the value. So she sat, watching Dang from afar, whilst giving the two others some much needed love.

She left the orphanage later than usual and it was past 6pm when she arrived back in her room. Whilst she'd promised Rich she would book a flight, she hadn't thought through how! Frankie was a whizz on the internet and had dealt with all the bookings. Laurie would have to try and work out what to do by herself and she was tired already so didn't relish the idea too much. She would have to get some lessons when she got home, she'd often noticed lessons being offered for free at their local library.

Another thing to add to her list, she thought. God, this list was going to become neverending! Maybe she could ask at the hotel reception, see whether they could help her.

And they had. A lady named 'Biu' took the time to show her exactly what to do.

Keeping half an eye on reception, she had sat down with Laurie for at least half an hour, guiding her through the booking process with incredible patience. There were many options for a flight home and she could have booked one for the next day very easily. But she didn't want to leave, not any day soon and there was no way she was willing to leave tomorrow, so, after taking some time to think it through, she had booked a flight home for Friday. That gave her two more days here. Not as much time as she would have liked but she didn't want to annoy Rich either. As he would so easily be able to check flight availability himself, she also knew she couldn't get away with any more time. So...Friday it was, she thought despondently.

She felt tremendously sad at the thought of leaving Dang, the orphanage too. She had become very attached to the place, as well as the whole way of life on offer here. She would be back, she told herself firmly as she thanked Biu profusely.

Yes, she was determined to keep that promise to herself.

She would add it to her list! God, her lists! she thought, smiling. But they certainly worked. They provided Laurie with the discipline she sometimes lacked, they banished her lethargy, that was for sure!

'Rich. Flight booked for Friday. Will arrive at Heathrow 7am Saturday. Could you possibly pick me up? Laurie'

Shit...she hadn't thought about the day she would arrive home. A Saturday was the worst possible day. She would have all weekend with Rich at home! Oh well, she told herself sternly. She'd put up with him all these years, she could certainly cope with one more weekend! Because that's all it was going to be!

'You having a laugh? Why would I want to drive all the way to the airport to pick you up? At that time in the morning, you must be joking!! Anyway, you got there on your own steam so I'm sure you can find your way home too. At least you've seen sense.'

Laurie read his email and felt the sting of tears in her eyes which she angrily wiped away. She shouldn't have been surprised, she knew what he was like but it was all just so sad and unpleasant. It highlighted how difficult life was going to get too. If he was so awkward now, she could only imagine his reaction when he realised she had left him!

Laurie looked at her in-box and noticed an unfamiliar name. Lucinda Wallis. Who is this? she questioned, opening it.

'Laurie,

Deborah has contacted me, asking if I would be able to represent you in your upcoming divorce case. I am happy to do so. I will need to speak with you as soon as possible, preferably face to face. Please let me know when you are back in the UK. Thank you in anticipation.
Lucinda Wallis.'

Crikey! No messing about there, she thought. Upcoming divorce case? It made the whole situation feel very real and more than a little scary!

'Lucinda,
Thank you for your email. I am arriving home on Saturday 24th September. I imagine you are far busier than I am so am happy for you to give me a date and time to suit you.
I look forward to meeting you.
Laurie'

'Laurie,
Monday 26th 2pm?
Lucinda Wallis.'

God! So soon! And in London. But she could get there by train easily enough.

'Lucinda,
Yes, that would be perfect. Thank you.
Laurie.'

'Excellent. My secretary will send you address and directions in due course. See you then. Lucinda Wallis.'

Right...Wow! Not only had she booked her flights now but also really set the ball rolling regarding a divorce! She felt full of trepidation. But she needed to stay strong. It was good really, she didn't want to talk herself out of leaving him and putting things in motion as quickly as possible was exactly what she needed to do. Frankie would be proud.

'Hey Frankie! Guess what??? Well, you'll never guess!!! I've only booked an appointment with a 'Lucinda Wallis'. Who is she? Only a shit hot divorce lawyer, that's who!!! Oh, yes, and I'm coming home on Saturday. And Dang is so much better too!! How are you? Laurie'

'Wow Laurie. Well done, that's great news. About time, I would say! I'm okay, still tired from the travelling but getting there. And dad's as well as can be expected in the circumstances. Great news about Dang. Have to go...dead busy here. Frankie xx'

The next two days went in a heartbeat. The same routine each day, with Laurie trying her best not to feel too disheartened by the thought of having to leave.

She had taken groups of children outside to play, including Dang and had relished watching Dang interact with the others. Dang occasionally looked over in Laurie's direction, smiling over at her but she was more engrossed in the play. Laurie could see such a difference in her, it was hard to see her as the same pitiful figure she had first met, lying listlessly on the hard floor.

And she was a fighter! She thoroughly enjoyed the 'rough and tumble' the others were engaged in, laughing often with them. She belonged here, Laurie realised. For Dang, this was home. Maybe she *would* miss Laurie, but not for long!

Deborah had already comforted Laurie by telling her that she would keep a special eye on Dang, even send her some pictures. And then very firmly told Laurie she was to keep in touch so they could arrange to return together next year. She was also insistent that Laurie was to stay with her for free...she would welcome the company.

Laurie immersed herself in the orphanage by day and yoga in the evening.
She felt quite despondent about Mike though. As much as she had tried not to hope, every time she decided to check her in-box, she couldn't help getting her hopes up, only to have them dashed.

She felt foolish. He obviously wasn't interested, she told herself, repeatedly. But why had he said he was? To Frankie? That didn't sound like the Mike Laurie had known! He would never say he was going to do something and then not! It just didn't make any sense to her.

Still... it was what it was.

She had e-mailed all three of her girls, telling them when she was returning and all about Dang. Not surprisingly, the only one that hadn't responded was Cara. She felt really bad about Cara. It would be good to get home, she decided. She needed to talk to Cara and face to face was always going to be the better way. Not that she was confident talking would make any difference! She would have to try though. That's all she could do.

Chapter 45

She was home! And shattered.

The flight had been fine but it had been a very long day.

Firstly, a flight from Chiang Mai to Bangkok, followed by a three hour stopover before an overnight flight to Heathrow. She had hardly slept.

She found sleep alluded her at the best of times, but, sitting up, her body cramped into a small space, a biggish bloke sat in the next seat, she had slept very little. Her eyes were dry, her head pounding.

She hadn't been surprised that Rich had refused to pick her up. Pissed off, yes, but, on reflection, it was probably a blessing in disguise. Just the thought of sitting in such close proximity to Rich for the long drive home would have made her feel very anxious.

So, here she was, sitting in a taxi! Costing a small fortune, but what the hell! She sat back, closed her eyes and tried to concentrate on her breathing, like she had learned to do in her yoga sessions, calming her thoughts as much as possible. She was *dreading* seeing Rich. She knew he was furious with her and Laurie hated confrontation of any kind. That was partly the reason she had ducked telling him she was going away! But she was well aware confrontation was going to be completely unavoidable, especially when this Lucinda got involved!

And, although she was so tired, she needed to be as clear thinking as possible. She looked at her watch, it was already 9.30am. It had taken an absolute age to retrieve her luggage. Sitting up, she leaned forward. "Is it possible to stop for a few minutes in the next town? I need to nip into the bank."

"It's your money missus," he answered with a cheeky grin.

They stopped in Oxford, the taxi driver dropping her off outside Barclays and agreeing to return in thirty minutes.

Looking over the counter at a young girl, a similar age to Cara, Laurie gave her the biggest smile. "Hello. I was hoping to make a large withdrawal today. Would it be possible?"

"Do you bank with us?" the girl asked in a bored tone, not bothering to look up from her screen.

"Not at this branch, no, but with you, yes. In Worcester."

"That's fine then," she answered, passing Laurie a withdrawal slip to fill in. Having completed it and passed it back, she noticed the girl's eyes open wider as she took in the amount. Peering closely at her computer screen and then back to the withdrawal slip again, Laurie could only assume she was checking her signature. "I'll be right back," she smiled, standing up awkwardly from her chair and disappearing into the back office.

Oh shit, what was the problem? Laurie felt her heart beating ten to the dozen as she waited. She needed to calm herself. She wasn't doing anything illegal even if it *felt* wrong.

"Mrs Wilson?" an older lady asked enquiringly.

"Yes?"

"This is a rather large sum to withdraw in cash. May I ask what you want it for?"

Thinking quickly on her feet, Laurie stuttered. "I'm buying a car with it."

"Right," said the lady slowly. "In that case, wouldn't it be better if we provided you with a banker's draft, it would be far safer?"

Laurie felt the sweat trickling between her breasts. "Er, no, not really. You see, I've come down this morning to see the car and I would really like to take it now. They have said I can as long as I pay them in cash." Laurie was impressed with herself. It sounded plausible as far as she was concerned!

"Okay, I won't be a moment. Would you mind taking a seat ?"

Laurie sat down and tried to keep herself calm. Slow breaths, slowly in, slowly out. She mustn't look panicky. She was doing nothing wrong! The account was in joint names, it was her money, they couldn't refuse her, the money she was requesting was hers to have after all...(and Rich's, she thought!)

And so it was with immense relief when she found herself back in the taxi, a large thick white envelope safely ensconced in her handbag. She could have cried! £10k in cash! That would keep her going for a while. And Rich could do nothing about it either!

But when he found out he would be apoplectic. All the more reason for Laurie to be on her toes and leave as soon as possible. There was no turning back now.

Taking her phone out and turning it on, Laurie hesitated. She needed to let the girls know she was back but didn't feel up to any of their questions right now. She was finding it difficult to even think straight and was feeling emotionally fraught. So she sent all three a blanket message letting them know she was back and all was fine but that she was shattered and was going to try to catch up on some sleep on her way home.

"Mum!" shouted Marie in excitement as she opened the front door for Laurie and gave her a huge hug. Laurie smiled. Oh, it was lovely to see her, she had missed her girls badly.

Just shy of three weeks, that's all it had been, but Laurie had never been away from them for this long. Not even from Sarah, who was always coming home at weekends. She had never left it three weeks!

"Oh Marie, it's so nice to see you. How are you?" she asked, hugging Marie back tightly.

"I'm fine mum. God, I've missed you though! Dad's been a bit off though mum, I haven't really known what to say to him, it's been really awkward here."

Laurie pulled a face. "I'm sorry Marie. Just leaving like that. Leaving you to deal with the fallout. And we need to talk. Just you and me, but firstly I could murder a cup of tea. How about I put the kettle on? Is your dad in?" Laurie asked, as casually as she could, walking into the kitchen.

"No, I don't know where he is... Just me here at the moment. Although I'm going out later," she added cautiously. "Is that okay?"

"Yes, of course it is! Anyway, I'm shattered, so I shall probably try and get some sleep this afternoon."

Laurie was immensely relieved. Rich wasn't at home, Thank God. Peace and quiet for now, at least!

"Well, let's get your case in and then we can sit down and have a natter eh? And you can tell me all about Dang too, I can't wait...and any photos? I presume you must have taken loads?" Laurie smiled. She loved how the girls could just chatter away, she'd missed this so much, she thought, watching Marie struggling with Laurie's case, plonking it heavily down in the hallway.

And they had talked...mainly about Thailand and Laurie's time at the orphanage but also a little bit about Laurie herself. Probably one of the first adult to adult conversations Laurie had ever had with her and she had been pleasantly surprised by Marie's reaction. Telling any child, however old, that her parents were unhappy together was never going to be an easy conversation and Laurie was well aware that Marie loved her dad too. She didn't want her to choose sides, that would be terrible for her. So she was very careful with what she said, trying to present a fair and balanced point of view. She told her about Mike...not much about him, but enough so that Marie would have a full understanding. She told her how guilty she had felt and that she could understand Rich feeling bitter toward her. She also told her about the impossible ultimatum.

She sighed deeply. "So, here we are now Marie, all these years later, and you three all grown up."

"Do you think you and dad will stay together?" Marie asked quietly, her eyes wide with trepidation.

"No Marie, I don't. And I'm so sorry. But I can't live like this anymore. I'm not happy and I don't think your dad is either. And, you know, longer term, maybe both of us can find some happiness. But certainly not with each other, we are only making each other very miserable. That's no way to live, surely you can see that?" she asked, her eyes imploring Marie to understand the situation.

After an incredibly long pause which seemed to last a lifetime for Laurie, Marie let out a long sigh. "Yes, of course I can. I wouldn't want to live with someone who made me miserable. But it's so scary mum," she added, tears streaming down her face. "Everything's changing and I don't want it to."

"I know, love," Laurie whispered sadly, touching her daughter gently on her cheek, wiping her tears away. "But it will be okay, I promise you. I love you still. Your dad loves you too and we always will, nothing changes there. Also you have your own life to get on with, you're happy with Adam aren't you?"

Marie smiled. "Yes, of course I am, I love him to bits."

"Well then! You concentrate on that, get on with living your own life and try not to worry about me and your dad eh?" encouraged Laurie as brightly as she could, trying, but failing, to stem her own tears. "God, we are both long enough in the tooth now to sort ourselves out!" she added, fingers firmly crossed behind her back, sincerely hoping this to be the case.

Left alone, Laurie sat down on her sofa in the living room. She was exhausted, mentally, physically and emotionally. She didn't actually know what to do with herself. She felt so bad, she didn't know what she needed either. Food? Sleep? Fresh air? All she knew for sure is that she felt absolutely awful.

Her conversation with Marie had gone as well as could be expected in the circumstances and Laurie felt proud of herself as well as her daughter. By telling Marie about Mike, she had thwarted any attempt from Rich to put his version to Marie first. That could only be a good thing. There was no right or wrong here. It was what had actually happened and at least now, Marie had the chance to sort things out in her own mind before Rich gave his version of events. Sarah was not a concern to Laurie, she was already aware there was trouble, Laurie just needed to fill her in regarding Mike. But Cara?...Yes, she was very concerned about her. She had no idea how she was feeling now, she hadn't responded to Laurie's text today and Laurie was worried as to how she would react to the split up. She couldn't control everything though, she would just have to hope and pray that Cara would understand over time, even if not straight away.

Laurie felt her eyes closing, the quiet in the house helping her to relax a little. Smokey had been absolutely delighted with Laurie's return and, after having had a mad half hour, was now curled up as close to Laurie as he could possibly get, his tail still wagging furiously.

The sound of a car on the drive startled Laurie out of her slumber. She knew it was Rich's car, he always swung in with such aggression, shingle crunching loudly beneath the tyres.

Shit! She had rather hoped he would be out all day. She presumed he had been playing golf, but as it was only

2.30pm, maybe not. The front door slammed and she heard his keys being thrown onto the kitchen worksurface.

"You're back then," he shouted.

"Yes," she answered, keeping her voice as calm as she could.

He strode into the living room and stood in front of their large fireplace, his hands on his hips, his feet firmly planted on the rug, clearly getting ready for battle.

He was quite an intimidating figure, being tall and broad. Adding to this, his ability to be verbally abusive, Laurie found herself feeling rather fearful. He was adept at this, she thought as she realised quite how much of a bully he had become.

Sitting down as she was also put Laurie at a disadvantage. But she was determined to stay calm. She mustn't give him any hint of her plans to leave.

"Would you like some lunch?" she asked, placing her hands either side of her, about to get up. "I'm not sure what's in but I'm sure I can rustle up something," she gabbled nervously.

Rich scoffed loudly and rolled his eyes "No...I don't want any fucking lunch thank you very much! Fuck's sake Laurie...what the hell's wrong with you?" he asked, his voice rising in incredulity. "You swan off saying 'sweet F A' to me. You delay your return. You ignore my emails. And now all you can say is 'do you want some lunch?' You're pathetic!" he shouted, spittle flying out of his mouth.

Laurie sat back down and raised her hands in a gesture of apology. "I'm sorry" she said in an appeasing tone. "Of course, you're right. I don't want any lunch either!" she added, in an attempt to lighten the atmosphere.

Rich looked over at her, his face full of loathing. "Fancy just going off like that. Not telling me. God, I felt so embarrassed! I mean, what must everyone be thinking? Firstly your fiftieth and then this! I've told everyone you're suffering with the *menopause*, only excuse I could come up with. But I just think you're fucking mad...crazy!" he shouted, his index finger making a circling motion by his head, his expression, one of utter contempt.

Laurie was just watching as he ranted, feeling a deep sadness as well as a healthy dose of fear. He was a dangerous man when angry, she realised. His bitterness over the years had just built and built inside him and he looked ready to explode. She didn't know what to say either. She couldn't seem to placate him anymore but saying nothing only seemed to be getting him more vexed.

"Oh yes, " he continued. "So, how did you pay for the trip eh? I've checked our accounts and there was no flight paid for, no cash taken out either so how *did* you pay for it Laurie?" His voice was dangerously low.

"Frankie booked the flights," Laurie answered, in an attempt to bide for time, give her a chance to think of what she could say.

"Well, yes," he said slowly as though he was talking to a complete idiot. "I worked that out for myself," he added sarcastically. "But you will have paid *her* for them won't you. So *how?"*

Laurie hadn't thought about this. Shit! She should have done. It was an obvious thing for him to ask. What did she say? She had no idea how to come up with a plausible explanation.

"Well!" he shouted. "I'm waiting!"

"I had some money of my own. I took it from there," she whispered, looking down into her lap. An ominous silence fell between them. And then came the full force of his anger.

He was upon her before she had a chance to move. His large hands around her throat and he was screaming at the top of his voice, his anger seemingly out of control. "Money of your own!" he screamed, squeezing her throat harder still.

Laurie was struggling for breath and his weight on her was rapidly squeezing the air out from her lungs. Her arms swung wildly around in panic, attempting to hit him or, at the very least, push him off her. Smokey was going berserk by this time, barking madly and Rich reached over and gave him such a kick, Laurie heard his loud whimpers as he ran from the room through into the utility room, seeking the comfort of his bed. But at least by kicking Smokey, Rich had removed some of his weight from her chest and released the pressure from around her neck. "Money of your own!" he sneered, before laughing raucously. "God, I could fucking kill you here and now," he said quietly, taking his hands away from her throat. "How *dare* you take MY money!" he shouted. "MY money, Laurie. Money I have earned, every last fucking penny of it. You *have* no fucking money of your own, you stupid bitch! It's all mine! And you have *dared* to squirrel some of my money away! Well, trust me, you won't be doing that again. Make no mistake. I've been far too soft on you all these years," he continued. "You fuck someone else," he shouted bitterly "And I stay with you. And what do I get in repayment?! You thieve my money. Wow! I've given you *everything!* What more could a woman want eh?" he asked incredulously, his hands gesturing around the living room. "A beautiful home, you have. Most women I know would *die* to be in your position. And what do you do eh?" his voice rising again in anger.

"I'm sorry Rich," Laurie cried, tears streaming down her cheeks. Her throat was burning where he had dug in his fingers and she was now really scared. Rich had always been verbally abusive, but never before had it moved to any kind of physical abuse.

He had now crossed that line and Laurie was very frightened.

But as quickly as Rich's anger had surfaced, it also dissipated and, with one last contemptuous look, he stood back from her and walked out of the room.

 Laurie was shocked. Her throat burnt, her chest hurt and her head was now pounding. She couldn't stay here, not even for one more night. She had to get away. But how was she to do that?

And poor Smokey, she thought, getting up gingerly to go and find him.

He was curled up, as tight as could be, in his basket, looking so sorry for himself, Laurie could have cried. Getting down on her knees, she talked softly to him, stroking his neck and his back, checking him all over as best she could. He wasn't whimpering now and didn't flinch at all as she gently pressed into his fur, checking his legs too. He was okay, thank God, she decided as she gave him a big kiss on the top of his head.

She guessed Rich would have gone into his study so she walked quietly upstairs and locked herself in their en-suite. Sitting down carefully on the loo seat, she tried to stem the tears. She needed to think...and think fast.

Oh my God! The cash she had taken out this morning!! Rich didn't know about that yet but judging by his earlier reaction, *that* would send him over the edge. And for all she knew, he could be checking their bank accounts right now on the internet! Would he be? She didn't know. Neither did she know how quickly the transaction would show. Was it overnight or immediate?

Her breathing was laboured as she began to panic.

She couldn't take the chance. She had to get away and fast. Think Laurie, she told herself firmly. She walked over to her jewellery box and grabbed all her mum's jewellery as well as some bits and pieces of her own that she particularly liked and threw them into her handbag. She couldn't risk taking anything else. But the family photos? No time for those, she decided sadly.

Trying to stay as calm as possible, she quickly changed into jeans and a light top, wrapping a colourful scarf around her neck to hide the fingermarks. Placing a jacket over her arm, she casually walked downstairs into the kitchen and picked up her car keys.

"Where are you off to?" demanded Rich, standing by the kitchen door, arms folded.

"I'm just off to get some food," she answered, marvelling at how normal her voice sounded, even though she felt so panicked. "I was going to do a lasagne for tea tonight and we need some minced beef. Do you need anything fetching whilst I'm gone?"

Rich was blocking her way and seemed to be thinking. Seconds passed. Did he believe her? She held her breath. After what seemed to be an interminable amount of time, but what was probably only thirty seconds or so, Rich moved aside, gesturing for her to pass. "Don't be long," he ordered as he walked back down the hallway into his study again.

Laurie didn't need telling twice! Looking regretfully at her suitcase, wishing Marie hadn't brought it inside, she opened the front door and walked as steadily as she could to the car. Sitting behind the wheel, she took two deep breaths. He hadn't suspected and she was leaving! Finally!

She turned on the ignition, took one last look at the home she never expected to see again and drove fast out of the drive through the electric gates, laughing a little hysterically.

A somewhat tearful Laurie turned up at Frankie's front door an hour later. On opening it, Frankie put her hands to her face in shock. "Oh my God Laurie, you're back! You look terrible, what on earth has happened?" she cried, ushering Laurie through into the living room.

"I've left him Frankie. We've just had the most awful row. It was vile! But I've finally gone and done it! And I've got nothing with me, no clothes, nothing. I didn't dare take the risk."

Seeing the mark's on Laurie's neck as she peeled away her scarf, Frankie put two and two together. "Come and sit down Laurie, you've done the right thing. And who needs clothes?" she added, laughing to lighten the mood. "I'll go and get us a nice cup of tea and you can fill me in. How does that sound?"

"Thanks Frankie. That would be great," she added, sinking into Frankie's sofa. This took Laurie back twenty years. Turning up unannounced, in a state! This was exactly what she had done then, she thought sadly as she waited for Frankie to return.

"Well, wow! You certainly did the right thing by leaving. He sounds unhinged!" remarked Frankie after Laurie had filled her in on what had happened. "Hey, I'm impressed though. Fancy you being so devious, you know, with the cash! You're right though. He *will* go berserk when he finds out."

"I know," said Laurie quietly. "And he'll be starting to wonder where I am too."

"That's true... and he might well turn up here," said Frankie, frowning. Reflecting on everything Laurie had told her, Frankie sprang into action. "Right...Firstly, let's put your car in the garage. Then if he comes knocking I can tell him you're not here. Secondly, I'm going to do you some food. Then, I suggest you get some sleep. You won't be able to think straight until you have. Beans on toast do you?"

"Oh Thank you Frankie. That sounds wonderful. Will I be okay staying for a couple of days, you know, just until I get myself sorted?"

"Of course you can. It goes without saying. Stay as long as you need. I've rather missed you this last week," she added, a twinkle in her eye. "It's been really quiet without you around, I must say!"

Laurie laughed. "You're only saying that to make me feel better, I know you, you love your own space. But thank you Frankie. Thank you so much. And it won't be for long, I promise. I'm going to find a place to rent as soon as I can," she added. "And it'll have to be dog friendly, there's no way I'm leaving Smokey with him!"

"That's it girl. Fighting talk, that's what you need," encouraged Frankie, patting her on the knee as she stood up and left the room.

Chapter 46

Sunday 25th September 2016.

Laurie couldn't believe it. She had slept soundly for fourteen hours! It was 8am. Waking up in Frankie's spare bedroom, Laurie allowed herself to think back over the events of yesterday. Well, it hadn't entirely gone to plan, that was for sure!

But she *had* left and she felt slightly euphoric.

Frankie had lent her some pyjamas yesterday but Laurie would need to get some more clothes today as she hadn't even a spare pair of knickers! Her throat was killing her, it was so sore and she could see a purplish bruise beginning to show all around her neck. Propping herself up on the pillows, Laurie grabbed her bag from the side of the bed where she had dropped it last night. She retrieved a pen and a crumpled piece of paper. Right...She needed another list! She found herself smiling. In times of chaos, her lists were becoming her 'go to,' always providing some semblance of order for her.

1) Phone the girls
2) Ask Marie to check Smokey was still okay
3) Buy some clothes
4) Email Lucinda- update her
5) Look on 'rightmove' for a rental
6) Find a job...No, she would scrap that for now. She had plenty to sort out and she could leave that for a week or two at least!

Hauling herself out of bed, she showered, taking her time. God, it felt so good. She had been so tired yesterday she had simply crashed out as soon as her head had hit the pillow, not even considering a shower, so she hadn't showered since leaving Chiang Mai and the water was deliciously hot.

She had actually done it, she kept repeating over and over, her face one huge smile. Free at last and it felt so good.

Having considered the time and the fact that her girls were not early risers and certainly not on a Sunday morning, she went shopping first. She didn't buy much. Two packs of underwear, two bras, one black, one white, two pairs of Jeans and seven tops. All from 'Next' as it was the closest store in a retail park only a few miles down the road from Frankie's. It would do for now and, anycase, she was hoping to get Marie to bring her some of her own clothes. She didn't want to waste her money needlessly.

"Well. What do you think?" she asked Frankie, doing a twirl in a pair of her new Jeans and one of her very practical new tops.

"Very nice," said Frankie "You've lost weight, I notice."

"I have, haven't I? It's all that yummy Thai food. Oh yes, plus yoga. Did I mention I'd become a yogi? I love it, it's so calming," Laurie said, pirouetting around Frankie's kitchen. "What?" she demanded, noticing Frankie's huge grin.

"You, that's all! You're bouncing from the ceiling, it's so nice to see. I haven't seen you like this since we were at 'Kays' together."

Laughing with her, Laurie had to agree. She felt good at long last.

She had finally surfaced from years of a nothingness. And there was no way she was going back!

"Hi Sarah...it's only your mum. I'm back and caught up on my sleep. How are you? Call me when you can. I've missed you. Love you."

Laurie put her phone down. She had tried calling Cara too, but she had not picked up and Laurie was reluctant to leave her a message. She really was feeling a desperate need to speak to her, see how she was doing. She was worried. Marie *had* answered however and was shocked by what her mum had told her. Laurie kept things as simple as possible, missing out the fact that her dad had been physically abusive. Marie didn't need to know that. She had simply told her that she had left and where she was staying, asking her to check on Smokey.

Again, to protect Rich, she had simply said that Smokey had been accidentally kicked. Although how anyone could 'accidentally' kick a dog, she had no idea, but it would have to do. She couldn't come up with any other explanation.

Sighing deeply, she tried Cara again. No answer. She was going to have to leave a message, there was nothing else for it. But she wouldn't leave a phone message, she decided to write one instead.

'Hey Cara...I've tried calling you but you must be busy. Just wanted to let you know I'm back. I'm not at home though. I'm at Frankie's. Please don't tell your dad though. I really would like to talk to you, I feel we need a chat. I love you so much Cara. Please call me, even if just to let me know how you are! Mum xxxxxx'

That would have to do. She had worried about whether to tell her where she was in case she told Rich, but she was willing to take that chance. She didn't want Cara not being able to come over to see her, should she want to do so. And, if Rich *did* turn up, which she doubted, she was pretty confident Frankie would send him away with a flea in his ear! Rich had never liked Frankie and Laurie knew it was because he was slightly unnerved by Frankie's strength. She could be a very formidable character when she wanted to be, Laurie thought, smiling to herself. Not for the first time,

Laurie thought how lucky she was, having Frankie on her side.

Right! Now, what else was there to do? Email Lucinda first and then set about looking for a place to live.

She was supposed to be seeing Lucinda tomorrow so she needed to book a train as she definitely wasn't up to driving into London!

'Hi Lucinda. I'm so sorry to email you on a Sunday but thought I needed to bring you up to date before tomorrow. I'm back in the UK, but not at home. We had the most terrible row yesterday and Rich was physically abusive. His anger frightened me so much, I felt I had little choice but to leave. I made the excuse I was going food shopping and am now at a friend's house. I know I probably didn't do the right thing by leaving like that, but, like I said, I didn't feel there was any other option. I'm also very concerned about our dog. Rich kicked him yesterday, quite violently and I've had to leave him there! Sorry, I'm gabbling now. Just feel very emotional. See you tomorrow at 2pm. Laurie.'

Within seconds Lucinda responded. Wow, she doesn't mess about, thought Laurie, opening her in-box.

'Laurie. Thank you for the update. You say physically abusive? Have you any mark's on your body? If so, please take photos as evidence. Your dog? Has your husband hurt him previously? If not, then he is probably going to be okay with him for now. If he has though, then I will call the RSPCA and ensure they pick him up. If you are scared of him, then ensure he does not know where you are staying. We will discuss the necessity of an injunction tomorrow. Lucinda Wallis.'

Laurie felt immensely comforted by Lucinda's reply. She was certainly a 'no nonsense' character, but pragmatic too. She had put Laurie's mind at rest about Smokey. Rich had never previously hurt him and logic told her he would be okay there for now. Photos! Laurie would never have thought about that but it made absolute sense. And an injunction! Oh my God, Rich would go ballistic!

Yes, Lucinda on Laurie's side could only ever be a good thing, she thought, hugging herself delightedly. She felt so much better and she also felt that, maybe for the first time, Rich would meet his match.

She needed to look on 'rightmove' too. She would write a list of what she required and in what vicinity. But before she did anything, she would do herself a cup of tea. God, she couldn't get enough tea since arriving home. It was absolutely true. There was nothing like a good cup of tea in a crisis.

Sitting back down, her tea in her hands, she decided to reply to Lucinda before looking on 'rightmove'. She hadn't cleared her emails either for a few days and she got so much junk mail, she had loads to delete. She clicked on her in-box. It was anal, she knew but she hated not having a clear in-box and it would only take a few minutes.

Scanning through her in-box, Laurie's heart missed a beat. She could hardly contain her excitement.

"SHIT...Shit...Oh my God," she said loudly, putting her hands over her face. She could hardly breathe. It was Mike! There was an e-mail from Mike. Sent yesterday! How had she missed it? She had given up looking, that was how! She hardly dared click on it.

'Laurie. I can't believe I'm actually e-mailing you! After all this time! You'll never guess where I am? In Chiang Mai!! I didn't want to message you, I wanted to see you and I'm gutted you're not here. I was at the orphanage this morning and they told me you'd left only yesterday

morning. I actually believe you were flying home as I was coming here! Anyway, please let me know how you are and please, please tell me you want to see me. Can't wait to talk to you.
Mike xxx'

"Frankie!" Laurie screamed at the top of her voice. "Frankie!" she screamed again. Running in, Frankie looked worried. "Oh my God Frankie. Look. Look. It's Mike! You'll never guess where he is? He's only in Chiang Mai!" shouted Laurie, jumping up from her chair in disbelief. "Here...read it," she said, passing her phone over.

"Wow!" Frankie was gobsmacked. "Wow Laurie. How awful! He's flown all the way over there to find you've already left!" she added in disbelief. "Why in God's name didn't he just e-mail you like any normal person would?"

But Laurie wasn't listening. She had given up all hope of Mike getting in touch. Not only had he got in touch though, he had actually cared enough to book a flight over to her! He obviously still loved her. And SHIT, If only her flight had been one day later, she wouldn't have missed him!

Grabbing the phone from Frankie, she replied immediately.

'Mike. I can't believe it! I can't believe it's you. And I'm so sorry. I didn't notice your email until now, what, with jet lag and everything. How on earth did you find the orphanage? Anyway, that doesn't matter. How are you? Tell me all about yourself. I want twenty years of your life in detail!! God, I can't believe it's really you. I'm fine...well...way more than fine now!! And yes...of course I want to see you. I can't wait!! Laurie xxxxxxxxxxx'

'Me you either! I'm just on the internet now booking a flight home. Frankie alluded to the fact you are unhappy with Rich? Is that really so? I hate to say I hope that's the case as that sounds really horrible. I only want you to be happy Laurie and if you are okay with Rich and Frankie's got it wrong, then I'll back off. Still love you though. Always will. Mike xxxxxxx'

'Mike. And I still love you too. Never has a day gone by when I haven't thought of you in one way or another. And No! I'm not happy with Rich. In fact, I have left him! Only yesterday! I'm staying with Frankie at the moment until I can sort somewhere to live. Oh, it would be so nice to see you again Mike. If only for old time's sake. Laurie xxx'

'Oh no Laurie. You're not getting away this time! Fuck 'for old time's sake'! I've booked a flight for tomorrow. For God's sake don't move from Frankie's. I'll get to you as soon as I possibly can. Mike xxxxxxx'

Laurie's beam spread from cheek to cheek.

'You might not fancy me when you see me!! Twenty years is a long time. Just giving you a 'get out' clause, that's all.'

'You could be 'ten ton Tess' for all I care Laurie. Its you I love, not how you look. Now, stay put. Don't you dare move. I'm coming to get you. Xxxxxxxxx'

Chapter 47

3 years later.

Sunday July 28th 2019.

It was Cara's 24th birthday and Laurie was busy in the kitchen. She was cooking a huge roast dinner and everyone was coming.

Mike came up behind her, putting his arms around her waist and hugging her so tightly she could hardly breathe. "Mmm," he said softly. "You smell so good."

"Thank you," she said, beaming as she turned around to give him a kiss. Just a quick one, she didn't want to get carried away otherwise there would be no roast at all!

"Yes. I know," he smiled softly, taking the hint and removing his arms from around her waist. "But you can't blame a man for trying," he added, giving her a wink. "Anyway, how's your list coming on?"

He took the mickey out of her on a regular basis about her lists, especially when he spotted her religiously crossing off things as they were done. "You can laugh," she replied, trying not to smile herself. "But if you want a nice dinner then I suggest you leave me to it, list and all!" she added for good measure.

There were nine coming over in an hour's time and Laurie had also got to wrap Cara's present. She had bought her a beautiful gold bracelet and hoped that she would like it.

Their relationship had only really got onto a better footing over the last twelve months, coinciding with Cara falling out with Tom. Her new boyfriend, Matt, seemed so much nicer, although Laurie hadn't met him often, but as far as she could tell, he seemed okay. Certainly better than Tom, that was for sure! He spoke to Cara in a much nicer way too which was a huge relief to Laurie.

Laurie had been delighted when Cara had agreed to come over for her birthday. It showed things were moving forward in the right direction. She was always careful not to put too much of a burden on Cara as she had always been a 'daddy's girl' and, as a result, was still very protective over him, understandably.

Laurie didn't see Rich now at all, ever since their divorce had been finalised. She obviously heard how he was doing from the girls though and, reading between the lines, he was not faring too well! He had suffered a nervous breakdown of sorts and had taken early retirement. She didn't like to probe too much but she wasn't at all surprised. He had continued to be as destructive as possible right through their divorce. He gave absolutely nothing away without a fight and had even burnt all of their family photos. An act which had devastated Laurie at the time, as well as deeply upsetting the girls. His behaviour however had helped Laurie get closer to all her girls again. That was the great irony.

It was Laurie they all turned to whenever Rich was kicking off. And Laurie who comforted them about their family photos. "They're memories, that's all and you have all those memories inside your head anyway. You can bring them out any time you want to. But now, you all need to look forward, make more memories of your own," she had added. And they had agreed, making far more of an effort when they were all together to chat about their childhood. They had many happy memories between them too. In fact, listening to them reminisce, Laurie realised what a wonderful childhood they had all experienced.

So, Cara was coming over with Matt, Marie with Adam and Laurie's delightful little grandchild, Maddy. Oh, she was an absolute treasure! Mike and Laurie looked after her every Sunday afternoon and they both loved that time spent with her. She absolutely adored Mike and would spend hours playing with him, taking his hand and calling "Grandad...come play" refusing to countenance the thought that he might actually say no to her!

Sarah and Maisie had travelled down last night, staying in one of their spare bedrooms. It had been a shock when Sarah 'came out' as gay. Laurie had had no idea, but, on reflection, she wasn't surprised. No wonder she had never been serious with any of the numerous boyfriends she had had! Maisie was a lovely girl and genuinely seemed to care for Sarah.

And that's all Laurie could ever ask for in life, she thought. For all her girls to find love...proper love...like she and Mike had. She crossed her fingers and touched the wooden table. Whoever knew though, she thought to herself. No-one on the outside could ever really know what went on in a relationship and only time would tell, she supposed.

Crikey, even Frankie had a partner now! Jim, he was called, and they had been together for just over two years. Laurie had been delighted for her. She had met him through work, only a few months after her father had died, a time when Frankie had been at an all time low and it had been a massive relief for Laurie. She wasn't used to keeping Frankie's spirits up. After all these years of it being the other way around, it didn't come naturally at all! And so Jim couldn't have turned up at a better time.

Humming to herself, she took out the gammon joint and began to baste the roast potatoes. They were going to have a wonderful day together, she decided. All the girls were starting to relax around Mike now too. Maddy had made the difference really. She had come into their family at the right time, with all the sweetness of angelic innocence and had somehow managed to blur the lines. New partners too, of course, helping.

She felt they were a family again, and, for that, Laurie felt an immense sense of gratitude.

Mike had had no family of his own and this was something Laurie felt guilty about, so to see him interact with Maddy and clearly be so taken with her was wonderful. He would have been fabulous with kids of his own, she thought sadly. But Mike had never settled down. He had lived with a couple of girlfriends along the way but had told Laurie that no-one could ever have measured up to her. And once he realised that, he had accepted he would stay single. He understood pure love, he said, and was not about to settle for anything less. Besides, he added, it wouldn't have been fair on anyone.

That was Mike! She loved how he comfortably wore his heart on his sleeve. Just like when he had flown out to Thailand. There were never any half measures with him. When asked why he hadn't simply e-mailed, his reply was simple. After twenty years, he said, he wasn't going to give Laurie a chance to slip away again. He wanted to give this his best shot and he'd believed that was by seeing her face to face.

The last three years had been the best Laurie had ever had. They had each vowed that they would never spend another night apart and held true to that vow, even when practicality should have dictated otherwise.

Mike had openly cried when Laurie had told him how she used to spend their anniversary (well...4th September) and he had agonized over it for weeks. "Oh my God," he remarked. "Why didn't I think of that?"

Laurie had smiled and put her arms around him. "Maybe it all worked out exactly as it was meant to," she had replied. "And anyway, even if we *had* met up, I would still have been in the same position. I still couldn't have left my girls!"

And Mike had agreed.

Laurie had been worried at first that Mike might have felt bitter about her decision to stay but Mike had hastily reassured her. It was one of the reasons he loved her so much, he had said...her obvious love for her children and he admired her for making such a tough choice as he saw it. But it hadn't been a tough choice for Laurie. She could never have left her girls with Rich. Crikey, she had even felt guilty splitting up the family when she did, despite all and sundry telling her they were all grown up now.

As it was, the divorce had taken its toll on Laurie. She had been determined to stand on her own two feet and had found work in a local nursery, work she loved. She had even taken her NVQ 3 in childcare. But it was a low paid job and she found the work physically exhausting, so much so, that she had recently dropped her hours down to twenty five each week.

So, Thank God for Lucinda. Without her, she wouldn't have had that luxury.

The divorce had been so difficult, Rich fighting her every step of the way and, without Lucinda, Laurie would have just rolled over and accepted whatever Rich had deemed reasonable.

But Lucinda was having none of it! "You might not want the money now Laurie," she would say, "but you have to protect your future. You earn very little as it is and you're getting older. I'm simply ensuring you get a fair deal and that you won't be on the breadline in your old age. And now, if you'll just let me get on with the negotiations in peace, I would be most grateful!" she would add.

"She's right Laurie. You never know what's around the corner. Just let her get on with it. That's what you're paying her for," Frankie would urge.

So, get on with it, she had. And Laurie had eventually received a cheque for £400k as well as an agreement that she received a third of his pension. Laurie had thought it was too much but had reluctantly taken it after speaking to Mike. "If you find you don't need it, then you can pass it on to your girls. But, for now, you must take it. Just in case."

With regards to the orphanage, Mike and Laurie went out twice a year, staying with Deborah as often as possible. All three were getting involved in all sorts of fund raising too and had started a fund which Laurie felt could be put to good use by ensuring they had more workers in the nursery every day with strict instructions that as much one to one as possible was to be given!

And Dang was turning into a beautiful little girl. She was nearly six now and would run up to Laurie, her arms open wide, a huge grin on her face, every time Laurie went out to see her. Mike and Laurie had even talked of adopting her but were in fairly early stages in their discussions at the moment. As there was so much red tape, Laurie kept telling herself not to get too excited. But...whoever knew? One day...maybe!

Sitting, drinking coffee after enjoying a superb meal, Laurie looked over at Mike. He looked tired today. "Are you okay, you look tired?" she whispered quietly, placing her hand gently on his forearm.

"Yes, I'm fine," he answered, smiling at her, before picking Maddy up to take her to the loo.

Marie was attempting to potty train and it was so hit and miss that she had assigned everyone to the task, having drawn up a rota so that every twenty minutes Maddy was given the opportunity to go! Way over the top as far as Laurie was concerned. Had it been her, she would have just stuck a nappy on her and be done with!

"Come on then, terror," Mike remarked, grabbing Maddy and starting to tickle her. Maddy screamed with delight as Mike ran out of the room with her and everyone around the table smiled.

A perfect day. She had nothing but perfect days now. She was so lucky.

She finally had the love of a wonderful, decent man. She had met her soulmate and she couldn't believe her luck!

Regrets? Did she have any? Well, how could she? Of course, in a fairytale world, Mike and Laurie would have met in their teens, had five beautiful children together and lived happily ever after, maybe winning the lottery too, along the way!

But in real life? No. No regrets. Had she not met Rich, she would not have had her three girls. And, had she chosen to leave, their childhoods would have been ruined, she felt sure of that. So, all in all, everything had probably turned out exactly as it was meant to. And now she was going to make damned sure she treasured every moment of her life from now onwards!

Chapter 48

Wednesday September 4th 2019.

Mike was dying!

If Laurie kept telling herself often enough, maybe it would sink in.

Mike was dying.

It didn't seem possible. They had both been in a state of disbelief since he had been diagnosed a month ago. Stomach cancer, they said. And a prognosis of 18 months left to live.

The signs had been there for a while, they realised. He had been feeling extremely tired and had been suffering on and off with bad stomach pain. Laurie berated herself for not encouraging him to go to the doctor sooner, but as Mike kept telling her, it would probably have made little difference. The tiredness, he had simply put down to getting older. It had only been the stomach pains which had finally made him go for tests and those pains had only come on badly recently.

They hadn't told any family members yet. They wanted to keep everything as normal as possible for as long as possible. That way, they could almost believe it wasn't happening. But they would have to tell family soon, they knew that. It would just make it feel too real though for both of them. They would need to dig deep, she told herself.

Mike's workplace already knew and Mike had been signed off from work last week as the pain had intensified. So things were already changing for them.

It felt so cruel! They had been expecting at least twenty years together and they had so many hopes and plans for

298

the future, it really didn't seem fair. But life had never been fair, Laurie reflected.

Since the diagnosis, they talked every night, way into the small hours, spooned together, the way they always slept. Mike was going to do everything he could to fight this, he said. He wasn't going to take it lying down and Laurie loved his attitude.

He was awaiting a date for an operation which he had been promised would come within the next week, followed by gruelling chemotherapy and radiation treatment.

Laurie was off work until Monday but had told Mike that she was going to talk to her boss when she was back in. She wanted to take some time off, unpaid of course. But she also wanted her boss to agree to keep her job open...she loved her job...the girls she worked with as well as all the kids, especially the babies and she would be sad to leave but Mike would need her in the next few months, maybe even longer and she had no intention of letting him down.

She would be with him, whatever. She'd already sussed out the hospital visiting times. Any time from 2pm through to 8pm! This had pleasantly surprised her. Far better than the strict visiting hours that had been in force when she had been in hospital with her girls!

So...2pm to 8pm it would be. And Laurie would stay with him all that time, every day he was in there. She would keep him company or simply sit by his side whilst he slept. They would have to kick her out of there every night. She would never be leaving voluntarily.

Hopefully her boss would keep her job open, but she was realistic too. After all, she had a business to run. If she couldn't, then so be it. Laurie would find other work at another nursery at the appropriate time. For now, Mike was her priority. Thank God Lucinda had fought for Laurie. At least she had no financial worries.

She realised how fortunate she was, being able to make the choices she wanted, not having financial concerns determine her decision.

And Laurie was determined to stay positive, just as Mike was doing. She had read in the papers only a few days ago of a lady who seemed to be defying all the odds, still alive ten years after *her* terminal diagnosis. If one person could do that, then so could Mike. They had to have hope...faith too!

But Laurie would look after Mike, come what may. Should a miracle occur, Laurie would be ecstatic, but should it not, then Laurie was going to do everything in her power to make each and every one of Mike's days as comfortable and pleasurable as possible.

She told him repeatedly she was going nowhere. He was stuck with her until he took his final breath, whenever that may be.

Not withstanding the sense of injustice, she also felt a strange sense of calm and gratitude. Gratitude that she was *in* this position...to actually be able to fulfil this promise to him! How things could have turned out so differently! She shuddered at the thought.

Yes...she was so lucky and she would be honoured to look after him and see him through his last days if it came to that. Their love ran so deep, she knew with a certainty she couldn't articulate that they would always be bound together.

Their souls were connected in such a way that death would in no way diminish it.

Picking up their small overnight bag, Laurie took Mike's hand. "Come on then love," she said, smiling. They climbed into her car, on their way to Stratford. Room no.5 booked as normal.

Kathy Kingsley can be contacted by email:
kathykingsley2020@gmail.com

Or you can follow on Facebook: Kathy Kingsley

Instagram: Kkingsley_Books

Printed in Great Britain
by Amazon

21199279R00172